winter
damage

Natasha Carthew

winter damage

BLOOMSBURY

LONDON NEW DELHI NEW YORK SYDNEY

Bloomsbury Publishing, London, New Delhi, New York and Sydney

First published in Great Britain in August 2013 by Bloomsbury Publishing Plc
50 Bedford Square, London WC1B 3DP

A CIP catalogue record for this book is available from the British Library

ISBN 978 1 4088 3583 8

Typeset by Hewer Text UK Ltd, Edinburgh
Printed in Great Britain by CPI Group (UK) Ltd, Croydon CR04YY

1 3 5 7 9 10 8 6 4 2

www.bloomsbury.com

For Evelyn

CHAPTER ONE

There was good in this world and there was evil but the young girl had not yet learnt the difference. She didn't have the time for noticing or wondering. Everything was just chores and more.

She sat with her face pressed hard against the thin scratched plastic of the windowpane, her legs bunched tight against the sill, and she counted the crows that bothered the crops in the upper sketch of field and the magpies that came into the yard. There were seven of them, gabbing their secrets to the chickens, who couldn't have cared less.

The girl banged on the window. She hadn't just thrown down scraps to have them eaten by the cackling devil birds.

Her breath fogged the fake glass and she drew a smiley, then smeared it clear and sighed.

Dad was calling from the other side of the trailer and she slid reluctantly to her feet.

'Ennor, you about, girl?' His voice pitched and split like a reed and Ennor pictured briefly how he used to be before, ordering her around the farm and laughing when she got things wrong, his little deputy, running three steps to his one.

The short hallway that led to his room was near dark in the morning half-light. Ennor had taken the bulbs from their sockets months ago to save on the leccy.

'Girl?' he repeated.

'Comin, Dad.'

She knocked on his door out of polite habit and went in. The room smelt of stale cigarette smoke and night-old pee and she crossed the room to draw back the curtains and crank open the window.

'It's cold.'

'I know, Dad, but you need some fresh air. It smells like rot in here.'

She went to the wardrobe and pulled out the spare blanket and stretched it over the bed. 'How you feelin?'

'Same as always.' He coughed and reached for one of the many cigarettes she'd rolled and stacked in a pile on his bedside table.

Ennor took the lighter from her jeans' pocket and lit his cigarette and one for herself, and father and daughter looked at each other while they inhaled, waiting for him to wake fully.

'So how's my girl this mornin?'

'Fine, Dad.'

'And the animals?'

'Fed and watered.' She smiled and sat down on the easy chair near the window like always.

'Good.' He nodded and flicked ash towards the heaving ashtray and missed. 'And that brother of yours?'

'Off to school, fed and watered just the same.'

'Good, good.'

They sat in silence, apart from the coughing. Ennor wanted to ask about money but she knew they had none. They'd had none for a long time now and she was running out of things to sell and places where shopkeepers weren't suspicious of her idle standing.

She cleared her throat and looked out of the window at the heavy tinted sky, knowing, from necessity as a farmer's daughter, that snow was heading their way. She leant forward to see if all four corners of the window were filled with cloud and they were.

'What is it?' he asked. 'I know you got somethin to say so just say it to have it said.'

Ennor looked back into the room with a start. She thought of the ways to say something without upsetting someone but then it just came out. 'We int got no food in the cupboards to speak of, the cattle are thin as bones plus we're down to the last of the silage and most of all we're eight weeks without rent and eight's our final warning. The landlord's bin knockin.'

'My.' He laughed and coughed at the same time. 'Anythin else?'

Ennor nodded and got up to stand at the window. 'Yep, there's a storm comin.' She held back the curtain and he looked past her at the yellowing sky.

'What should I do, Dad?'

'Close the bloody window for starters and get your old man a cup of tea. Can't think without tea.'

Ennor stood beside the bed and crossed her arms.

'Don't be like that, girl. Dad always comes through with somethin, don't he?'

Ennor shrugged. She wanted to disagree but you weren't supposed to kick people already way down in the dung heap.

'Yes, Dad.' She smiled. 'Only don't be expectin strong tea cus the bag's already bin through twice this mornin and the milk's powdered.'

She left the room and went to the kitchen to get the tin kettle and she carried it to the outside pump to fill it, then brought it to the stove and banked the fire with clumps of offcut wood she'd scavenged from the barn.

The weather was getting colder and she refilled the five-gallon milk churns at the pump in case it froze and dragged them inside the makeshift porch that someone at some time had bolted on to the trailer.

She stood with her hands in her pockets and leant against the stove and saw by the clock on the wall that it was nine o'clock. Class would be starting around about now and she wondered if she was ever missed in the town's small school.

Since the phone had been cut off the welfare officer had visited only once and that was three months ago. A lot had happened in those three months, things had fallen apart and gone wrong and were just plain busted and broke, but Ennor still stood in the kitchen that smelt of woodsmoke and chicken fat and watched the kettle boil same as always. She went and looked out of the window like she had a hundred times before, watching the seasons change and scanning the horizon and the leaves for colourful signs of hope. There was nothing but white, a blank-page stare and a laughable routine.

The kettle sent sudden spits of steam towards the ceiling and momentarily lifted the linoleum on the wall into blisters of warm air, moving mouths of gossip followed by tight lips.

Ennor loosened the tea in the damp tea bag with a pinch and poured the water in, pressing and stirring this way and that until the liquid hinted at colour. She added a dip of the powdered milk to make it look better.

She returned to the bedroom to find that Dad had drifted back to sleep. His cigarette lay in a burnt hole in the blanket. She put the butt into the ashtray and checked the hole wasn't smouldering, then pulled the blanket around him before taking the mug of tea to the bedroom she shared with her brother, Trip.

In the squat room she put on her mother's old Loretta Lynn CD and sat cross-legged on her bed, listening to the lyrics for clues to her own miserable life and wishing she knew the reasons behind all the things she didn't understand.

She sipped the tea and its dryness caught in her throat and tickled her ears, the brief hit of warmth heavenly on such a cold morning.

Out of the window the sky fixed heavy with mood and a few sparks of sleet flicked against the pane like bad reception in a news report from a war-torn country, fussing her reflection into a messy scowl. She stood up and sighed because work never had a line put through it. She clicked the misery mute button inside her head and went to the porch to put on her hat and coat and the ripped wellies with the posh buckles.

Outside the easterly wind caught against her cheek like a well-placed slap and she lifted her coat collar as she ran across the yard and through the gate that led to the field.

The cows were still at the silage she'd dumped there that morning and Ennor swore at herself for not listening to the weather last night. Not only would she have to lead them down to the barn, she would have to bring down the silage too.

She opened the gate and they glanced up, puzzled, briefly concerned for the young girl who fed and cared for them, then continued eating.

'You got the life, int you, girls?' She patted one of them on their hindquarters and winced as her hand cupped the knuckle bones that popped through the skin like studs on a leather jacket.

If the cows didn't survive the winter, she'd have no calves in spring and no money coming in except Dad's social, and their carcasses would be taken by the knackers to be minced into dog's dinner.

Since the last outbreak of foot-and-mouth things had turned worse from the top of the country to the bottom. Ennor didn't remember it all so well. She was only seven at the time and losing the prize cattle was the least of their problems once they had lost the farmhouse and the land and her dad went half mad with the misery and then the drugs.

The half-dozen cows, a barn and the field that caught the worst wind were all they had left, and them a rope-run of farming kin that went back to the day dot.

She stood with the wind pushing against her back and rubbed her chin like the old men in the village and she wondered whether to bother moving the silage and decided against. If the cows were hungry, they would more than likely have it eaten before the snow came proper and, besides, there was nothing but fumes left in the ancient tractor, not even enough for sniffing.

She leant into the wind and took some comfort from its support as she watched the grey muck landscape get scrubbed and cleaned white. A transformation that hid the unfertile truth: this land was a hopeless scuff of nothing.

She gripped her collar to her jaw and ran from the cover-up hill back down the path to the trailer and sat by the stove in her outdoor clothes until heat seeped back slowly into her bones.

Ennor pulled out the tiny plastic table that was meant for outdoor use and swung it in front of her. She set a biro and her notebook square in the middle.

She sat flat-palmed like she used to at school and clicked the radio on for company and hummed along to a tune she didn't recognise, looking to the window for creative inspiration and, when inspiration didn't come from the cold, she watched the embers of the fire for sparks.

Another song came on and then the news headlines and talk of the weather and instead of poetry Ennor wrote 'Things to do' at the top of the page. She under-lined it three times to compound its importance and wrote one to ten in the margin of the notebook, circling the numbers and drawing smileys in each corner of the page.

An expert on the news was telling Cornwall to brace itself for the worst winter since 1978 and Ennor laughed as she connected the smileys with chains because they said this every year. She looked at the radio and told it that it knew she was right.

The newsreader rattled on about 1978's Winter of Discontent and history repeating itself and when he listed the latest riot hot spots Ennor clicked the button to shut him up.

She'd rather have no company than bad company.

Talk of the looting and strikes was everywhere but Ennor fancied there were other things that might be important besides doom and gloom, like hope. Without that they'd all be close to swinging out in the barn like her friend Butch's dad. He was lucky they found him before he choked, though she supposed he didn't see it that way.

She ripped out the 'Things to do' page and wrote 'Things I'd like' on the fresh page, making the letters bigger than before.

She started the list in order of importance, beginning with a proper house of their own like backalong and, despite knowing the facts, she wrote that she wanted her dad to get better in all ways. She added she'd like to buy herself and Trip horses so they could ride out in the fields together, and she underlined the word 'buy' to show whoever it was that presided over wish lists that she was serious and not asking for straight doley handouts.

With the radio off she could hear her father stirring in his bed in the other room and she huffed and pushed the table back to fill the kettle again.

'Comin, Dad.' She knocked at his door and went in. 'Kettle's on.'

She straightened the bedding and went to the window.

'Leave that and come and sit down.' He patted the bed and Ennor did as she was told.

'Just bin thinkin bout what you said, money bein tight and all, and I remembered there's this bloke in town who owes me a few quid. I'll put the word out, see if I can't get him to pay up.'

Ennor put her hands deep into her pockets to keep them from fiddling. Niggling suspicions had a way of making her rub them and scratch, and she'd been training herself to be calm.

'Honest?' she asked.

'God's honest.' He smiled.

'How much?'

'Enough for Christmas, enough to treat my kids I'd think.'

Despite herself Ennor was warmed through by his moment of lucidity and fine words. She looked at the bootlace ring that lived around his neck and it winked. Mum's ring.

She wished she could take that warmth with her from his room and carry it around like a kitten all day long but there was one fat spoiler she had to ask.

'What about the rent, Dad? We're massive behind.'

The smile on his face dropped a little and he tried to edge forward as if he were about to whisper in her ear.

'Forget bout that, I'll take care of it.' He brushed the hair from her face with the hand that didn't shake so much and painted a smile across her face with his thumb. 'That's my girl. Go and get your old man a cuppa.'

Ennor wondered if what he'd told her was true. She jiggled his words about in her head and decided it was because he never really lied. Sometimes he twisted the truth but that was because of his medication and not really his fault.

She made a pot of tea with a fresh tea bag and gave it time to steep while contemplating a Christmas list. Not wanting to jinx things like usual, she decided she'd write the things needed for a proper Christmas on lines, top to bottom, in her head. She started with the list for food, which was kind of a shopping list, working backwards from sweet to savoury because really she was still a kid and couldn't think about what you needed for cooking when in her mind's eye she could buy cakes and ice cream and ice-cream cakes.

She made the tea and carried the two mugs into her father's room and put one on his bedside table and carried the other to the chair.

'So who's this friend then?' she asked.

'A long lost, you wouldn't know um.'

Ennor watched him pick up the mug with both hands and despite its heat he took a big swig and winced as he swallowed it down. 'That's good.' He smiled and she nodded and sipped at her own.

They drank in silence and Ennor watched his hands cradle the mug like a broken bird, still calloused and scarred from a lifetime in the fields, and she looked about the cramped room and wondered if he ever missed the outdoors and she wanted to ask but didn't know how.

Around the room in dusty glassless frames were photos of prize bulls and favourite horses. Rosettes and trophies lined the shelves among collected crap and scrap from years of hoarding.

In his day her dad had been a proud man with a prize-winning Simmental herd to show. That time was like jelly in Ennor's memory and in all probability was gone from his.

She wondered if there would be a little money in the pot to pay for a few bales of silage from the farm in the next valley, but this was something else she kept to herself.

'Bucket needs emptyin.'

'I know, Dad.' She put her mug on the bedside table and looked at the bucket and sighed, then picked it up and carried it carefully across the room.

'Don't spill none.'

Ennor looked at her father and shook her head in disbelief. 'Int like I'm goin runnin with it now, is it?'

'Give up the cheek, girl. You int too old –'

'For the belt, I know.'

She set the heavy bucket of waste down in the hall, then closed his door and propped open the trailer door and the one in the porch before carrying the bucket through. She returned to close up behind her.

Outside the snow fell in thick muffling strips like

sheets on a washing line, and fixed blown to the hedges and fences that surrounded the farmland.

She put on her wellies and coat and stepped out into the white with the bucket swinging and threatening below. The slop pit was close enough for regular trips but far enough not to notice its stench back in the trailer and Ennor knew the path so well she could follow it easily despite the white. She held the wire-and-string handle tight and it cut into both her hands.

The pit was annexed to the side of the barn they used to house some of the furniture from the old house, stuff she couldn't flog, plus the cattle in bad weather.

She climbed the concrete block that acted as a step up to the walled hollow and found her footing on the shallow dome of ice that had thickened there, counting to three and praying to God all at once as she lifted the corrugated lid and swung the bucket up and over the side.

The familiar stink filled her nose and her mouth and throat and she gagged the same as every day and she wiped her eyes with her sleeve and jumped down into the muddy snow. She headed back towards the outside tap to swill the bucket before the water finally froze but it was too late and she kicked the tap and then the bucket. A great urge to fall back into the snow engulfed her but she swallowed the want to be a child back down into her belly with a gulp.

The snow was falling like in a full-on Christmas card

and Ennor knew the cattle would need to be brought down to the barn as soon as possible. She returned to the windy field and as she walked she snapped snow from the twine that was strung out between the hedges to guide the cattle and obediently followed the pink lines as if she too were some dumb animal.

Her gloveless hands were butcher red and the skin on her fingers shiny tight and she put them under her armpits and blew on them and hung them useless by her sides. If she had a mother, she would have been reminded not to forget her gloves when out in the cold, but she didn't and there was no point in dwelling on it.

She called out to the cows on approach and snapped a stick from the hedge to poke them from the circle of silage, glad she'd not bothered to move it because they'd eaten it gone and the soil beneath was already frosting with ice flakes.

The cold made steel-blade peaks of the hoof-tilled land that surrounded her. Snow settled all around and over the hedgerows so that she could no longer see the dark trim of moorland beyond.

'We're goin walkies,' she told the cows. 'And I don't need no nonsense so just move along now.'

They followed her out through the open gate and down the track to the barn and Ennor told them they were good girls because they were. She pushed them through the barn door and bolted it, one and two, with thoughts of the cosy stove inviting her back indoors, then she wondered about Trip and if she might go to meet him because his lift was near enough due.

Along the track Ennor looked up to see Butch in the upstairs bedroom window of the farmhouse.

This was the room that used to be her parents' in the house that had harboured her family all the way back to the man who built it, her great-great-great-grandfather.

She waved and he waved back. 'You comin down?' she shouted.

Butch nodded and he put one finger to the rattling top pane, which meant 'Wait a minute', and she nodded and went to sit in the woodpile. She slumped against the seasoned wood and settled on one of the upended logs they used for seats, watching the snowflakes fill the potholes in the dirt track and thinking all things Christmas.

'Now you know why I suggested my old man put a roof on that thing.'

Ennor smiled when she saw Butch approaching. 'It's cosy enough.'

He sat down and undid the buttons on his parka and Ennor knew he was up to something because of the glint in his eye. 'Look what I got.'

'What?'

'Home brew. I found it in the pantry. Bin there for ever.'

'Why int it drunk?'

'The olds must have forgotten bout it.'

15

He passed the bottle to Ennor and she inspected the hand-written label. 'What flavour is it?' she asked as she wiped the dust away with the heel of her hand.

'Elderflower.'

'I hate elderflower, don't you?'

Butch nodded. 'Like soap.'

'Tastes like sick and more.' She dug at the cork with her penknife and took a swig and then nodded. 'Bad.'

Butch laughed and Ennor saw him wince with pain.

'What is it?'

'Nothin, just muscle strain or somethin.'

'You don't do nothin to get muscle strain 'cept read. Maybe it's liftin too much books.'

'Don't be daft.'

'Is it your chest?'

'Just leave it, would you?' He took a sip of the wine and then another. 'That is bad.' He nodded and poured the liquid into a bubble in the snow.

'Don't need no booze anyway. I've got celebratin on my mind,' said Ennor.

'What kind of celebratin?'

'The Christmas kind.'

'What you got to celebrate bout Christmas?'

Ennor smiled and linked his arm. 'Dad says he's got money comin and he aims to spend it.'

'And you believe him?' asked Butch as he pulled away.

'Why not?'

'Cus hello?'

'He don't lie. Just circumstance turns up bad some days.'

'Like a bad penny.'

'Just like it. Why you on a downer?'

'I'm not.'

'Seems that way.' She rolled herself a cigarette and passed the tin to Butch.

'You heard the news recent?' he asked.

'Heard enough of it.'

'Bad int it?'

Ennor shrugged and lit up and held the flame for him. 'I'm not worried. Don't affect us so much out here in the sticks. Things are bad here anyway.'

'No fuel, no food, no government even. I dunno, it just might.'

'You reckon? I hope not, just gettin used to a nice thought in my head.'

'What's that?'

'*Christmas*, silly.'

'Thought you had rent due.'

'Big time, but Dad said not to worry.'

Butch shook his head and Ennor ignored him. 'The power of positive thinkin.' She nodded.

'Maybe you should be careful. You're sweet and all but gullible as –'

'Don't even know what that means. Is it a good thing?'

'Means you believe everythin anyone's got to say, no matter what.'

'Like trustin?'

'Kind of.'

'Nothin wrong with trustin.'

Butch laughed and drew his hand up to his chest 'Till it brings trouble.'

'I int stupid, Butch.'

'Just sayin.'

'Well don't. I was lookin forward to tellin Trip bout Christmas and now you've gone peed on me fairy lights.'

'Don't be daft, just watchin out for my best friend.' He smiled.

Ennor liked it when he said things like that. 'You don't think Dad's gonna pay off the rent?'

Butch shrugged. He looked tired, in pain.

'Cus if he don't we're buggered, homeless and everythin.'

'You can live here in the woodpile.'

'We got the barn but I'm not livin with a load of snippy snappy rats.' She shook her head and then looked at him. 'Things will be all right, won't they?'

Butch changed the subject and asked about Trip.

'Fine, spose he is anyway. School's closin and stayin closed. Trip thinks it's great cus, you know, he don't like it for the teasin. But school's a good thing. It's a right thing when everythin else is wrong.'

Butch nodded. 'Learnin's the only thing we got as a get-out. So what bout Christmas, you made your list yet?'

Ennor smiled. 'Course.'

'Got your mind on all things fancy, I bet.'

'We int had a fancy one ever. Just a few nice things I'm plannin, for Trip, make some nice memories. I got a few of um myself in regards to Christmas.'

Butch said nice memories were better than a fancy Christmas and Ennor put her hand on his arm and then took it away. 'We gotta make the best of it, don't we? Whatever we got, one way or other.' She leant forward to look at him, to see if he wanted to talk about his stuff the way she always did about hers but his mouth was on the fag and his mind had wandered someplace else.

At the crossroads she rested on the wooden signpost and rolled a cigarette and settled herself to smoking and waiting. She kept her eyes fixed on the grey dust horizon and continued with the shopping list from earlier, with everything hot and fatty and of gargantuan proportion.

Headlights flashed occasionally through the trees and Ennor ignored them, loading an imaginary table with heavy food until an ancient Land Rover slowed to a stop in front of her.

'Ennor.' Mrs Trewithick climbed out of the front seat and levered it forward for Trip to scramble from the back.

'Wow, miss, how many you got in there?'

'Sister, the car was skiddin. We nearly died.' Trip linked his hand into the loop of his sister's arm and jumped for attention. 'And there's no more school, ever.'

'Hi, buddy, looks like you're gonna have a long Christmas. Is that right?' she asked.

Mrs Trewithick nodded. 'No fuel. No heating. Best thing is to keep listening to the radio. I'm sure things will be back to normal soon enough.' She smiled and passed Ennor a letter and she looked like she was on the brink of crying.

'And look, Mrs Trewithick gave me these hikers.' Trip kicked snow into the air to show off his new shoes.

Ennor crossed her arms and pulled up proud. 'There's no need for that, miss. We was goin shoppin soon enough, weren't we, buddy?'

'They were my son's. Honestly, he barely wore them. Grow so fast, don't they?' She closed the car door on the screaming children and took a step towards Ennor in an attempt at privacy.

'Well that's great, Mrs Trewithick. Thank you, really.'

'You look after yourself, Ennor.' She smiled and nodded towards the letter. 'It won't be for long.'

Ennor smiled and said something about winter not being a for ever thing.

She told Trip to thank his teacher again and she pulled him off the lane towards the track.

'You've got my number, Ennor. If there's anything I can help with, please let me know.'

'Thanks, miss.' She pocketed the letter and turned to put an arm around Trip's shoulder and she told herself not to think badly of Mrs Trewithick because she didn't mean to interfere.

'Fine boots you got there, buddy. Winter boots, int they?'

Trip smiled up at her. 'It's gonna be like a real Christmas, snow and everythin.' He danced out into the powder that had banked against the verge and and his heels kicked happy hope towards the storm. Ennor skipped after him. She tried to recall what it was like to be a kid but it felt unfamiliar to her, a briefly glanced at movie starting with the slaughter that led Dad to drink and the baby that led Mum to leave.

They raced down the track to the courtyard in front of the farmhouse and Ennor hinted more and more that it was going to be the best Christmas ever.

'Like how best?'

'I dunno, best food, best pressies, a snowman out in the yard.'

'I don't like snowmen. They scare me.'

'Well whatever you like.' She scooped two handfuls of snow into a ball and threw it at him as she ran to the trailer.

'Hey!' Trip ran after her but when he got to the porch she was already inside and she refused to let him in until he threw the snowball he held behind his back into the wind.

Trip sat by the stove and stripped to his vest and pants while Ennor hung the wet clothes on the line that drooped from one end of the cramped room to the other.

'You need to take them boots off too. You look a right sight in your undies with them big boots stickin out.'

Trip laughed and bent to undo the laces and Ennor helped.

'Miss tied um double-knot tight.'

'You need to stick some sheets from the free ads into the toe, ball um up tight and leave um be and they'll be dry in no time.'

Ennor made them mugs of hot squash and took down the tin of oat biscuits she'd been saving for the end of term. 'These are a bit soft so dunk um in your juice and you won't know the difference.'

They sat close to the stove and Ennor quizzed her brother about his day as he petted his boots, turning them in his hands like found objects.

'Fine boots.' He smiled to himself.

'And what happens if you look after your boots?' his sister asked.

'They'll look after you.'

'That's right. Never dry straight without paper and a good dab of wax if you got it.'

'And leave the wax on for an hour.'

'That's right, buddy, you got it.'

'And what if you don't have wax?'

'Rub a banana skin over it.'

This answer always made Trip laugh. 'We int got no bananas.' He grinned. 'Not since a long, time, sister. Shops are closin and everythin.'

'We don't have a lot of things and never have so never mind bout that. What I tell you bout listnin in on older kids talk?' She lifted his chin to show she was serious.

'Don't,' he answered.

'Don't is right. It's gossip and it's rubbish and worse. Shops closin or no don't mean a thing.'

Ennor emptied his school bag to add it to the washing line and she was glad to see he'd brought home reading books because reading was good and she laid them out on the little table along with the plastic horse he carried everywhere and his jotter and pencil case. Then she remembered the letter and settled back in the chair to read it.

Letters used to be about school trips and term dates but not any more. Ennor read them and kept them in a card file in a box under the bed but she knew this one was different as soon as it was pulled from the envelope. 'Social Services' was writ large at the top of the page and Ennor read the words over and then 'Trip', 'institution' and 'vulnerable' and she balled it and shoved it deep into her pocket.

She looked to see if Trip had noticed the letter but he hadn't and she watched him show his horse the new boots. She would not give up her baby brother no matter how bad things got and she wondered why social services were bothering with them when there were a million families in the same situation and worse with the men street fighting just for the sake of it and everyone without money and roofs. What kind of an institution was it anyway?

At least her dad was a man allergic to trouble. He'd know what to do. Ennor knew he was no angel but he had wings enough to get them out of trouble in the past and she wondered about social services and if telling him was a tick against good or bad. She pushed the biscuit stodge around in her mouth and pretended that everything would be fine, but her stomach churned and she spat the lump into her hand and ran outside to be sick.

CHAPTER TWO

The cramped fold-down bed where Ennor lay was full of loose springs but it was her bed and she loved it. She stared up at the ceiling and wondered this way and that, her head a buzz-bulb full of impossible questions and unfeasible answers. She knew Trip was awake because she could hear him whispering to his buddy horse beneath the sheets and she knew he was talking about Christmas by his cheerful tone.

'Mornin, buddy. I can hear you over there, you know.'

Trip giggled. 'And buddy horse.'

'Mornin, buddy horse.' She smiled.

'Mornin, sister. Mornin, Ennor. Is it breakfast?'

Ennor rested up on her elbows. 'Well I guess so. Porridge OK with you?'

Trip peeked out of his bed and pushed his nose up against the window. 'It's stopped snowin. Can I go look for eggs, please?'

'Well good luck in findin any but OK we can go take a look.' She counted to three before leaping into the cold damp room and she added layers of clothing to the ones she'd slept in. She told Trip to dress quickly so they could look for eggs straight off and she looked in on her dad, like she did every morning to stop the worry that had her restless each night.

Out in the porch Ennor made Trip put on his wellies and not the hikers and they put on their dirty work coats.

'Weather got worse in the night,' said Trip as they trampled fresh snow in a pattern towards the barn.

'A right little genius you are, int you?'

She pulled his bobble hat down past his ears and they continued on their way.

In the barn the cows slumped on the dirt floor chewing and the chickens sat startled and at odds with the sudden change in weather and were everywhere awkward. Heads and necks sprang from crates and broken bits of machinery, each one of them up and over and out of reach.

'Why do they always do that?' asked Ennor.

'Do what?'

'Roost everywhere but the coop when you're hankerin after an egg.'

Trip shrugged. 'Cus they don't like sharin. Don't worry, I'll get um.'

Ennor watched him disappear into the wall of junk and she shouted for him to be careful.

The wind outside was close to gale force and it raged through the barn's loose panels and filled the place with a thousand whistles that crawled up Ennor's spine like fingering boys.

'You found anythin?' she shouted above the noise. 'Trip?'

'I see somethin,' he called back.

'What? Better be eggs or we're goin in.' She crouched to the ground and peered into the hole.

'There's a load of old clothes.'

'Any eggs? I'm startin to freeze to the spot here.'

Trip pushed himself further beneath the machinery and Ennor bent her head to look where his legs had been.

'Eggs,' he exclaimed. 'I knew it, the little buggers, there's loads.'

'Hey, no swearin.'

'You do.' He reached out a twist of rag with seven eggs piled against each other and handed them to Ennor.

'Good work, buddy.'

'Seven, that's lucky right?'

'Lucky when you're hungry. Come on out now.'

'There's a load of old stuff in here.'

Ennor stood and counted the eggs over and waited for him to reappear.

'We could sell some of it.'

'Everythin worth anythin has been sold already. Now come out.'

'What about this?'

Trip reversed out of the hole in the junk wall and handed her an old picture frame.

'Is it gold?' he asked.

Ennor's fingers twitched like triggers as she stared at the faded photo of Mum and Dad on their wedding day.

'It int gold,' she said.

'We could sell it on the internet.'

'How'd we do that? We don't have a computer. Anyway there's no internet no more.'

'We could ask Butch to help.'

'Butch int allowed usin the computer.'

'Why not?' He grabbed the frame from under Ennor's arm.

'Cus his dad's a bastard but you dint hear it from me.'

Trip held out the frame in front of him to look at the photo. 'He beats him, don't he? You don't have to say, cus I know.'

'All you need to know is you got a good daddy at home there and you should thank the Almighty for that.'

They retraced the circle of footsteps through the snow and Ennor clutched the eggs to her chest like a newborn.

'Who's these in the photo?' he asked.

'Dunno.'

'How many eggs we got?'

'Seven.'

'Two each and one for buddy horse?'

'Maybe.'

'Why maybe?'

'Cus buddy horse don't like eggs and always gives it to you.'

'Then I eat three.' He smiled up at his sister as they entered the porch and she told him it was good to be smart but not with her.

They flicked off their boots and coats and Ennor carried the eggs into the kitchen and placed them on the side still wrapped in her mother's old shirt.

'Go see if Dad's awake, will you? Ask him if he wants a boiled egg.'

She gathered an armful of wood from the pile in the porch and carried it to the stove, thinking about the photo as she stacked the oddments into a higgledy wall. Her mother and her father reunited as clear as black and white. It was a sign; it had to be.

There were whispers riding on the wind and the words lodged dead in her ears. A tumble of maybes and what ifs coming through the open door and she closed her eyes to the speed of things because sometimes ideas came too fast. Ennor needed to shut them out, rake over what had been planted, see what had seeded as a good idea. She slammed the door hard and slid the bolt to stop the rattling push and in that moment she knew what seed had been set. She could feel it split and multiply inside, a good idea growing into an even better plan, and she put the eggs into the pan and held the shirt close to her face. 'Mum,' she whispered.

'He's awake.' Trip appeared in the doorway and stood leaning on the flimsy door frame.

'What mood's he in?'

He shrugged.

'What?'

'I showed him the photo.'

Ennor sighed. 'Why'd you go do that for?'

He shrugged again and shook his head. The down-turned mouth warned her that he was close to crying. His tears were always accompanied by shouting and throwing and a full day of stubborn silence.

'Never mind. Go get buddy horse and I'll set the table for three.' She winked at him and waited to see if he would go down to the bedroom and he did.

'Thank God for that,' she whispered and she watched the eggs bounce about in the everyday pan she used for most meals. The last thing she needed was one of his tantrums when thinking was on the agenda.

She made a pot of tea and took a mug down to her father, placing it on the bedside table. She could see he was settling into one of his moods.

'Got some eggs on.' She stood with her hands on her hips and waited for him to look up.

'Want any?'

When he didn't answer Ennor left the room with a bang of the door that had the trailer rocking like a storm-tossed boat.

Back in the kitchen Trip set three eggcups on the table and sat down with the toy horse beside him.

'Buddy horse says he might have an egg this mornin.'

'Just one?'

'Says he might try one.'

'Would he like some fried toast with his egg?'

'Nope. Horses don't eat toast.'

They laughed and Ennor scraped the circles of mould off the last inch of stale bread and heated butter to fry it.

'I love breakfast.' Trip smiled. 'I love everythin you cook me.'

'Well that's good cus the maid's off sick and the chef's on holiday.'

They ate five of the eggs and kept two back for Dad and Ennor put the radio on so they could listen to the weather report.

'More snow comin.' Trip nodded towards the radio. 'Gonna get worse even.'

'Well we'll see. Can't go worryin just yet.'

'I int worryin. I like snow, don't you, sister?'

Ennor sat opposite and closed her eyes to the taste of sweet egg and the homely memory of fried bread. 'Don't like the cold it brings.'

She told him to stop talking and eat while things were hot and half turned an ear to the news headlines.

'What's "economy"?'

'Money and stuff.'

'What stuff?'

'I dunno, maths and that.'

'Like mental maths?'

'All maths is mental if you ask me.'

'You like countin.'

'That's different, that's just numbers for the sake of um. Now eat up.'

There was a knock on the kitchen window and a shadow passed and entered the porch and then the trailer door and shouted if anyone was home.

'What the hell?' Ennor jumped to her feet and prayed it wasn't social services, not yet.

'Who's that?' she shouted. 'Doors are for knockin and waitin, not enterin.'

She found the man grinning in the dull narrow hallway and he held his hands in the air as if she had the cross-hairs of her dad's rifle pinned upon him.

'It's Ennor, int it? Turned into a right handsome beauty, dint you? Just like that mother of yours, all dark and broodin.'

'You with the council?'

'Are you mad?'

She looked him up and down and was glad the cut of him was anything but official.

'Dad home?'

Ennor nodded. 'He's always home.'

'Heard he's not well. Come to pay my respects.' He smiled.

'He int dead yet, why you smilin?'

'He's an old friend and I'm here to settle an old debt.'

Ennor guessed this was the old friend her father had been talking about. 'Did he ring you?'

'Yeah, somethin like that.' He tipped his hat and she turned and knocked on the bedroom door.

'Dad, you got a visitor.' She showed the man into the room and she minded her manners and offered him a cup of tea and he accepted.

'Who's that man?' asked Trip when she returned to the kitchen.

'Friend of Dad's. Nothin to worry bout.'

'I don't like him. He looks mean.'

'Well looks int everythin. You bin taught that.' She told him to clear the table and help dry the dishes and to hurry up because she needed to talk to Butch about something.

'He's your boyfriend, int he?'

'Butch? Course not.'

'You're always over there.'

'That's cus he's my friend. Now hurry up and you can go see the horses in the stable.'

They cleared away the dishes and wiped the sides and Trip put the eggshells in the compost bin outside while Ennor took the cup of tea to the stranger and she told her dad she was going up to the farmhouse.

Butch's bedroom was backalong familiar. The high ceiling with the pattern wrapped round the light fitting and the ugly red carpet that bounced when you walked was lodged someplace in her memory. She sat on the edge of his bed and waited for him to make coffee in the kitchen downstairs and tried to remember something about her early life the way you might remember a book, but her mind buzzed and fizzed with other things.

The bed used to be in the far corner of the room, she remembered that much, furthest from the window and furthest from the door. A well-sprung bed, where she supposed all her dad's family had been made and born and loved until putting-out time. Somewhere in the house there was a room that had been hers but she'd never bothered asking and she never went looking. Half-cut memories were best left that way, half fantasy and the rest a blur not worth bothering.

It was just a house after all, just granite blocks and stone and slate.

Butch stood in the doorway with steaming mugs of coffee and he handed her one and sat down beside her on the bed.

'How you feelin?' she asked.

'Same as.'

'Chest playin up?'

'It's this weather. Makes my lungs wet or somethin.'

'That's a bummer. Weather's gonna get worse.'

He leant back against the ornate footboard and held the mug to his mouth so he could breathe in the steam.

'You don't look too bad – not like before.' Ennor

wondered if he believed her because in all honesty he looked washed and scrubbed like an old rag. 'Where's your mum?'

'Dunno.'

'Your dad?'

'Out shootin.'

'What?'

'Whatever he can. Deer, I guess.'

'How's he doin?'

'Dunno. Don't talk much, does he?'

Ennor propped herself up against the pillows and crossed her legs. 'How's he healin?'

'All right. Wears a scarf mostly so you can't tell.'

'Lucky you found him when you did.'

Butch shrugged. 'Don't' know what's so lucky bout it. What's this urgent thing you got to ask me? Saw me yesterday, dint you?'

'It's a favour.'

'Go on.'

'I'm goin away for a bit, short notice like.'

Butch took a sip of his coffee and waited for her to tell him where she was going.

'Gotta get to the north moor. Gonna look for Mum.'

'When you decide this?'

'Just.'

'What bout Dad? Trip?'

'I gotta go for them. Mum can help us, protect us even.' Ennor slouched into the duvet and waited until she could rely on herself not to cry. 'That's kind of why I'm here.'

Butch didn't speak and he rolled them a cigarette with all the time in the world laid out between them. She watched his big blue eyes that were almost too big for his neat face stretch with added worry and she wanted to tell him it was just a joke but it wasn't. She needed someone to look after Trip and that someone was him. Butch was the only person her brother trusted apart from herself and she knew he would be OK. He had to be.

She watched the only friend she had in the world light the cigarette in his mouth and he sucked hard until his lungs gave way to coughing and he passed it to Ennor.

'It's just a few days. I'll be back before Christmas.'

'Why are you goin at all? She left you, dint she? I thought you hated her?'

'I do, did, but there's bin a change, an emergency.' She told him about the letter from social services and that they would take Trip if she didn't have family to look after them. 'They'll stick Dad in a refuge. He int much cop, the way they see it.'

'They'll take you and all.'

Ennor sat up and looked at him. 'Say's it's an institution. What kind of institution?'

Butch shook his head and said he didn't know what to say.

'Say you'll do it. A few days tops, promise.'

'What about your dad?'

'He int up for much, don't worry, the odd cup of tea and Trip will empty the slop.'

'What's wrong with the bog?'

'No water.'

Butch nodded as if remembering she'd told him this before. 'If my dad gets wind, he'll kill me.'

'He don't need to know. You can sneak round, you do anyway.'

'He'll have me in the ground is what he'll do.'

Ennor waited for the answer she was banking on and she watched him get off the bed and stand by the window. 'Just a few days, right?'

She nodded.

'How'd you know your mum will help?'

'She will. She's me mum, int she? Besides, it's Christmas, she liked Christmas.'

'Where you gonna look? The moor's a big place on foot.'

'I've got a great-aunt who lives not too far west. Not seen her in years but she's Mum's aunt, she'll know where she is.' Ennor slid from the bed and stood beside him. 'Don't go worryin bout me, if you are I mean, I'll be fine.'

'You could take my motorbike, if you can get fuel to put in it.'

Ennor shook her head. 'Fuel's scarce. Nobody got

much and we int got any. Anyway your dad would go mental if he knew your bike was missin.'

They stood loose and wondering and Ennor asked again if he would do it and he nodded.

'You better look after yourself. Don't want no part if it blows up.'

'It won't and I will. You look after that brother of mine. He's all I got in the world. Promise?'

'I promise.' He tried to smile and she could see there was more he wanted to say but he turned away and everything was as usual just friends and solemn between them.

They walked down to the stables and stood and watched Trip as he finished up the story he was telling the horses from his perch on an upturned bucket.

'You're lucky,' he said to Butch. 'You got your own horses and they're real and everythin.'

'Course they're real. Wouldn't get far on a pretend one. Maybe I'll take you out ridin when Ennor's away.'

'Where you goin, sister?'

Ennor made a face at her friend and crouched to the ground beside Trip.

'What? You were goin to tell him, weren't you?' asked Butch.

'Course, in my own time.'

'Where you goin?' Trip asked again.

Ennor tried to explain that there was one thing she had to do before Christmas and then she kind of said it with just hints but to an autistic boy of seven there was only one way to say a thing and that was truthfully.

'I'm goin to look for Mum.'

'Mother?'

She nodded and waited for the whys but he shrugged and asked Butch when they were going riding instead.

'One of the days,' said Butch.

'Tomorrow or the next day?' asked Trip.

'Maybe,' he said.

'Butch isn't very well at the minute,' said Ennor.

'Which one?' Trip demanded.

'Tomorrow, maybe.'

Trip turned to Ennor to tell her he was going riding tomorrow and she wondered if he'd forgotten she was going away, but as they walked back to the trailer he asked if she was going to get Mother to bring her home.

'That's the plan. I'll ask in any case.'

'No harm in askin.'

'Nope.'

They took their time as if both had things they needed to say and Ennor put her hand on his tiny shoulder and pulled him close.

'You'll be all right, won't you, buddy? Just a few days tops, I promise.'

Trip nodded and his copper brown eyes that were like her own flashed amber in the bright white. 'If you promise.'

'And you'll have Butch stay over to look after you.'

'We're goin ridin tomorrow.'

'That's it and there's one more thing you gotta remember in all of this – you can't tell Dad.'

'I know that already. It's cus he'll flip.'

'How'd you know that?'

'Cus he always flips with Mother things.'

Ennor stood with hands on hips and looked at him in disbelief.

'Did I say somethin wrong?'

'No, buddy,' she smiled. 'You said everythin right.'

Ennor sat at the table in the kitchen and ripped the lists from her notebook and tore them into tiny squares. Where she was going there would be no place for them. She would find her mother no matter what it took.

She tossed the bits of paper into the bin and turned on the radio. That way Trip and Dad would think she was about if they woke, and she put on her coat and wellies and hooked the torch from off the peg in the porch and squeezed it a million until the dynamo spun enough sparks to light her way. Outside it had stopped snowing and she asked God to keep it that way and she asked seven times for luck. In the barn the girls were sitting in a steaming clump and they watched Ennor with the usual suspicion, their eyes following her every move and the torchlight as it bounced like a beach ball between them.

'Don't look at me like that,' she whispered and she

told them not to try changing her mind when a couple of them answered back. 'I got concerns bigger than you. Bigger and bigger still.'

Ennor climbed over them to reach the back of the barn and she told them not to bother moving and they didn't.

'It's out here somewhere,' she said. 'Someplace among the crap.' She was looking for an old rucksack she hadn't seen in years. It had belonged to one of the farmhands who used to work the farm in summer, in the days when irrigation ditches needed digging and fences needed fixing, back when Dad could pay for the privilege of hired help. She remembered the rucksack because it was left with her in mind, some travelling lad who moved into the village and didn't need it any more. Maybe he saw something in the young girl, some wild mustang spirit when really she was just showing off.

There was nothing about her but dreaming and the day to day. Wishing and dreaming and counting and praying; four things about Ennor Carne, just about. She climbed the ladder to the loft of 'nothin but more junk' and sat cross-legged on the floor. Most things weren't even boxed and that was fine by her. She pumped the torch until her hand hurt and placed it on the floor beside her.

This kind of rooting and nosing usually made her sentimental but not tonight; tonight she was looking for the destiny rucksack.

She dragged the junk from one side of the space to the other and tied the torch around her neck with an old tie to go hands free. 'Load of rubbish,' she told herself. 'Everythin useless or mouldy or both.'

Standing with hands in pockets she scanned the corners of the loft. There was one last bin bag she hadn't checked and she tore at it until the rucksack fell free and she threw it down into the barn and climbed after it.

Ennor sat on the chair nearest the fire and looked the rucksack over. It was bigger than she remembered, way bigger, and it was heavy with metal tubing crawling up the back like a kiddie's climbing frame. She told herself it was sturdy. Sturdy was good and, if all else failed and the snow kept coming, she could always use it as a sledge.

Closing her eyes she tried to picture herself out on the moor. Walking for real and not just the usual A to B. She wondered if she should be worried, because she wasn't. The world was busted and damned yet Ennor buzzed with big-bang excitement.

She listed the everyday essentials: porridge oats, tea, the everyday pan, matches. What else? Her penknife, tarpaulin for sitting on, warm clothes, a blanket. She'd also bring a pack of playing cards and her notebook for writing, maybe even bring the picture frame, for proof.

She crept about the trailer, finding things and adding them to the rucksack, and when it was full she emptied it on to the kitchen floor and started again.

She knew heavy things went on the bottom because that was common sense, but what if she needed some things more than most? The tarp she'd taken off their miserly woodpile was the most important thing, it was also the heaviest.

She stood at the sink and looked at her reflection in the window and she wetted her hands and scooped them flat against her hair. Butch would arrive soon to go through her plan and although she didn't have one she'd agreed because it was nice to have company besides family in the trailer. She filled and set the kettle ready on the stove and banked the fire to roasting, then sat down. The rucksack sat next to her and she looked at it and sighed. If there were things she'd forgotten, it was too late now. It was packed to bursting and she had no thinking left for it.

The moor and all it had got was out there waiting for her in the dark, a cold rock thing, hard as nails. She got up and went to the airing cupboard in the hall. There was one last thing she needed to bring with her, a 'just in case' thing that she hoped never to use, but with all things upended in the country, something she just couldn't leave without: the shotgun.

CHAPTER THREE

Ennor shifted the heavy rucksack on to her back and shrugged it into place between her shoulder blades. The weight of her world was packed tight into pockets and swung jangling from baler twine and the rifle sat jabbed through the straps of the bag like a yoke.

She walked with purpose despite the uneven weight and didn't dare look back at the trailer once.

Before she left she'd sat Trip down to explain things over and she was honest with him like always. She told him it would only be for a few days and she and Mum would be home for Christmas and when he'd cried she told him he was made of strong Carne stuff and she kissed him and called him 'buddy' one last time.

The snow had stopped falling and despite dense cloud the morning was awake with a sudden clarity that lifted Ennor's spirit to bursting and she made a good pace through the fields towards the track that led to the moor.

She had plans written by Butch and plans written in her mind's eye but a girl used to life's underhand knew plans for travel and actual journey were two very different things.

The one link that would lead her to her mother lived less than five or so miles west and Ennor hoped to reach the cottage before nightfall.

She passed through the kissing gate that marked the end of the farm boundary and hiked up the gradual incline north-west. When she reached the top of the hill she stood in the thick snow-laden ground to settle the urge that grew in the well of her stomach – the urge to look back at the farm one last time before the landscape swallowed it up.

Her father would be calling from his bed around about now, his weak voice breaking to finish her name. Perhaps he'd be wondering the why and the where, perhaps he knew something was up, perhaps he did not. Ennor wanted to turn and say goodbye to something, something she was losing, something she had already lost, but she held off the melancholic fog and reached into her shirt pocket for her tobacco tin, rolled herself a cigarette and moved on.

Ennor Carne told herself there was no room for crying in this new world: it would be the one guarantee she could put in the box stored at the back of her mind labelled 'sure things'. It was a small box, there wasn't much she was sure of to put in it, but the not crying thing and the getting on with things were packed in tight.

When the track she followed leant full-tilt west she looked out at the whitewashed landscape and a bump of excitement bubbled and burst from her insides and pulled at the corners of her mouth with a smile.

The following few days would be hers and hers alone. No chores and no demands to bog her down; these would be her freedom days. She dug her heels into the frozen ground and kept an eye on markers and monuments to stop herself from straying. The standing stones and tin mines she knew so well had become unfamiliar pointers in the snow. The stones wore thick broad hats as high as boxes and skirts that drifted into her path. Ennor felt as if she were being lifted gracefully towards her destination.

Her great-aunt's cottage sat stitched into a tangle of gorse and bracken, as far as she could recall. She and Dad had visited it once when her mother first went missing, but the scramble of texture and colours had stayed with Ennor, and she was sure once she found the cottage she would be on route to finding her mother.

All around her the moor rose higher and the land below melted and broke away like icebergs. She imagined herself setting sail towards unknown territory and fancied herself something other than a dumb kid. She thought about the country crumbling slowly to ruin and wondered if it was as bad as the news made out.

There was a part of her that wanted to see a little of the crazy stuff, find something to prove that she wasn't the only person poor and searching.

She stopped occasionally to study the way the land played out and she painted everything in summer colours to match that in her mind's eye and she counted out the skeletal trees half fallen like matchsticks all higgledy from a box and counted them back in with a nod.

An even number meant God was with her and she continued on her way.

Ennor liked to talk to herself and she raced through the list of things she needed to ask her great-aunt and numbered them one to five. These were her main questions. There would be other questions, but they would be labelled 'spontaneous' and couldn't be numbered.

When the opportunity arose she introduced herself to a hawthorn tree with her hand outstretched and she shook the branch with a firm practised grip.

'You might not remember me.' She smiled. 'But I am your great-niece, Ennor Carne.'

The branch shook her hand and the tree swayed indifference and Ennor moved on.

Question number one was, 'Do you remember me?' Question two a plain, 'How are you?' Three was, 'Do you know where my mother is?' And numbers four and five were, 'Could you tell me?' and 'Can I stay the night?'

She asked the questions in her head and she said

them out loud to feel the words like sweets in her mouth and she moved the sequence and the words about with her tongue, adding new ones for the flavour, before changing everything back.

There was also a set of questions saved for when she met her mother and she kept these quiet and separate from the others so as not to get them all scrambled. She settled her mind squarely on the thought of her missing parent. She recalled the last time she'd seen her she was seven years old, seven years back. Lucky numbers, but not for Ennor. Her mother had been standing with the baby in her arms and crying like often and always, except this time there was something different about her, a streak of defiance and decision that danced in her tawny eyes, replacing resignation.

She must have planned and schemed all summer long before she ran away, pulling the baby from her breast and leaving the only other love apart from God's behind.

Ennor remembered the Christmas Mum was pregnant. Sitting bundled by the fire toasting chestnuts they had foraged in autumn. The Christmas before the baby came, when they were a family of three, a happy trinity.

Despite abandonment Ennor did not resent her. She knew she might seem naive to others but she didn't hate her because her mother had been sick in the head and sick in the soul. She had told Ennor on leaving that only God could save her and one day Ennor would understand. Each day she looked into her beautiful brother's eyes she did not. Every time she made a meal from scraps and emptied the slop she did not. With her dad sick and dying and her brother a kid, and perhaps herself too, she did not understand. But still she didn't resent her, didn't pity either.

She traced the skyline with her finger and the ribbons of cloud knotted and tied together, hanging like heavy bows close to clipping the countryside and they were like nothing Ennor had ever seen. She wondered if she'd seen the last of the snow storms because the clouds looked menacing and she stamped her boots all ways for the patterns in the snow and tiptoed and went wide and looked back at the yellowing swirls like hoof marks.

The route Butch had numbered one she knew like the back of her hand because he had worked it and fiddled it a hundred times last night, but there was another route that stuck in her mind, a rough sketch of maybes, and this was route number two.

Route number one took terrain and variants into consideration and route number two did not. Number one was part track and leant into the moor as if driven by a guiding hand all the way to safety. Number two was a straight line and had no regard for safety but was direct and fast.

Ennor knew, given the time, that one meant getting there sometime tomorrow. Two meant getting there tonight and, despite all the reasoning Butch had given her to stick to his plan and all the promising and everything, the path less travelled meant warmth and a hot meal. It also meant talking about Mum and planning out and doing the list numbering for the next stage of her journey.

A seagull called out to her on the passing wind and she scanned the skewed sky until she spied it and counted it, one, and when it joined its flock she counted the rest in a panic and got only halfway before they dropped from the horizon. A bad sign she chose to ignore and she continued to follow route number two.

Seagulls meant many things to the Cornish. Inland they meant either rain or ploughing and in winter just rain, but in the cold like today seagulls just meant seagulls passing through. Perhaps they were journeying coast to coast, south to north like Ennor. They were the lucky ones: an hour on the wing and they'd arrive, fishing for lunch and whatever else seagulls did.

Every now and then she stopped to adjust the rucksack and each time a little voice told her it was time to eat. Her stomach fisted into a rubber-band ball and her mouth rinsed with the thought of food but this was not the time for weakness. If she was to have any luck on her journey, she'd have to make sacrifices along the way, pretend this was hard even when it tickled her into thinking it was fun.

Simply put, luck was long overdue; it owed her big

time. Ennor believed in it and indulged it and gave it life, helping it to exist by holding tight and loading faith into it like a reusable carrier bag. There would be no hitches or snags on her journey, the snow would not return and she would complete her mission in time for Christmas. If luck was paying up, she'd have it bagged in a heartbeat.

She wished there was a way Butch could have come with her. He wasn't the type for sport and doing, but it would have been fun for the company, a bit of chat to pass the time.

Ennor stopped to survey a granite outcrop of rock that had bubbled into view and she wondered whether to climb it or go around. She imagined Butch whispering for her to take the long way and she smiled and clambered to the top and cleared a circle of the snow to sit.

He had made her a stack of potato cakes and a flask of milky coffee as preparation for her trip into the wilderness and she ate a little and drank some coffee and thanked him and she meant it. She looked up at the sky. The brightness of morning had been rubbed and washed with hues of grey and orange and a slight breeze was picking its way from the north-eastern slopes of the moor.

The rest was welcome, but idle sitting felt awkward to Ennor, her mind raced everyplace wrong.

Bad thoughts rattled her and fear stalked the tor

where she sat. Leaden fear with doubt whistling sense-less through its teeth.

She sipped her coffee and thought about home. If she went at it fast, she'd get back in time for the goodnight and have everyone forgetting she'd ever been gone. Turn the radio on and off and make a proper cup of tea, climb into her bed, bundle up and dream.

Ennor knew in two, maybe three hours the snow would return and she finished off her coffee, cleaned the mug with snow and packed the flask and plastic box of potato cakes back into the rucksack.

She stood up and brushed herself down and swung the pack on to her shoulders, careful of her footing as she climbed down.

With the snow tagging and threatening behind her, she moved on and picked up speed as best she could. The straggling brightness had been eclipsed by thicker cloud and Ennor took to humming to keep her mind from wandering further than each new step she stamped in the snow. She stamped over fear and its nibbling questions and was happy to be moving to keep the chatter at bay.

The afternoon came and went and with its passing came the crossover of time and light that was twilight. Ennor stopped to make a cigarette and she scratched her head and reached inside her coat for the map Butch had given her.

She crouched behind a disgorged stack of granite

blocks and opened the map crossways from the wind and stroked it flat with the palms of her gloved hands, retracing her footsteps from the morning's walk with her fingers. The realisation that she was a little lost dawned on her slowly; her mind had been settling on too many other things to pay attention to the basic detail of this way and that.

Maybe she was enjoying herself more than she should have been. Perhaps Butch was right, she had not thought things through.

Flints of wet snow were dashed by the increasing wind and Ennor resigned herself to the fact that she would have to take shelter until it passed. She replaced the map and dipped her head as she continued on her way, occasionally sharpening her eyes to the horizon in the hope that she might spy a familiar run of farm outbuildings in which to stop.

Darkness came knocking and menacing shadows crept about the moor. The heavy snow built towers out of specks and arched in frozen waterfalls from skeletal trees.

She twisted the cuffs of her coat round her fists and cursed the woollen gloves that scratched between her fingers and she narrowed her eyes to trace a faint outline of trail that led to the gash of a small quarry.

The carefree attitude from earlier had now deserted her and she could feel the choke of tears tightening in her chest like a slow snapping rubber band. The quarry was an ink blot compared to the higher ground and she stumbled as she stepped down, fingering the rock for anything that might resemble a roof for shelter.

Inside the belly of the quarry the void split open to reveal a mountain of thick granite slabs heaped together like fallen cards. Ennor took off her rucksack and stuffed the ridiculous frame into the largest hole.

She lifted her collar to the wind and pulled at her hat until it rested against her eyebrows and wedged herself as far down into the dank crevice as she could without getting stuck.

Ennor thought about the future and she punched out at the darkness in frustration, her fist hitting rock with a thud, and she let the pain warm her like something reassuring brought from home.

The quarry and the moor were silent with the black of night and white of snow and she thought she might go crazy with her heavy breathing bundled into damp clothes and her heart beating out loud and threatening in her ears.

She thought to look at her watch but didn't want to know that it was maybe early teatime and she convinced herself that it was later to shorten the entombed sentence, lighting a cigarette to make good with doll's house light and heat.

She sucked the backwash dregs of tepid coffee through her teeth to make it last and she swished it and sniffed it and was reminded of Butch and his sweetness.

When there was nothing left to smoke but the glowing ember of butt and the flask was tapped dry Ennor settled bony and crushed against the rucksack and sighed. She closed her eyes to the dark and painted her eyelids with a bright blue sky and a sun as warm as embers and she put people she loved into the mix with laughter and dance and everyone summer drunk.

Her mother waltzed into her dream with her sanity intact and happiness for everyone was a given. A sure thing before the decline of little things unnoticed.

Ennor danced with her mother while in her imagination Loretta was singing a whole lot of lovey-dovey; a little girl standing barefoot on her mother's, singing and giggling with the stretch and awkwardness of things.

The merry flight of fantasy soon turned shocking and unbearable and Ennor sat balled and cold and insignificant to the world, the past hanging like an old damp coat hooked to the back of a door, lifeless and rotten. She pressed her hands over her eyes and dug her fingers in close to popping, pinning what couldn't be explained to the back of her mind to stop herself from crying.

A reluctant dawn loped across the moor and tapped at the young girl's shoulder until she woke and opened her eyes to the funnel of grey half-light that split the rock in two.

She lifted her face to the gentle breeze and the salt smell of sea air indicated the wind was now coming from the south and she heard the double drip of melting snow outside.

She stretched her legs as best she could and startled herself with a yawn that ripped her mouth wide with a wild howling echo, then she slid from the shelter and pulled at her rucksack until it dislodged from a snag in the rock and she stood to slap the dirt from her clothes.

Sunlight was sudden and bright through a hundred layers of cloud and the quarry rocks moved with shifting snow. The landscape changed around her and Ennor sat on a corner of rock and pulled the rucksack between her legs and she untied the tin mug from the tubular frame and went and held it beneath a run of melting snow.

When the mug was inch-full she swallowed it down and refilled it and splashed the iced water over her face. She took off her hat and wetted her hair into some kind of tidy, itching at the rib-lines on her forehead with relief.

Her empty stomach turned somersaults and she tried not to think about the last of the potato cakes. Saving them would stave off a 'no food' panic so she could think about other things.

Even so, the flat fried potato nested in her mind and she thought she could smell them as she tied the mug to the frame of the rucksack. She told herself no and, when her stomach wouldn't listen, she shouted it and waited for the quarry to echo its agreement, realising that in that snow hole she would be waiting a long time.

She did star jumps to warm up and jiggled the stiff from her legs until her knees no longer snapped with the cold, then crouched to wiggle the rucksack on to her back.

Outside the quarry Ennor sensed the creeping, coming daylight and she loosened her scarf and folded her hat back into a wide turn on the crown of her head in anticipation.

Today was the first proper day of her adventure and she was determined to forget last night and make good progress. She would get to her great-aunt's in a matter of hours and tomorrow she might even end the day standing at Mum's door.

Ennor pulled the map from her pocket and she held it out of the wind to study and tapped her finger on the creased paper at the shading that represented a quarry. She looked out across the moor with newfound authority, deciding the quarry on the map was the quarry where she'd spent the night.

Map reading was easy, it was useful too and she strode out to kick at slushy heaps of snow with soldier pride as if battling a war she'd already won.

She thought about Dad and Trip without the usual melancholic pull, and imagined them all together at Christmas, not quite a big happy family, but some kind of family of four, equal.

Ennor hoped Trip was coping best he could and she told herself he was fine because anything else would have fear back snapping at her heels.

She made herself think about the potato cakes to take her mind off home. For now her shadow walked in front and this other self gave comfort in the lonely landscape, a silent friend looking out for her, testing the unmarked ground one step at a time.

She knew the sun wouldn't be out for long. The horizon concealed the clouds but she knew they were circling, planning their line of attack. She was in the eye of it.

If she kept to the present, settled on the one foot two foot, things would rattle into place. She sang songs learnt at Sunday school and songs half-eared off the radio and she mashed them together into a continuous stream of lust and condemnation.

Her impromptu entertaining and carrying on turned the moorland foreign the further she walked. Places she would have recognised in summer or on Sunday visiting in better days were nothing to her now. The shadow picked up speed and Ennor followed in obedience. She would walk for two hours and at midday she would stop to eat the remaining potato cakes and light a small fire to heat water for tea.

She walked on through thawing marshland and fell into a labyrinth of trenches that had her stepping in every direction but forward. The smell of rotten vegetation caught at the back of her throat and she coughed and spat into the wind. Following her shadow towards a firm footing, she sat damp to the ground and told her shadow to go on without her. The potato was salty and fat on her lips and she stuffed the potato cakes gone, then licked the paper clean and chewed it like a wad of bubble gum to get the last of it.

Ennor sat back and took out her baccy tin to roll herself a cigarette and as she smoked she blew smoke rings at the splashes of mud that weighted her jeans and stiffened her boots and attempted to pick at the sleeves of her coat that were stitched with nature's barb. She leant back on to her rucksack and clipped her fists beneath her chin. She was lost. Fear crawled up her spine and blew cruel damp words into her ear. She was lost and cold and hungry.

She unfolded the map and scanned the horizon and sighed. There was nothing left to do but take a short cut across to a granite ridge that bumped the yonder skyline, hoping the vantage point would settle her mind on some kind of course.

At the foot of the granite outcrop she shunned the weight from her back. She dug her toes into the rock as she climbed and called out at the wind to catch her when she scrambled to the precarious summit. The moorland stretched out for ever below her, immersed in low licking fog. Ennor turned to look to the south to see the last column of sunlight get snipped by scissoring clouds and she watched the sun's reflections bounce across the cradle of sea, everything sucked of colour and spat out in a smudge.

Ennor knew rain would replace snow and she counted out the time it took. Ten quick-step seconds before huge droplets began to fall from the sky. She hurried to check the diminishing landscape beneath her against the contours of the map that softened in her hands. If there was ever a time for hope, this was it. Faith, hope and courage stood beside her and together they looked out into the wind and together they saw it. A square of stone nestled dark and deep in the valley below; a house, her great-aunt's cottage.

She climbed from the rocks with her heart playing ping-pong in her chest. As she ran, the wet rocks tripped and tricked her and Ennor jumped to keep from stopping, battling forward until the toe of her right boot shunted and wedged itself into a crevice and her left foot skidded by. Head over heels, she fell from the tor and back into the snow and she waited for pain to come and when it did she nodded with congratulation and raised her head to watch the map she had been holding catch in the wind and bellow into a sail, escaping to the sea.

Her ankle was hurt. Just how badly, she didn't know. Part of her wanted to bed down in the window of time that was ignorant bliss and just stay put, but this was it, this was her test, her trial. She felt around in the wet snow for anything that might resemble a stick and her fingers pulled at the dead root of a gorse bush and she wrenched it from the ground. The pain in her ankle made her nauseous and she swallowed to keep the remnants of food from leaving her stomach. She waited for the pain to numb to a fizz and hobbled towards her rucksack and she punched it into a secure holding in the rocks. There was no way in God's name she was carrying that damn thing through the snow. She would have to collect it tomorrow when she was better and she hoped above anything else that her leg wasn't broken because if it was all hope of finding Mum before Christmas would be over and worse was that she might never see Trip again.

Ennor lodged the stick beneath her arm and edged around the tor. Each step had her near to fainting and she cried out a little from the pain. The heavy rain clamped her hat tight to her head and loose hair stuck to her face and fingered her neck in a stranglehold. Everything itched and everything was weighted with water and at times the stick became a paddling oar. Ennor's boots sank into the boggy snow and she yanked her injured leg out of the suck with a hand beneath her thigh. She looked for things to count to keep her mind from going under but the rain had the world blurred and painted wrong. Raindrops filled her eyes and there were times when she thought she might be crying, though there was no way of knowing because everything stung and hurt inside and out.

Ennor hardly knew which direction she was heading but she knew there was no alternative but to keep moving no matter how slow the turn. The weight of the storm felt like a landslide collapsing on top of her. If she stopped, she would weaken and fall. She would be nothing but a dead thing and she counted herself in the ground, one.

The cottage was set in memory's muddle and no place else. A pretty square with sunshine windows and a twist of smoke circling the chimney. She told herself she was nearly there and in reality maybe she was.

Sometimes she closed her eyes and when she opened them was amazed to find she was still walking, the cottage getting closer, vivid. When doubt kidded that maybe she was seeing things and the landscape dipped and altered suddenly she sped up and winced with each painful step. Time slowed and stopped and did not matter until finally she fell against the cottage gate and shouted through the storm, waiting to be heard.

The cottage was not how she remembered it on that rare visit; the overgrown garden had things that looked wrong and so did the dark netted windows.

She unhitched the gate and pushed into the thorny briar, its claws snagging her clothes and stealing her hat like a school bully.

She banged on the door with the crippled stick and bent to call through the letterbox but it was welded shut and she fell back on to the path and cried until her insides were out.

The rain fell in fast, heavy drops and she felt it smother her face and soak into her clothes and she let it puddle her eyes blind and fill her ears deaf.

Ennor Carne was alone in the world and she would die alone. This was her truth, her destiny.

CHAPTER FOUR

The room that Ennor had been assigned was cramped and dark and smelt near enough to her own home.

She looked at the cracks in the ceiling and the curls of flaked plaster that were close to falling. She knew every imperfection as if it were the ceiling in her bedroom. There was not much else in the room besides the bed and the stool where the old lady, who may or may not have been kin, occasionally sat with the medicine or a spoon of tasteless soup.

Through the curtains she could see daylight and she rubbed her wrist and the indent where her watch used to be. She had a bad feeling she'd been in bed some time and she wondered if Christmas had been and gone.

Under the weight of hospital blankets and military coats she stretched out her legs and lifted the covers with her good foot to make a tent for looking and she circled the bad ankle and waited for the pain to come but it didn't.

She guessed the medicine that tasted like earthy bread mould had worked. She sat up next to the window and pulled the damp net curtain around her shoulders like a cape and rubbed the wet from the pane expectantly. The snow that had covered the moor however long ago lay thick and solid on the path and had part melted and refrozen into thin needles of ice that dangled like sugar bells on the jumble of foliage.

It certainly looked like Christmas to Ennor and she called out in a panic because she needed to get going. She looked about the room for her rucksack and shouted for it to be brought and her head banged with sudden exertion.

There was a thump and a draw back of chairs in the room next to hers and a brief thinking silence as the house went stone-cold quiet.

'Hello?' she shouted. 'I need to speak to you.'

Footsteps came to the door and backed away and were followed by the old lady's slipper shuffle, then the door opened.

'What's up, birdy?' the old lady scuffled to the side of the bed and lowered her face close enough that Ennor could smell the sour stench of recent meat on her breath.

'How you feelin?' she cuffed a rough hand over her forehead and up close Ennor could see stranger's eyes.

'Who are you?' she asked.

'You still got a temperature, bird.'

'You're not my great-aunt.'

'Never said I was.'

'What you done to her?'

'Done nothin with nobody besides lookin after you. You're welcome, by the way.'

Ennor wanted to ask about her rucksack. She remembered telling someone something about its whereabouts but details were blurred and then she noticed the old woman was wearing her woollen cardigan.

'Hey, that's mine. You're wearin my cardy.'

The old woman stood at the door and wrapped the cardigan about herself in a snuggle and she gave a little spin, smiled and skipped from the room.

Ennor lay back in the bowed and broken bed and listened to the voices in the other room and the occasional splinters of laughter angered her. She swung her legs out of the bed and placed her feet, one and two, on the filthy wooden floor. They looked silly and white compared to her ruddy rest and she bent to take a good peek at her injury. She peeled back the rag bandage and the herb poultice stuck like dried nappy poo and she ran a finger over the paper-thin skin and pressed.

The swelling had gone down but the area was sore enough to tell her not to keep touching. Her clothes lay in a heap in the corner of the room and she reached for them and was grateful to find that, while not clean, they had been fire dried and cleaved of mud.

Ennor dressed and the cold of whatever time gripped her skin tight like swaddling to her bones and she pulled a small red army coat from the bed and hung it across the shoulders of her own and, bootless, she stepped with consideration for her weak ankle from the room and into the next.

The old woman and a boy about her age sat face in to a roaring fire and when Ennor entered the room they remained fixed to the heat.

'I need my boots,' she said.

There were no other chairs in the room but the two that were occupied and she stood back against the heat for attention and warmth.

'I need my boots,' she said again and she looked at the old woman's feet.

'Take them off,' she shouted. 'Please, I need to get goin.'

The old woman coughed out a splattered laugh and she made a face at the boy. 'Bossy little madam, int she?'

'Please, I'm grateful for your care and all but I got things I need to take care of. Important things.'

'Just like that, is it?' the woman stood up and pushed the chair back against the slate tiles.

'Eat our food and take the only good bed existin and you're off now with no regard.'

She was taller with anger in her, a good head and shoulders taller than Ennor's great-aunt from what she could recall.

'I got regard and I got grateful too. Dint I just say as much?' She pulled herself to full height but felt tinier than ever without her boots. 'Please, you can keep the cardy, but I need me boots.'

The old woman laughed wet spittle into her face and she sat back down with a humph and the boy laughed too. 'Only kiddin, birdy. Tell her, Rabbit, only kiddin, int I?'

The boy nodded at Ennor and as he smiled she saw two long thick teeth sticking crazy from his gums.

'Only keepin um warm for you, int I? Ready for the get go, birdy bird.' She held each foot in turn across her lap and unlaced the boots with melancholic eyes and Ennor could see she really liked them. She watched as she kicked them into the grate and stretched her sticky bare feet towards the fire.

'Whatever, don't matter. Your socks are hangin by the back door in the kitchen. Rabbit's bin usin um for double gloves, int you, boy?' The woman ordered him to fetch the socks and she beckoned Ennor to sit in the vacated chair.

'Long time since we got visitors, see? Things get a little lonely out here on the moor. Only lost souls like yours and farm folk wantin me gorse wine. Drives men crazy but it's warmer than a fat slag, or so they tell me.'

Rabbit appeared with the socks and Ennor put them on and held her feet to the flames until roasting.

'How long have I been here?' she asked the woman.

'Not long.'

'How long?'

'Couple days, couple nights. Not long.'

'Damn, I gotta go.' She pulled on her clammy boots.

'So who's they in the photo, bird?'

Ennor looked up.

'Don't worry. Rabbit's packed the bag back the way he found it out in the snow. Strange place to leave your belongins by all accounts.'

"Cept the cardigan,' said Ennor and she laced the boots loose and stood and tested her full weight on the ankle.

'Only I seem to recognise them from someplace, someplace long past. Them faces, there's somethin there.'

Ennor steadied herself with a hand on the back of the chair and she looked long and hard at the woman, Butch's words about her being gullible ringing ding-dong in her ears.

'Knew your great-aunt too. Dint live but a stone toss away. Sad when she passed, she was one of me best customers.'

'Nana Burley?' asked Ennor.

'Poor old Nana. Had a cottage much like this un, dint she?'

Ennor nodded but she was unsure of which way lies and truth were tied and what she herself had said with the mouldy wine medicine that was probably clouding her memory.

'This is crazy, int it? Me knowin Nana Burley and you half Burley yourself, turnin to me door in your hour of need?'

Ennor scratched her head and she found herself sitting back by the fire when she really wanted to leave and she asked what the woman knew about the people in the photo.

'Well, let me think, it's been a long time but I recognise the girl all right. She visited Nana once or twice.'

Ennor sighed and leant into the chair. She was not sure if the woman knew her mother or not and the giddy curl of hunger twisting in her stomach had her head as light as a lantern.

'Got soup on the stove.' The old woman nodded as if reading her mind. 'You'll stay for some soup, won't you? Maybe I'll even tell you the quickest step cross the moor to find that mother of yours.'

'I told you bout that?' asked Ennor.

'No. Rabbit read it from that notebook in your bag. We've bin havin a right laugh, int we, boy?' she sat forward and grinned. 'Just teasin you, girl. Where's your humour?'

'You pullin me bout my mother? Tell me honest cus I int got the time.'

'Course not. Her name's Eleanor, int it? Don't say that in your notebook now, does it?'

Ennor shrugged. She couldn't remember much of anything. 'I lost my map,' she said. 'Lost me map and now I'm lost meself.'

'Bless.' The old woman smiled. 'Now you eat. Let's see if I can't get you back on track.'

Ennor supped at the unidentifiable soup and she listened to the old woman as she walked them across the moor, sketching everything into her mind's eye and scratching notes with her pen to make sense.

The woman sat low and heavy in her chair and with eyes half closed she visualised everything in detail and sometimes she smiled and pointed out things of interest to Ennor as if she were part of the memory.

'Not far now. Brown Willy just to our right, see it, girl? Always keep it to your right, biggest tor on the moor, you keep him in sight and you won't go wrong.'

The woman fell silent and Ennor sat forward in anticipation. 'What is it?' she asked.

Suddenly a magpie slammed into the front-room window with a thump, causing them to jump and Rabbit got off the floor to go outside to look.

'There it is, good-sized house on all accounts, small village tip-top north of the northmoor. What's it name? Treburdon, I think, and there's that yellow door. That's the house you want.'

Ennor looked at the old woman and asked her how she knew all this.

'Your nana told me.'

'Really?'

The woman shrugged.

'And you int pullin me?'

'Why would I do that, birdy?'

Ennor thanked her because maybe she really was telling the truth and if she was she didn't want to seem rude. She underlined the words 'Treburdon' and 'yellow door' and closed her notebook.

The front door slammed and Rabbit stood grinning with the magpie swinging and its feet sticking like pegs through his fingers.

'That's bad luck,' Ennor and the old woman said in unison.

'I'm gonna stuff it.' The boy grinned and he ran to the kitchen with a squeal.

'Please excuse the kid. He's fifteen but a life lived out on the moor with nobody but his old gran has him turned backwards a little.'

Ennor wondered about the rest of his family but before she could open her mouth the old woman told her they were dead.

'All of um dead,' she repeated. 'In the ground one way or the other, burnt or bones, but it don't really matter, does it?' She offered up more soup but Ennor declined. The sound of knives chopping in the kitchen and the talk of death had turned her off it.

'I gotta get goin, while it's still day.' She stood and went to take off the red coat and was told to keep it like a swap shop and she thanked the woman for everything and let her put the rucksack on to her back and fuss her a little.

'Got your hat here somewhere. Found it danglin in the bushes like a poor dead thing.' She took Ennor's hat from a nail in the back of the door and tucked her hair tight and bulbous into it.

'Don't forget us now you hear, birdy bird? Come back knockin when you're passin. One or other is always here.' She called Rabbit out from the kitchen and they stood and waved her from the house like long-losts and then from the path and finally from the ridged horizon.

Ennor stopped once to wave and then twice and when her path was close to dipping from view she waved a third and final time and shouted thank you into the wind towards them.

Things were going to start moving now. Ennor knew she was a day away from finding Mum and then they would be home and dry for Christmas.

The sky was bright and the sun lay low and blinding on the horizon, barely up, almost down. Ennor looked at the time and she stopped to push up her sleeve. 'Damn,' she shouted. The old woman had stolen her watch and she would now have to make estimates by this and that and by the rare occasions the sun appeared because there was no time for backtracking. She stood and looked about her and up at the flat bright sky and guessed at the time being somewhere around two o'clock. She had two hours of daylight walking time ahead of her before stopping to set up camp.

She narrowed her eyes to the smear of sun and followed its arc to where she thought it might fall, that was west. She would keep the sun sitting on her left shoulder as she headed north and when it was elbow high it would be time to stop.

Ennor counted her steps to make up a minute and then an hour and by hour number two the sun had set someplace other than her guessing and the cold that replaced it slapped her clean across the face. She tried to ignore it because she liked plans to go her way but it was later than she had first thought and dark was racing towards her like a hit-and-run.

Ennor looked about for anything that might resemble a shelter and she walked close to blind with the dynamo torch crunching and stalling in her hand until she saw the familiar turned and bundled wall of a cairn. She went to it with a whoop and threw down her rucksack and laid her square of tarpaulin across the damp ground.

Outside darkness hammered down on her as fast as she could spy twigs for lighting and she realised she would not even have a small fire to look at tonight let alone to cook, and she returned to the stone hut defeated and sat with the dumpy coat heavy across her knees and told herself red was a lucky colour despite it sitting in the unlucky black of night.

Through the half-tumbled doorway Ennor thought she saw movement of light and she rubbed her eyes to check if she was seeing things and watched as the swish of colour and warmth crawled up on her.

'Who's that?' she shouted. 'Got a shotgun here.' She picked up the gun and held it in the pool of light, the realisation that she hadn't loaded it dawning on her slowly, but it was too late.

'Don't shoot bunny rabbits, do you?' laughed the light.

'Who's that?'

'It's me, silly. It's Rabbit.' He flicked the beam on to his own face and the shadow complete with horror fangs pinned itself to the cairn wall.

'What the hell – followed me, did you?'

Rabbit continued to laugh. 'Mother told me to come lookin so I come lookin. Knew you wouldn't get far. Forgot to pack you a meal and all. Here, hold this.'

He passed her the torch and swung a bag off his shoulder and a bundle of sticks tied up in rope.

'Thought she was your grandmother.'

'She is.'

'And your mother?'

Rabbit shrugged in the torchlight. 'I dunno.'

Ennor didn't like him and didn't much want him to stay but she was intrigued as to what was in the bag and she asked him.

'Spuds and meat.'

She kept the light gripped on him. He had a smile that said one thing and eyes that said another.

'You my babysitter then?' she asked.

'Just goin to light you a fire is all. Mother would never forgive herself if she heard you'd gone hungry or cold or worse.' He looked her over and smiled and told her that was all it was.

When the fire was lit and growing Rabbit set about preparing the meat and he lifted it lovingly from the fold of newspaper it had been placed and speared it with two butcher's hooks he produced from his bag.

Ennor asked what meat it was and he didn't know and she asked if he'd brought anything to drink and he had – the dreaded gorse wine.

'You like that stuff?'

'Not much.'

'Why'd you bring it?'

'Mother made me.'

'Why?'

He ignored her and continued to tend the fire and as it grew it decorated the cairn walls in splashes of orange and pinched her cheeks into a hot flush.

The meat cooked slowly on a stick looped high above the flames and the smell was loaded with memories of her home kitchen and her mouth watered in anticipation. She felt the heaviness of thought and worry fall from her and she remembered her manners enough to thank the boy for the fire and the meat and she said she supposed he could stay to eat for one hour tops.

Rabbit sat at the edge of the tarpaulin and he leant on one knee to worry the fire or turn the meat occasionally and his face was flat and ungiving like a soft-faced doll.

'You got a dad?' Ennor asked.

'Nope.'

'Got anyone else besides?'

'Not that I know of.' He pulled his bag into his lap and pulled out the bottle of wine and asked if she had a cup.

Ennor untied her metal mug from the frame of the rucksack and put it on the floor and let him pour the cloudy liquid to the brim.

'You got parents?' he asked.

'Bit of both.'

'That don't sound right.'

'I got a dad but he's sick and a mother but you know bout that.'

'You think you'll find her?'

'I'm sure of it. Tomorrow, defo.'

'How's your dad sick?'

'He's got cancer in the lungs but he's sick with drugs.' She took her baccy tin from her pocket and rolled two cigarettes and passed one to him.

Rabbit thanked her and he asked her if her father had ever worked and what at.

'Farmer all his life and before probably.' She nodded and took a too-big gulp of the wine and swallowed it down hard.

'So you got your own farm? Land and everythin?'

'Not no more. Foot-and-mouth was the start of that and now with times tough and breakin and all . . .'

Rabbit nodded in agreement 'No jobs. No nothin.'

'Strikes,' added Ennor.

'No job prospects. What we sposed to do after school?'

'I don't go no school.'

'Exactly, nor do I.'

'All closed in any case.'

Ennor finished her drink while Rabbit drank from the bottle and they both nodded into the fire like old souls chewing over the fat.

'Nice gun you got there. Saw it back at the cottage.'

Ennor reached for the double barrel and passed it to him 'Don't worry it int loaded. Only a fool would point a loaded gun.'

Rabbit smiled as he balanced the rifle in the palms of his hands and he felt the weight of it. 'Looks heavier than it is. What you killed with it?'

Ennor shrugged. 'Tin cans and water bottles mostly but I'm keepin my options open.'

She laughed and Rabbit joined her and his teeth glowed fluorescent and menacing in the firelight.

'Why you called Rabbit?' she asked.

'Cus when I was a baby I was always jumpin bout like a bunny.' He jammed the gun to his shoulder and aimed it at the cooking meat and then at Ennor when she asked him his real name.

'I told you. Rabbit.' He closed one eye and traced the barrel from her face to her chest and back.

'How old are you?' he asked.

'Old enough to have a gun.' She grabbed the barrel and twisted it from his grip. 'Stop messin.'

'Just askin your age.'

'Why?'

'Just to ask.'

'I'm fourteen.'

'You look older.'

'Well I int.'

'Got a mouth on you for a fourteen-year-old girly, int you?'

Ennor finished her second drink. Her head lifted and spun a little way out and away from her and she ignored it and waved her mug at the boy for a top-up.

The alcohol set a fire in her belly that carried her close to sleeping and she smiled at the meat and at the fire and maybe she even smiled at the boy with a look that was mistook for saying something more than just smiling.

The heat and the wine smelted Ennor's event recollection into molten mush and she could not fasten one link of the chain to the next. One minute she was sitting with contentment in her lap and the next she was running hard and fast. She ran until she thought her lungs might rip apart and her weak ankle swelled tight and bloodless in her boot and as she fell she palmed a bullet from her pocket, loaded the gun and pointed it into the dark ether but nobody came. She shouted for the boy to go ahead and try it and see what he got but there was no sound but the painful cry of a fox transporting its hunger across the moor.

She got to her feet and held the gun so tight she thought her fingers might bust through it and she pulled back the hammer and stood, trigger ready.

She could see the glowing orb of the cairn in the distance and the smoke still idling against the night breeze and she called out and kept calling as she turned and made her approach.

There was a part of her that wanted to shout some kind of apology but she knew this was just a deep-down habit girls were accustomed to doing through bullying and embarrassment so she called out his name and nothing more.

When she neared the cairn she shouted a reminder that she had the gun and it was loaded twice and she tapped the metal against the stone wall.

'You in there, Rabbit boy? Better be sittin on your grubby little hands, I'd say.' Her voice was small and it wavered slightly but she continued to talk and she asked him to push her rucksack through the opening if he knew what was good for him.

She waited to see movement in the dying firelight and listened and waited some more.

A thought passed over her that maybe he had

scampered back to the cottage and she loosened a little and thought briefly of the meat and hoped she hadn't kicked it over in the scuffle.

She told whoever was or wasn't sitting in the stone hut that she was coming in and she one-stepped into the opening. The boy was still there and she stood over him and her shadow crushed him to the ground.

Blood from his head had squiggled into a thin string line down his face and had knotted around his neck and his teeth peeped loosely from his mouth.

'Rabbit?' Ennor poked him with her boot and when he didn't turn she kicked him hard in the hope of some movement because him not moving was bad.

'Rabbit, you dead?' She put the gun to the ground and bent to listen for breathing.

'I won't touch you,' she shouted. 'I won't get into trouble for your crazies.'

She pulled the tarp from the ground and rolled it into her rucksack and put on her gloves so she could settle the wine bottle into his lap without leaving clues and cleared all trace of herself.

Ennor Carne's destiny had led all roads to this. A dead carrion boy left to rot on the snow-blown moor.

The journey would now take her deep into the night to escape the scene and she walked with the meat in one hand and the torch cranked in the other and the gun hanging prepared and ready from its strap across her chest.

Darkness stayed with her for what seemed like for ever and the cold tightened her bones with such breaking force she was glad to be walking because if she stopped she would die.

She walked blind but for the small puddle of light that she stepped into and into and into. The moor beyond the puddle was an evil being standing and watching, its ancient eyes fixed on her, and the fear snapping, urging her to keep going round in circles, laughing her mad.

Ennor wished she hadn't left home in the first place and she didn't care if God heard and she shouted at him that if he was listening to please return her from this hell-wheel she was treading.

CHAPTER FIVE

In the desperate morning light Ennor stopped to smoke a cigarette and she watched a family of moorland ponies sketch silhouettes on to the horizon and move gracefully like oil riding water.

She wondered if this was a sign of hope or impending doom and as they passed she saw their bellies bloated with hunger and the bone-impaled flesh of their hindquarters. She looked down at her cigarette and fingered the lean tobacco strands in her tin and she took her time with the one she smoked and made it last down to her fingertips.

The ponies edged a little closer and she counted them and wondered if they remembered the recent past when folks leisured out on the moor and kids fed them ice cream and caressed them like pets.

She put away her baccy tin and surveyed her surroundings and wondered if she should change her path any which way from the one she was on. What if the boy was found with a hit to his head in the shape of a double barrel? What if the old woman got on board with her clever tongue and the police got involved? What then?

The whole county out hunting and the news headlines wondering how things had got so bad, children murdering children, whatever next? She was a fugitive now, a murdering fugitive.

Throughout the morning Ennor occupied herself by spying bits of wood that peeped through the frozen snow and she tied them into a bundle with the rope Rabbit had used. Her head still swam from the gorse wine and she promised herself a pan of tea heated on a fire of her own soon enough.

The collected wood was nothing but a few damp sticks and she eyed each patch of shadow that stretched across the high looped plains ahead for anything resembling trees. The search paid off when, in a sprawling cut of valley, she saw the green-white canopy of a pine forest.

Ennor knew forests were dangerous places; the hostile forestry commission protected them from theft and she made sure to step just once past the boundary to scan for fallen limbs.

Her ankle throbbed and occasionally buckled when she bent a certain way and she kept herself going with thoughts of warm fire and hot tea.

She hauled what wood she could manage far enough away from the forest to not be seen and dug a snow circle with her boot, lighting some of the dry gorse she carried in her shirt pocket and feeding the fire in an orderly manner until it was big and smiling and she smiled back.

Snow was boiled to water and then to tea and she sat on the tarp and savoured it and thought about the boy with his rude hands and his teeth snipping at her flesh like a wild thing and the strength in her bones weakened to a brittle snap and she thought she might sink down into the snow and peat earth and never be found.

Tears bubbled in her eyes and ran into the corners of her mouth. She licked them away and washed the salt down with the tea and lay close and tangled to the fire and closed her eyes to the rising dawn.

Sleep came in an instant and the young girl clung to this other world that was safe and familiar and she pulled the stillness into a place of covered thoughtlessness.

In the passing hours while she slept the sun came and went and with its passing it pulled a drag of heavy cloud from the east which held a new kind of darkness.

Ennor woke with a start and she called out into the abyss that was isolation. The fire was long gone and tiny flakes of ice caught on the wind and landed on her face. The snow had returned.

Fast as a bullet she packed up her few belongings and

chased the path she'd made crossways to the valley and towards the forest for shelter.

Beneath the canopy of guarding trees Ennor felt as if she were among friends and she caught her fingertips on the tall trunks as she idled. The smell of rotting pine needles fixed in her throat and smelt like funny foreign tea and she pulled fresh needles from a lower bough and put them in her coat pocket for when teabags became history.

At first the snow did not come into the forest and it was as if another set of laws ruled the place, something set in the granite shift of stone beneath the light-bounced surface.

She took out her notebook and followed the winding route of words she'd written and forests were written here and there and everywhere with confusion and she snapped the book shut. All she could see was an imprint of the yellow door that would lead to Mum.

As Ennor walked the forest came to life with whistles from its duelling boughs and she thought she heard music and smiled and marvelled at the trees and the wind and perhaps the brilliance of her imagination.

The comforting music became louder as she walked and, further still, voices joined the music and the raucous singing threatened to lift the canopy of trees clean off the ground.

Ennor stopped stony dead and she turned an ear to the sound and stared hard and fearless into the fading light. She squinted at things that weren't there and crouched to the ground the way a wild animal might, her ear still cocked against the noise of trees for better listening.

The flicker of light was occasional and jagged, turning off when movement eclipsed it with dancing shadows, erratic flicker-book acrobatics that nobody could see but Ennor. She rubbed her eyes and looked again and her instinct was to run but the fire and scent of happiness hooked her closer and she sat huddled in the dark shadow of the trees and watched the colourful strangers. The music fattened her ears until she was full to the brim with sugary pleasure and she dropped mindless into the exotic dream.

'You dead?'

Ennor closed her eyes to the early morning rise and hoped the voice was in her imagination.

'Hey, I'm talkin to you.'

A sharp kick against her shin made Ennor lurch forward and she opened her eyes to a pair of split and restitched biker boots.

'That hurt.'

'It was meant to. Good to see you alive and not the other. Thought I'd have to spear you and roast you cross the fire.'

Ennor sat up and rubbed her leg as she looked at the dark-eyed girl squatting beside her.

'You're not a spy, are you?'

Ennor hugged her rucksack into her arms away from the girl.

'Leave me alone.'

'Why the hell? You're on *my* property. What you got in your precious big bag?'

'Nothin, I gotta go.'

'That's a whole lot of nothin.' The girl started to laugh and she told Ennor she'd have to bring her in on account that she was trespassing. When she stood up straight, Ennor noticed she was a way big girl and not with fat but big with muscle and bone.

Ennor gathered up her blanket and tied her boots as fast as she was able because the girl was everything that meant trouble and more.

'Don't worry, I int gonna steal your crap. Not just yet anyway, hell.'

She sat down on the snow beside Ennor and was close enough for malice if she tried to run.

'You see a gypsy girl and what you think? You think criminal intent.'

'Dint say that.'

'You don't have to say somethin to think it.'

Ennor prepared herself for some shape of a beating and she asked God if he was punishing her for killing the boy. She clenched her teeth to a bite and counted seconds. One, two, three . . .

'I'm Sunshine.' The girl slapped her hands to Ennor's

cheeks and searched her eyes for fear and she gave her chin a little pinch and laughed. 'Pleased to meet you. My friends call me Sonny and so can you for starters but madden me and we're back to Sunshine and a whole lot of whip-ass.'

Ennor told the girl her name and Sonny laughed some more and got up again and headed towards last night's fire and shouted for Ennor to follow if she was hungry.

'Where we goin?'

'To meet the others. You're mine now.'

Ennor followed the girl out of the forest and past the smoking embers and she shouted that she really had to be on her way.

As they walked through the camp the gypsy girl shouted to everyone who might be listening that they had a visitor and she spat out Ennor's name like it was poison.

Some faces looked up from their doings but most did not. Ennor smiled just in case but nobody paid her much attention.

She looked skyward and a lone magpie caught her eye and she counted it, one, as it flew against the snow clouds and settled on the roof of one of the trailers.

'That's bad luck.'

'What is?'

'That magpie.'

'It's just a dumb bird. There int no such thing as luck and bad luck. Nobody ever tell you that?'

Sonny led her to a stack of upturned crates that circled another smouldering fire and told her to sit.

'What if I don't?'

Sonny laughed and shook her head to indicate she thought her crazy and she set about refuelling the fire with pine branches that were stored beneath a plastic sheet.

Sonny sat back and nodded into the flames with a satisfying grin. 'You like coffee? I could murder a cup of coffee.'

Ennor nodded.

'Well that's tough for the both of us cus all we got is tea.'

She disappeared into the trailer with the magpie glaring down from the roof and Ennor took a moment to take in the higgledy camp.

Some of the trailers were without wheels and bracken had fingered its way into hub spirals and cracks and holes where things used to be useful out on the road.

Paths had been railroaded through the snow to connect the homes to where Ennor sat. The surplus snow was banked into ice walls for both privacy and orderly living.

She reckoned people had been settled there a long time. They had grown into the fabric of the moor as if patchworked into place with remnants of a forgotten land.

Their lives looked as though they hadn't changed in for ever and the end of the world had not hit them because they were self-sufficient and lived close enough to poverty in any case. Like Ennor they didn't have so far to fall and there was comfort in that.

Sonny appeared behind her and she splashed a mug of tea into her lap and sat with a bounce on the crate beside her.

'My dad wants to know if you're from the fascist forestry commission, one of their kids or somethin.'

The girl stared at Ennor. Her skin and eyes and hair were like Ennor's own only darker, and her accent thicker with a hundred other accents mixed and spiced within.

'Cat chewin on your tongue?' she asked.

'No.'

'No what?'

'No I'm not with the forestry and there's no cat eatin my tongue.' She gulped at the tea and it was sweet and strong and tasted like the fruitcake once made backalong.

'My dad thinks you're a spy.'

'Well if I see him, I'll tell him I int.'

'Dad?' Sonny shouted 'The forestry spy wants to talk to you.'

'Not got time for your games right now, girl,' he shouted from inside the trailer and Ennor couldn't help herself and started to laugh.

'Lucky for you,' Sonny snapped. 'Personally I think

you're guilty in some way all right. Like you got somethin to hide.'

Ennor glanced at the woodpile and Sonny followed her look.

'That's all found wood sittin there, so mind you don't think otherwise.'

'I'm not. Just lookin round.'

They drank their tea and looked about and into the fire and Sonny peppered Ennor with friendly fire questions and with every answer given she laughed and declared it nonsense.

'No way you out on a nature walk. Got a lump on your back like a snail movin home. I think you're a pathological liar, is what I think. A regular bar of fruit and nut.'

Ennor didn't know what 'pathological' meant and wasn't about to get into an argument over it and she told the girl to believe what she wanted.

'I gotta go in any case.' She drank the tea down fast, then flicked the tea leaves into the fire and set the mug down on the crate where she'd been sitting.

'No you int. Where to?'

'What's it to you?'

'You'll miss the party tonight.' She got up to block Ennor's path and the look on her face suggested a fight hug mix-match.

'Looked like a good enough party you had here last night.'

'That was impromptu. Today is the shortest day party,

the twenty-first. The proper one.' She put her hands on her hips and looked Ennor up and down. 'There's a storm comin back, worse than before, they say.'

Ennor thought about the storm and she counted out the four days remaining. Four days to find Mum and get back to Dad and Trip. She looked at the girl with the non-stop chat.

'What?' she said.

'I said even spies have one day off occasionally. You hungry?'

Ennor shrugged. 'A little.'

'I got Coco Pops. You like Coco Pops?'

'Never had um.'

'They're mine. I nicked a box from the village shop before the wire mesh went up, hell.'

She grabbed Ennor's hand and pulled her towards the trailer and into the kitchen.

'Wow,' said Ennor.

'What?'

'It's like a proper kitchen. Like in a house, I mean.'

'Of course it is. Well it would be if we had the gas to work anythin. Sit down, would you?'

Sonny stomped about the kitchen opening and closing cupboard doors. Ennor sat quiet and rocking and secretly coveting the full-size cooker and the washing machine alongside it.

'I do all the washin by hand.'

'What's that?'

'At home I do all the washin by hand.'

'The dishes?'

'No the clothes. Out the back of our trailer we got an old tin bath. I do it there.'

Sonny laughed and pushed a huge bowl of cereal on to the table. 'Milk's fresh from the goat, none of your shop-bought swill.'

'You got cows too?'

'Nope.' Sonny sat across from her and watched her eat with the excitement that a new toy brought, excitement and devilment gleaming in her eyes.

'We got cows. Used to have Simmentals but Dad lost those to foot-and-mouth and now we got a half-dozen Friesians.'

Sonny nodded and made a face to pretend she was interested while indicating she wasn't in the least. 'Foot-and-mouth was a bummer. There were fires all cross the moor. Mountains of cows with their feet pokin up and out like sticks. We had to keep movin sites to keep from the stench.' She sat back and smiled at her new friend and Ennor thought it was her, if anyone, who was crazy.

'Enjoyin the Coco Pops? The best, int they?'

Ennor nodded.

'Well don't go wild after um, hellfire.'

'They're nice, *really*.'

'They are, int they? That's the last of um. I'll have to go shoppin someplace else after Christmas.'

'What village you go to?'

'Minions.'

'Don't they recognise you?'

'Ha, now that's the fun of it. Go in disguise, don't I. Got wigs and hats and all sorts. You can come with me next time if you're that intrigued.'

'So you're the spy.'

They both laughed and Ennor finished the cereal and drank the chocolate milk from the bowl and when she had finished she wiped her finger around it to mop up every last drop.

'That's it, girl. Get it down you.'

The two girls sat steady and looked at each other with suspicious curiosity and it was Ennor's turn to ask the questions.

'How old are you?'

'Fourteen.' She smiled.

'You don't look fourteen.'

'What can I say? I'm mature for my age unlike some. Next question.'

Ennor tried to think of something clever to ask because the girl thought her stupid and green. 'Have you always travelled?'

'What kind of a question is that? I'm a gypsy, int I?'

'Some of your trailers don't look like they seen tarmac in a while.'

'Well they int my trailer. What else you got?'

'Any brothers and sisters?'

'Nope.'

'You go to school?'

'Borin, nope.'

'Ever bin another country?'

Sonny thought for a minute. 'No but I'm plannin on it, once my career takes off. You?'

'I've never bin cross the bridge.'

'Never bin out of Cornwall? Hell.' Sonny started to laugh and she held her sides for added effect. 'Call the doctor. Gonna bust a gut here,' she screamed.

Ennor shifted in her seat and decided she wanted to get going. She wondered how to say it without the girl bullying her to stay.

'What career you plannin? World's on the brink or dint you notice?'

'Bare knuckle fightin. Look at these.' She smacked her hands down on the table and Ennor leant forward to look at her scabs and scars. 'Want a demo?'

Ennor shook her head. 'What's the money like?'

'Good. Just cockfightin with kids really.'

'Who d'you fight?'

'Townies, travellers, used to fight emmets till they stopped comin and I fight boys as well as girls. I int no baby.'

Ennor was unexpectedly impressed and she found herself saying as much and she swallowed what she was going to say about leaving back down into her belly.

The girl scared her as it was and she was now showing off her arm muscles.

'What you think of these?'

'Nice.'

'Nice? Is that all the word you got?'

'No. I've also got thank you and goodbye.'

'Well that's just great. After you troughed the last of me Pops.'

'You gave um to me.'

'Dint hear you complainin.' She got up and settled herself into a wide stance and was about to say more when a woman's voice from elsewhere in the trailer shouted for Sonny to keep the noise down because they were filming.

'Filmin what?' asked Ennor.

'A film. Don't mind um. Most days there's somethin or other goin on. Where'd you think this fancy kitchen come from?'

Ennor got up and she put the empty bowl and spoon into the sink. 'How'd they let you fight?'

'It's all money, int it? Don't worry, they make a pretty penny off me out on the ropes. I'll teach you some moves if you want.'

'I really got to get goin. Got to get somewhere and back before Christmas.'

'Where?'

'I can't say.'

'Secret, is it? You know my life story. All I know bout you is cows and not much else besides.'

'I don't know where I'm goin exactly.'

Sonny shrugged. 'So how do you know where you're goin if you don't know where you're goin? Don't go yet. We're havin fun, int we? I could teach you to wrestle, self-defence and all that, and we got the party tonight.'

Ennor was under the impression that there hadn't been much jollity at all and she asked why she wanted her to stay.

'Are you kiddin? Hell, look at this place. It's Boresville with a capital bore.'

Ennor went outside and lifted her rucksack up on to one of the crates. She wanted to go and she wanted to stay just the same. The camp swung an invisible cape around her shoulders that was safe and warm, a womb. She thought of Mum. 'I have to go.'

'Don't say that. Stay for the party, we'll get up to pranks and all sorts. Please?'

Ennor thought the idea of doing things for the sake of it was strange and wasteful in time and purpose, but she was fourteen and could count fun times on the fingers of just one hand.

'Well?' asked Sonny. 'Only I int got all day.'

'OK. I'll stay. For one night and that's it and I've got to get up early in the mornin.'

'I know,' Sonny laughed. 'You gotta get somewhere and back before sundown or somethin. We'll go nick some booze from the other trailers later.'

She threw Ennor's rucksack into the door of her

bedroom and told her to follow and not to worry about anyone because they were either busy or sleeping.

'You gotta help me out.'

'Why?' asked Ennor.

'I'm in a fix. Bin given the task of settin traps all over the place and I can't remember where I put the buggers.'

'What's that got to do with me?'

'You want to eat tonight, don't you?'

Ennor shrugged. 'I guess. What you usually catch?'

'Nothin,' she laughed. 'This is my first time. I begged Dad to give me somethin worthy to do and now can't remember where I put um. Not all of um anyway.'

'That's dangerous. Could catch a kid, maim um even.'

'Know that, don't I? Hell, I'm lookin for support here.'

Ennor said she'd help Sonny find the traps. The camp was a safe hole in which to hide for a day and night, a place the police would hopefully avoid to keep the peace. She could forget about the boy, if only for a little while.

'Come on, girl,' shouted Sonny as she set off down the track. 'We gotta do this while it's light, you know.'

Ennor ran alongside her and the faster she went the more the snow clumped to her feet and stumped her in her tracks.

'Where d'you think you put um?' she asked.

'Mostly in the forest but, hell, maybe I got carried away a little. I remember thinkin and plottin all sorts of ways.'

'How many you put out?'

Sonny shrugged. 'Ten of um, roundabout.'

'Ten? What they look like, the traps.'

'You a farm girl and you don't know what traps look like?'

'I know they're all evil and snappin, but there's all kinds, int there?'

'How the hell do I know? You ask some dumb uns, don't you?'

Ennor looked across at Sonny and shook her head. There was something scary and something striking about her, the way she looked and the way she spoke, with arrogance and swagger kicking out from under her badly fitting clothes.

They entered the forest from a low split in the track and it was a clamber to get to the ridge without sliding backwards. Ennor wanted to ask why they hadn't just walked through the woods by the camp and when she fell headlong and frozen into the snow for the third time she shouted out the question.

'Why d'you think?' asked Sonny.

Ennor lay on her back and she stared up at the nothing sky. 'Surprise me.'

'Cus this is where I put the first one. I remember this one.'

Ennor rolled on to her side and got to her feet. 'Let's go back to camp.'

'Hell, you got a right moan runnin through you.

Where's your sense of fun? You're like an old bird squabblin and squallin. Now come on.'

The forest was familiar to Ennor from wandering through it yesterday, but only in the way of smell and form and the way it made her feel. The pine trees in this part of the forest were freakish tall and their trunks were thick and good for hugging. Living, breathing things, they had even guided her to the gypsy camp last night, she believed that.

The girl up ahead was going on and roundabout, her mouth beaking like a baby bird and her eyes bursting with all the things she wished and thought she'd seen. The world to Sonny was a sudden pleasant surprise, a constant revelation.

To Ennor it was a rope-tie of let-downs, knot upon knot of confusion and restraint and fear.

She could see the boy's bludgeoned head everywhere she looked. She could see his face etched in the pleats of tree bark and it merged with her dad's and she imagined him dead the same.

'You listenin to anythin I say?'

'Course.'

'What then? What I just say?'

'You were sayin bout the traps.'

'What about the traps?'

'Bout them bein well hidden for a reason.'

Sonny stood facing her and she jammed her hands on to her hips. 'That's a lucky guess.'

Ennor smiled. 'See I was listenin.' She wasn't.

They walked further into the forest and Sonny screamed when she saw her own handiwork. She fell to her knees and was careful to dismantle the wigwam of sticks and pine fronds that disguised the trap.

'Anythin?' asked Ennor.

'Shush.'

'Why shush? It's either dead or int nothin there. Which is it?'

'Nothin there, hell.'

Ennor crouched beside her and looked into the trap. 'Looks like somethin got the bit of meat.'

'No they dint.'

'How'd you know?'

'Cus there weren't any, I forgot.' She sat back on her haunches. 'That's what I was sayin bout.'

'You got others though, right?'

Sonny started to laugh. 'Nope, none with gristle. Anyway I lost um, int I?'

'What you gonna tell your dad?'

'Nothin. Say they was all empty and whatever.'

Ennor stood up and a little bit of herself felt sorry for the big-mouthed gypsy girl. There was a lot of talk and bluster to her but she knew there was a reason for that. It was the same with Butch.

'Let's go back. I'm freezin and there's no point to bein cold when there's a fire goin.'

'Can't,' said Sonny as she got to her feet. 'Not yet.'

'Why not?'

'Gotta put a little time between us and the day. Don't want to look failed even if I failed.'

She started to walk and Ennor followed.

'Where we goin?'

'Vantage point.'

'What's that?'

'You'll see.'

'Can't we just go back to the trailer, please?'

'Not yet. I'll build us a fire, so just shut up.'

'You're not very nice, are you? Someone who wants a friend to knock about with and all.'

Sonny didn't answer her and she didn't look back at Ennor to see if she was following.

She led them through the corner of forest and up a bank of carpet pine until they stood high up on the cone of a silt stack.

'This is what a vantage point is, see? Over there you can see the clay mountains. Somethin else, int it?'

Ennor nodded. 'St Austell.'

'Right. You know how high we are?'

'No.'

'Neither do I, but it's high, really high.'

Ennor walked a little way out on the man-made ridge. The silt underfoot was frozen solid and she stabbed the toes of her boots and climbed it up and down like a ladder.

A great middle chunk of Cornwall sprawled below her and she closed her eyes and winged her arms like a bird. She heard buzzards fighting and she imagined jumping in to join them, a dance of wing and claw and love and hate, a flamenco. A great leap towards freedom, a fleeting one-chance opportunity.

'I gather wood when I can,' shouted Sonny. 'Whenever I'm up here I stack it up.'

'Why?' shouted Ennor and she walked back to where Sonny was crouching out on a level spot.

'For fires, hello?'

'Why you have fires up here on your own?'

'Why not?'

Ennor sat on one of the thick quarry slates that were positioned beside the fire and watched Sonny tend and pet the coming flames until they grew and smoked out on the wind.

'Bin comin up here for weeks. I'm callin it my relaxation spot.'

'You meditate or somethin? Put your legs behind your ears?'

'Don't be daft.'

'You come up here every day?'

'No, just some days.'

'Why?'

'When I gotta escape.'

Ennor shrugged. 'Int you got things to do? Other things beside.'

'Nope. Everyone tells me I'm just a kid so here I am bein just a kid.'

Ennor wondered about the 'just a kid' bit and thought about her own life. She supposed there was something comforting about the routine drudge no matter how hard the work and she wondered whose life was better and whose was worse. Hands worn from fiddling as opposed to idling made more sense to her; there was point to it, a reason. Maybe she herself wasn't such a dumb kid after all.

'So what you think of the view?'

Ennor looked down into the cavity and her stomach lurched. She was no longer a lifting bird but a tumbling rock, fear rolling her all ways towards lower ground.

She looked at the falling fire, a crucible of scolding heat bubbling within the void as it tried to lure her in. It would put her into the ground and into hell, for ever buried and burning with the grizzly toothed boy.

'Hellfire,' said Sonny. 'Some view, int it?'

'I feel dizzy.'

'No you don't.'

'I do. I feel dizzy and I can't breathe.'

Sonny laughed and she punched her in the arm. 'I knew you'd like it.'

'I did but not so much now. I feel sick.'

'Lay back a bit then. You scared of heights or somethin?'

Ennor sat with her back against the woodpile and she tried to focus on something solid, then she closed her eyes but that was worse. The light of fire danced before her and she opened them again quick snap.

'You gonna get sick?' asked Sonny. 'Hell, if I knew you were a scaredy cat at heights, I'd have come on me own.'

'I just don't feel so good.'

'Well whatever. Show you my secret hideout and this is what I get.'

The fire sent sparks into the sky and Ennor watched holes burn dark in the grey that threw down snowflakes in return. She had killed a boy. She really had killed a boy.

All around flashes of white circled the girls and landed on their faces and Ennor caught them on her tongue and licked the ice gone.

'It's snowin,' she said. 'It's snowin and everythin's gone wrong.' She started to giggle.

Sonny looked at her and shook her head. 'Maybe we should get goin after all. In a minute we'll be in a snow cave and not of our choosin.'

Ennor looked at the fire and watched Sonny kick it over and she looked at the view as it filled with white fuzz.

'It's snowin,' she said again.

'Really? You don't say!'

'I gotta find my mum before the snow comes back.'

'Snow's back.' Sonny pulled her to her feet and started to walk towards the forest and Ennor followed.

They walked for what seemed like the longest time and Ennor looked at her wrist and wondered again where her watch was. 'What time is it?' she asked.

Sonny shrugged. 'Afternoon maybe.'

The forest echoed a dim light that was both night and day. Shadows were slow to disappear but movement of some kind sloped between the slats of trees and Ennor's eyes were caught and pinched between them. She looked down at her feet and saw them walking, one and two, and she tried to count her footsteps to keep her mind off the shadows but fear was everywhere.

Snipers watched her from the trees and she gripped on to Sonny's arm and speeded up to keep the target moving.

'You OK?' asked Sonny.

She nodded.

'You don't look so good.'

Ennor ignored her, not because of reasons but because fear had bitten her tongue and scabbed her mouth shut. The dead boy was everywhere.

'You can have a rest back at the trailer. I don't mind.'

Ennor nodded again.

'You can have the bed if you want. Just till you settle some. Spose sleepin rough int the best for spirit. Still feelin dizzy?'

Ennor shook her head. 'Not so much. What you gonna tell your dad bout the traps?'

'I told you, nothin much. Just zip it.'

When they got to the trailer Ennor lay on Sonny's bed and she listened out for anything that resembled argument but there was nothing but the whirr of campsite laughter and she slept with the comforting cloak of another world wrapped tight around her.

CHAPTER SIX

The two girls sat on the bed and emptied the rucksack of Ennor's worldly goods and they replaced them with cartons of homebrew.

'You feelin better?' asked Sonny.

Ennor nodded. She supposed so; an hour of sleep had her numbed a little. 'You carryin that on your back?' she asked, pointing to the rucksack.

'Why not?'

'Looks heavy.'

'Well it int. Hell, anyway we won't be luggin it for long, will we?'

Sonny looked over Ennor's things and laughed and she picked up the gun with a shrug.

'Spose this is quite a fun thing for a girl like you to be carryin.'

Ennor stood up. 'Give it here.'

'Quite a strange thing in fact.'

'Just pass it.'

'What's it for? Or shouldn't I ask?'

'Huntin, whatever. Give it.'

Sonny tossed it on to the bed and narrowed her eyes towards thinking something.

'I thought you said the party was out of camp?' said Ennor.

'It is. The stone circle other side of the site.' She picked up the photo of Ennor's parents and weighed the frame in her hands. 'This is worth a few bob, I reckon, without the borin photo obviously.'

'Give it back.' Ennor snatched it from her hand and put it with her other things on the table by the bed and she warned Sonny she'd better not touch anything because if she did she'd be dead meat and she meant it.

'Big arms or no, just leave my home stuff alone.'

'Calm down, little one. Just lookin.'

Ennor thought about Trip and she suddenly felt sick to her sides with worry. She hoped Butch was doing OK. Trip's autism was mostly under control but he had his colourful days.

She pictured his face when she had said goodbye. He had tried to be strong because that was what she had asked of him; his mouth had turned down and his eyes filled with tears but still he smiled, his sister's brave little boy.

Sonny told her to snap out of wherever she was drifting because she'd volunteered to help with taking wood

110

down to the party site and she was now volunteering Ennor.

'Means we get on the men's side.' She jammed the stuffed rucksack under the bed and pulled Ennor outside when her mother appeared in the hallway in her dressing gown.

'You int got much respect for your mother, have you?' Ennor said.

'I give her plenty, girl, but it's a two-way street and, besides, there's no way I'm goin into the family movie business so, hell, I'm forever dodgin bullets one way or other.'

'She looks nice.'

'Yeah, well, looks can be deceivin.'

They walked up towards the forest and Sonny made Ennor promise that what she might see she'd keep to herself.

'Don't want the forestry on us. Aggressive sods, they is.'

'You cuttin down trees then?'

Sonny smiled. 'We like to call it thinnin. Trimmin and thinnin.'

'What if I was a forestry spy?'

Sonny shrugged. 'I'd have to kill you I spose.'

Some of the men were pleased to see Sonny and they tussled her hair and pretended to fight and she introduced Ennor and told them she could be trusted.

'She's good, I promise. Not from any rivals or nothing. She's on her own, int you, girl?'

A dark leathered man beckoned Ennor towards a clearing where they were sawing trunks into great wedged logs with a giant two-man handsaw. He asked her name and her father's name and when she told him he nodded as if the name meant something to him and she wondered if he'd ever kept Simmentals.

'What's a pretty girl like you doin walkin the moor alone?' he asked and Ennor tried to tell him in a roundabout way and it came out like a car-crash lie and he told her to be mindful travelling alone because things had gotten worse about the county and some places were turning into war zones.

Ennor went to answer but he'd turned his back and was shouting for them to load the wheelbarrows.

'He's one of the bosses. He likes you.' Sonny grinned. 'Pretty girl like you. Int that sweet?'

They loaded the logs into two corroded wheelbarrows and followed others carrying wood down to the stone circle.

'It's gonna be great. Dad got us a pig from somewhere and we're gonna roast it over the fire, like a ram roast but with pig. You eat pig?'

'Course.'

'Not a Jew or Muslim then? Only you got a bit of somethin holy flashin hot in your eyes.'

'I'm Methodist, was brought up Methodist.'

'Knew it. Makes you mad, don't it? All that gotta do this, gotta do that.'

'Not really.'

'Yeah really.'

They walked in single file with Sonny leading the way through the newly settled snow.

Occasionally Ennor's wheel got stuck in a drift and Sonny laughed and said maybe she should ask God for help. 'Loads of people have gone holy recent with the country fallin apart. They think cus you believe somethin all a sudden it's gonna save you. I tell you somethin, prayin won't put food on the table. Won't rid us of snow either.'

Ennor watched the girl push ahead with the barrow, her long dark hair knotted in the wind and her mouth shouting and singing and going on, and she wondered if she ever shut up. If she was honest, there was something she liked about Sonny; she was everything that Ennor wasn't.

'Come on, slowcoach, hell! Or shouldn't I say that?'

'You say it all the time. Why should I care?' Ennor gave the barrow an almighty push and its contents veered into the snow and she fell after it.

'There is a God,' laughed Sonny as she pulled Ennor to her feet. 'You're a regular disaster zone, int you?'

Down at the stone circle the women were arranging crates and car seats in among the standing stones and the girls handed over the wood.

'Cigarette?' asked Sonny.

'Hey, that's mine.'

'Mine now. Let's say it's payment for the Coco Pops.'

Ennor couldn't be bothered to argue. Her bum hurt from falling and she was trying not to think about all the grown-up things she should be putting her mind to. She wished she had some of Sonny's bouncy madness. The girl didn't seem to have one care in the world and she hoped a little of the fizz would rub off on her. Ennor nudged her and told her she needed a drink.

They returned to camp to collect the drinks stash and they got themselves ready by sharing a two-pint carton of scrumpy and rolling the last of the tobacco into as many cigarettes as it would stretch.

'Seven each.' Sonny nodded to herself. 'Plenty and don't go offerin them to nobody.'

'Like who? I don't know anybody.'

'You'll see. Smoke um sneaky so you don't get asked.'

They stepped out into the hard-bitten twilight and listened to the singing that spiked and carried on the wind and they followed it down to the party.

'We'll sit high so nobody can see the booze. You need to be sneaky with that as well.'

'Don't worry, I'll drink it quick enough.'

'Thought Methodists dint drink.'

Ennor ignored her and held on to the rucksack that was pinned to Sonny's back and she followed her into the black-and-white night. 'What we celebratin anyway?'

'The shortest day.'

'Why's that worth celebratin?'

'I dunno, it's pagan or somethin. You can stop with the questions now, you're borin me.' She sped up and Ennor nearly fell and she shouted for her to slow down because she couldn't see through the falling snow.

'I can't. The bag's dictatin.'

The two girls slipped and slid down the hill into the crowd and they fell laughing head over heels to the ground.

Ennor lay for a moment and turned to watch the flames of the fire lick and snip at the dancing feet and she felt its warmth soak into her veins.

Sonny was shouting something to her and she realised she was still holding on to the bag and this made her laugh even more.

'Get up!' Sonny pulled her to her feet and she shouted above the noise of singing and drums to follow her.

'We need to find a high point away from everyone. Stop draggin your heels.'

They climbed the other side of the scoop of land that surrounded the stone circle and the gigantic fire within and sat on a bumped slab of granite and dug their boots into the ground.

'Scrumpy or beer?'

'Scrumpy.'

Sonny opened the rucksack between her knees and she glanced about to check for eyes and then asked Ennor what was wrong with the beer.

'Nothin, just a bit soapy.'

'Beggars can't be choosers when it comes to home-brew. Anyway the boys are only makin scrumpy now cus of the apples we bin storin.'

She passed one of the plastic milk cartons to Ennor and watched her drink.

'It tastes like summer.' She smiled. 'Summer and heaven all squished into one.'

Sonny laughed and took the bottle and drank without swallowing.

The dancers had joined hands in the dip below and they circled the fire as one and Ennor asked if Sonny was related to everyone.

'Not all. The pagans and the travellers are from down west. More their thing than ours all this worship crap but a party is a party, init?'

'What about them other fires?' Ennor pointed towards the horizon at the small jewels of dancing flames flashing out in the countryside below.

'Wait a minute.' Sonny reached into the black leather bumbag she wore strapped around her waist and she produced a compact telescope.

'What's that?'

'What you think it is?' She crouched behind Ennor and rested the telescope on her shoulder and told her to hold steady.

'Maybe it's other pagans?'

'Shut up, would you? I'm tryin to focus here. Ah, got the buggers.'

'What is it?'

'Cars, burnin cars on the edge of the village. I'm guessin somethin must be goin down.'

'What kind of somethin?'

'The crazy kind. People are goin mad roundabout with the hunger and the cold, I swear they are.' She passed the telescope to Ennor and sat back down. 'Guess I should tell me dad.'

Ennor looked through the lens and she walked it from one fire to the next and back and counted them one to five. 'There's five cars burnin. Why burn five cars?'

'Useless I spose. Int bin no petrol or fuel oil for two months or thereabouts. Don't you listen to the news?'

She took the telescope off Ennor and stuffed it into the bumbag and took out another bottle of scrumpy. 'If we drink enough, we won't care one way or the other soon enough.' She unscrewed the top and drank while Ennor finished the other carton.

'You bin livin under a stone or somethin?'

'Course not. Dint think things were all that bad. Spose I thought it was just us.'

'Well it's gettin that way. Gotta keep your wits more and more these days, hell.' She sat forward and pointed into the crowd. You see everyone here? Dad and the boys know every single face, every name.'

'Apart from mine, I'm a stranger.'

'No, *strange* is what you are.'

Ennor laughed and repaid the compliment and when Sonny asked her why her life was so bad she surprised herself by telling her about Dad and Trip and the trailer and in a roundabout way she told her about Mum too.

'Let me get this straight. You're trekkin out in the snow to the north moor to find a mother who may not even exist?'

'Oh she exists, I'm just not sure where. I've got no choice, got to get our lives on track before the social take Trip and Dad dies and I'm left without a home.'

'What's up with your dad?'

'Cancer.'

'Bummer, hell.'

'I need someone to take care of us before the social split us up.'

'Really?' Sonny started to laugh a little. 'Like they really care bout things like that, with everythin goin on.'

Ennor shrugged. 'Got a letter to say as much. Sounds like they got a prison waitin for us.'

Sonny nodded and said her getting somewhere and back made sense. They drank the scrumpy and then the beer and, when the sky cleared to moon and snowflakes became stars, they danced out with the others and sang along to songs they didn't know.

Boys of all ages danced around Ennor and they took turns to dance her around the fire and for a moment she forgot herself in the spin of things.

'Who are these boys?' she called out to Sonny in passing.

'Cousins, each and every one of them.' She told Ennor she was meant to marry one of them soon enough and she made a face like she was going to be sick.

Ennor didn't think they were all that bad. They had manners and praised her on her dancing, smiling and winking as if they found her in some way special.

'Don't be taken in,' shouted Sonny on her next passing. 'They're only after one thing.'

Ennor nodded but she didn't believe her and she thought briefly about Butch and how maybe he was supposed to be the one. She blushed when she thought what he might think of her dancing wild with a gang of strange gypsy boys and this made her suddenly sad and she said she had to sit down when Sonny next came laughing around the fire.

She sat back from the crowd on an upturned crate and lit a cigarette. When people smiled at her she smiled back and she tapped her hand on her leg so as not to seem rude but her mood had changed abruptly.

The drink and the boys and Sonny made her fit back into the place where she should by rights be, a fourteen-year-old girl out having fun, careless and carefree. She wished she could stay cocooned in the party for ever because life and the changing world around was just plain wrong. Nothing fitted as it should, all and everything square pegs in round holes.

There was one boy who kept looking her way and smiling and finally he had courage enough to come over. Ennor told herself that this was the way things were done. The girl was supposed to sit and look and the boy was meant to stand and look and, when he found some nerve down there in his pockets where his hands were stuck, he came over. In truth the long looking made her nervous and, besides, there was a lot more than one boy to look at.

He stood in front of her and asked if he could sit down beside and she nodded and smiled and stubbed out the cigarette she'd been smoking and put it in her pocket for later.

'Good night.' He smiled.

Ennor nodded.

'You a friend of Sonny? She's my cousin.'

She shrugged and looked him over, noticing the family resemblance. The thick black hair and black-pebble eyes, the type you might pick up off the beach.

'You want a drink?' he asked. 'I can get you one.'

'I got one, thanks.' She picked the plastic bottle up off the ground and passed it to him. 'I don't mind sharin.'

He took the bottle and drank some down and wiped his chin with the back of his hand where it had spilt.

'You go to school?' he asked. 'You look like the type of girl who goes to school.'

Ennor nodded. She wanted to look like that type of girl.

'Where'd you go?'

'Just in town.'

'You like it?'

Ennor nodded and then shrugged.

'You?' she asked.

'Not really.' He smiled again. 'Never did really and now I'm sixteen so that's the end of that.'

They watched the others dance about the fire and Ennor thought what question to ask next and she folded her arms to stop herself fidgeting.

'What do you do?' she asked.

'This and that.' He shrugged.

Ennor wanted to ask him his name but the chance had come and gone. She looked out for Sonny but she was leaping about the flames with the rest of the revellers.

'My name's Gary by the way.' The boy extended his hand and she shook it hard like a grown-up and he asked if she wanted to walk a little way from the noise.

'We can talk easier.'

'OK.' She smiled and she hoped this was the way to behave with grown-up boys.

They walked with a little distance put between them and Ennor talked about school and her life like she was reading from a book and in a way this was exactly what she was doing.

She told the boy she was top of her class and that her favourite subject was English because she liked to write and she told him she lived in a big house with both her parents and she knew that she was drunk because she enjoyed spreading the lies way too much.

'We put up the Christmas tree this mornin.' She smiled. 'Put it up in the hall by the grand staircase so guests can see it when they come to the door.'

Gary nodded. 'You must live in a big house.'

'Yep, big enough.'

'That's nice.'

Ennor nodded and agreed and she thought how nice it really would be to have a mother and a father and a nice big house.

Gary asked her question after question and Ennor answered without the usual reserve because she was making it all up. She jazzed up her replies with flair and bright sparks and the boy's eyes grew wide with wonder. Maybe he could picture himself someplace in Ennor's world, smartly dressed and nervous at the dining table on Christmas day, trying to make a good impression and failing. He was no Butch.

Ennor laughed. If the boy could see her father and the trailer, he'd laugh too. He'd probably turn around and leg it without a goodbye or a thank you.

'What you smilin at?' he asked.

'Nothin.'

'Don't look like nothin.'

'Just a funny thought, nothin.'

They had been walking for quite a while and they

turned and stood to watch the party unravel below them.

'We have some crazy parties,' said the boy.

'I can see that.'

'Spose it's different for your kind. From what you know, I mean.'

Ennor agreed, it was, but not for the reasons he thought.

They stood awkward against the wind and Ennor worried that now was the time they were supposed to do something. 'Shall we go back?' she asked.

The boy shrugged. 'You want to see somethin really cool?' he asked.

'Is it far?'

'Not far at all.'

'How far?'

'Just up to that quarry a bit.' He started to walk and Ennor followed and she laughed when she slipped.

'Where you takin me?'

'To the quarry. Come on.'

She followed him up the incline and she wanted to go back but didn't know how to say it without sounding like the fourteen-year-old girl she was.

'Here we are,' he shouted as they followed a path towards the pit.

'What is it?' she asked, squinting into the dark.

'Christmas come early,' he laughed.

Ennor stood next to the boy and looked towards the

crater of rock and the circle of frozen water that flattened there.

'Summit else, int it? We come up here in summer, just swimmin and muckin bout, but this is summit else, don't you think?'

Ennor nodded and she stepped forward and tapped her toe on the thick ice.

'Spect someone like you bin skatin enough times.'

'Not really. Is it safe?'

'Hard as rock.'

'You sure?'

'Come on. I'll show you.'

He took her hand and led her out on to the rink and Ennor found herself suddenly skating in a fairy tale of forbidden love and long-losts and happy-ever-afters.

Gary was guiding her and pulling her close and she laughed when he spun her in his arms. She was at a school dance and the world was watching, cheering 'Good on you' and 'Go, girl, go'.

She let go of his hands and swung out on her own, holding her breath to keep the moment from dying. The ice below her dancing feet sparkled like summer sand and she let it carry her up through the cloud and snow and to the moon and back. She grabbed at the stars and put them in her pockets for the warmth and bent low to the ice as she skated to touch the amber orbs beneath her. Eyes just like her own and like her mother's, looking back and flashing bright like fires in the snow.

'You're a natural,' shouted Gary as he caught up to her. 'You defo done this before.'

'Maybe.' She smiled. Alcohol ran riot in her veins and she was of a mind to do and be a million dazzling things. This was what it was like to let go and she picked up speed and called for the boy to chase her.

'Hell,' shouted Sonny from the path divide. 'What you done with her, Gaz?'

'Sonny!' screamed Ennor with delight. 'Look, I'm ice-skatin.'

'I can see that.' Sonny put her hands on her hips and waited for them to come over.

'Where did you find her, cuz?' asked Gary. 'Bit posh to be your friend, int she?'

Sonny shrugged. 'I guess.' She looked at Ennor in the half-light and raised her eyebrows. 'She's as posh as I don't know and that accent, hell, it's like chattin with the Queen.'

'She's bin tellin me bout her life.' He grinned.

'That's nice.' She smiled again.

'You don't have to look after me,' giggled Ennor. 'I'm fine.'

'I'll be goin then, only with your screamin and goin on.'

Sonny turned to go and they followed her. When they got back to the party Gary left them and joined the other boys.

'He'll be tellin the others he had you,' said Sonny.

'No he won't, he was all right.'

'Really?'

'Really. Why? You jealous?'

'Of my cousin's attention?'

'Of any attention.'

'Girl,' Sonny laughed. 'You got a lot to learn bout life, int you?'

Sonny went to get them food and Ennor sat and lit the half-smoked cigarette and she smoked it down to her fingers and apologised that it was her last to anyone that asked. The singing and dancing stopped and gave way to some kind of worship and all of the gypsies and some of the travellers sat back from the fire or went to the roasting pig that cooked over a small fire pit beyond the stone circle.

Dining chairs were thrown into the pyre to keep it burning and a wooden rocking horse was added and it sat dumbstruck, riding out the flames.

'Hope you're hungry,' shouted Sonny as she approached with dripping hands. 'We got pig in a blanket,' she laughed.

'What's the blanket?'

'Some kind of barley flatbread, who knows. It's no hotdog but you get used to it.'

Ennor thanked her and said she'd spent the last few days mostly eating potato cakes. The meat had been barbecued to within an inch of its life and tasted of charcoal and rotten flesh and she wondered how long the pig had been dead.

'Tasty, eh?' grinned Sonny through fatty lips.

'The best,' lied Ennor and she swallowed it down and chased it with flat coke Sonny had found. She rinsed it through her teeth like mouthwash.

'You want another?'

'No, I'm good thanks.' She patted her stomach to indicate fullness and pretended to be engrossed in her surroundings so Sonny wouldn't push it.

'Who are they?' she asked, pointing to a group of men standing across from them at the far side of the fire.

Sonny squatted beside her. 'Where?'

'Over there, I int seen um before.'

'Damn.'

'What is it?'

'The uninvited. I knew there was somethin I had to tell Dad.' She told Ennor to stay put and she ran up the bank to where her dad sat and whispered something in his ear.

Ennor's heart pounded and her ears rushed with the charge of blood. Maybe they were looking for her. She kept an eye on the strangers as they kicked about the fire and put the empty rucksack on her back so as not to leave it behind. A few men were having words with the strangers and Ennor knew by the cut and swagger of them that peaceful celebrating was not on the newcomers' minds.

The chanting stopped and raised voices could be heard and they echoed about the standing stones and caught in the branches of trees and snagged in the briar.

A sudden hand on her shoulder made her jump from the crate. 'Come with me. You need to help take the children into the forest.' Sonny pulled her to her feet and they ran drunk and stumbling to where the children and woman gathered.

'Head back to where they were cuttin trees this mornin and stay away from camp in case they try to trash it. They'll try and head there for sure. They'll see what they can steal and burn the rest.'

Ennor held on to the collar of Sonny's leather jacket to steady herself. 'Who they lookin for?'

'Nobody in particular.'

'Where you goin?'

'Fightin.' She jumped from the bank and went towards the beginnings of a brawl and Ennor wanted to pray and she wanted to run but instead she followed the others in a convoy of raised voices and some of the children were crying. In the forest clearing the tarpaulin sheets were patterned together like patchwork on the floor and the children sat at odds and angles to the outside world.

Ennor sat on a tree stump and pulled her legs up under her. It was cold after sitting by the fire and the drink was wearing off. She thought about the boy and she smiled and let herself be drawn into the dance once more, her innocence intact no matter what he told his friends.

The women eyed her as if she were perhaps some kind of decoy and after a while she felt pushed enough to stand out at the edge of the forest. She looked to see if the fighting had trailed up to the camp but it hadn't and she ran.

Inside Sonny's trailer she took up her things and packed the best she could considering and she was about to take a little food from the kitchen when she saw Sonny standing against the door frame.

'Goin somewhere?'

'No, I dunno. I'm scared.'

'Of what?'

'Out there, the fightin.'

Sonny laughed and kicked off the biker boots and lay down on the bed. 'You're bonkers, know that? You'd rather be out there alone in the dark with the crazies at it than safe in camp.'

Ennor sat at the edge of the bed and listened to the many voices returning and circling the clearing outside. 'What happened?'

'Nothin much, really just a let-down in the end, a right anticlimax.'

'Are they gone?'

'Slapped and gone with their tails beneath. Hell, I was lookin for a bit more of a put-up if you want to know the truth.'

'Will they come back?'

'Not unless they want more of the same.'

'You got a black eye.'

'No biggy. Do what you want, guest and all, but you can get off my bed. Have the floor if you want.' She tossed Ennor a pillow and told her to turn off the light.

Laughter had returned to camp but the comfort of community no longer reassured Ennor.

She unlaced her boots and put them next to the rucksack by the door and knelt to sandwich her blanket against the floor. She got in with the pillow plumped and listened to the shrill voices of tired kids being led to their beds and the murmur of drunken songs bringing the camp back to life. Ennor closed her eyes and tried not to think about the killer inside and she thought about home. She didn't know which was worse.

'You awake?' she asked.

'No.'

'Goodnight then.'

'I'll try for one, if someone stops natterin.'

Ennor turned left and then right and she settled on her back and watched the flashing flames through the window turn the ceiling into moving marble. She thought about her bedroom and she told herself to be positive because what else was there? She closed her eyes and thought about Butch and in her close-to-dreaming state she had him dressed in a suit and he was spinning her around on an ice-rink. She fantasised that they were together and in love but as sleep came settling she was soon back to dreaming the one foot in front of the other. Ennor Carne walking circles into the snow, nothing but a dying father and fading brother and a dead boy stranger to her name. Dreams had become life and the cold and the snow were everywhere, inside and out. It sucked her blood while she slept and chewed her down to rime bone, a dusting on the land.

CHAPTER SEVEN

'You awake?' asked Sonny.

'I was, thought you wanted to sleep.'

'I did. It's mornin, dummy.'

Ennor got up and pulled the curtains from the window. 'It's still dark.'

'Is there a fire goin?'

'Yep.'

'Is there a little old lady pushin pots and tendin?'

'Yep.'

'Then it's mornin.'

They got dressed and shuffled out into the fresh slap air and sat at the fire with blankets close across their shoulders and drank sweet tea while Sonny's grandmother petted a great pan of porridge strung high above the fire.

'You should be doin this, Sunshine. Show the boys you got more strings than just fightin.'

'Yes, Nan.' She made a face at Ennor and shook her head. 'Always tryin to matchmake, int you, Nan?'

'It wouldn't hurt to turn your hand at women's work now and then, learn the jobs you should be learnin.'

'When I'm makin heaps of money I won't hear no old biddy complainin.'

'She lives in la-la land.' The woman smiled towards Ennor. 'So what's your name, cutie?'

'Ennor, pleased to meet you.'

'Pretty name, pretty girl. Got a boyfriend?'

Ennor thought about Butch. 'Kind of, I don't know.'

'Well you either do or you don't.' She sat up close and flicked a calloused finger under her chin. 'If he's a good un, he's your boyfriend.'

'You ever gonna serve up, old lady?' shouted Sonny.

'You do it. I gotta see a man bout a horse.'

Sonny sighed. 'Gotta do everythin yourself round here. Porridge?' She crouched at the fire and slapped two bowls to the brim and sprinkled sugar straight from the jar.

'No Coco Pops today. Somebody ate um all.'

'You're so funny.'

'Know that, don't I.'

They ate in silence and others came to the fire and helped themselves to the pot and conversation settled on the previous night.

Some people didn't think the celebrations were spoilt much but others thought they were spoilt a lot and a bat-and-ball banter aced across the fire.

Ennor had never known such morning spirit. They made her smile and she nodded in agreement and thought how easy it would be to just chop her heels, one two, into the ground and stay put.

She finished her porridge and took another mug of tea and she watched the stars fade and blue come into the sky in a slow drag from left to right and her life turned with it, upwards and backwards in a timeless drift of changing skies.

Most trailer doors were open to the rising sun and people came to the fire with wood and food and news as urgent as the last.

There was talk of the storm heading out towards the Atlantic and promise that it would not return. Ennor hoped they were right.

'I gotta get goin after this tea,' she said.

Sonny ignored her.

'I'm behind in my schedule and you know I am. What you lookin at?'

'Look over there,' said Sonny.

'What?' Ennor looked across camp. A police Land Rover pulled up through the trees and she wondered if guilty was detailed somewhere across her face.

'What do they want?' she asked.

'That's just what I was just thinkin.'

'Bout last night?'

'It's not usual. Don't care one way or other is usual.'

Ennor sucked her tea to the leaves and she watched

Sonny join some of the others as they collected around the car and when she was the only one left sitting at the fire she swung the rucksack on to her back and headed into the canopy of trees.

The forest chewed at her and ate her up with its silence but Ennor could still hear voices and she ran until nothing but her thumping heart filled her ears.

She had no idea where she was or in which direction she should go and she breathed hard against the wall of ice which was early morning fog.

Within twenty-four hours she had become used to big rising fires and company and food turned by the hand of others and she had become used to a little piece of easy life.

She thought of the look that might now be on Sonny's face when she realised she had gone, and she wished she had said goodbye and thanked her right because she really was grateful for the hotchpotch hospitality.

Truth was she couldn't take the risk in regards to the police and their wormy questions. There was a dead body out on the moor and it was her hand that had killed him and she would answer to God and nobody else because she didn't have time for prison.

She stopped to adjust the rucksack because the straps had jiggled loose from the running and she took a minute to decide on her route. She had entered the forest in a different place from where she'd exited and needed to get back on track and she settled on a straight line in the direction she was going because there was no other choice except backwards.

The pine needles underfoot were frozen solid with the wet, cracking occasionally as she walked and the echo snapping between the trees like a stranger's footsteps.

Things caught her eye as she walked, a quick-dash shadow or something thrown into her path and she tried to ignore her quick-trip mind but sometimes it was all too much and she'd stare, then jump, then run.

Her dad always said she was full to the brim with imagination and his words rang in her ears now when she edged and twisted her way through the forest half-light like a fawn.

'If he could see me now,' she whispered, 'scared of my own shadow.' The dead boy fear reignited and melted with the police fear and was now red-hot fever fear fused with loneliness as big as heaven and earth.

She imagined faces popping mad from trees and the red and the blue of police cars everyplace she was heading.

She covered her face with her hands and held her breath, counting to ten to steady her nerves, and for good measure she kissed the silver cross that hung around her neck.

Ennor kept her eyes closed and prayed for strength of nerve. She prayed for guidance like she did most days and she told God that she was in his hands in all ways possible.

The boy was dead and she was sorry about that and now the police were after her and she was sorry about that too. Maybe they had bigger things to contend with than a teenage runaway boy-killer. If they knew the facts, they'd understand, but she didn't have time for explaining and not much for being maudlin either.

She slapped the fretting from her cheeks and settled herself on one direction, her eyes fixed three steps in a line ahead and she counted them over, one two three. She counted in her head and sometimes out loud and paid no regard to the bump of a tree trunk or scratch of a branch, keeping to the line like a dumb heifer. One two three, one two three.

She heard a distant call and then maybe her name and the hunt call of a buzzard indicated she was near open land. Ennor picked up her feet and hurried towards the call and she counted its squawking cries and thanked God because it was nature calling her out of the forest.

Out in the open she took off her rucksack and bent in half to catch her breath and the cold air was painful in her throat and lungs.

She drank a little of the water she had left and crouched to watch the buzzard circle and fall against the white of sky and land and she realised the blue hint of morning had been wiped clean by the stupid clouds. The gypsies were wrong; the storm was returning.

Up ahead the cut of a tin mine silhouetted black on the horizon and Ennor decided this was where she was heading if she wanted any kind of shelter.

She collected what wood she could from the forest floor and swung the pack and set a course direct. Every so often she glanced back at the forest and she laughed in its face because she'd walked it safe and really it was just a bunch of trees.

In the comfort of ancestor-built walls Ennor set about pushing a circle clear in the snow and she pulled hand-sized rocks from the ground and circled them neatly round the fire pit. She used seven for luck. She knelt with her back to the rising wind and lit the last of the gorse tinder and added twigs then sticks into a wigwam of fire. Clean snow she clubbed into her pan and she set it to boil for tea and built back fallen granite bricks into a wide seat and sat with her back against a wall. While the water boiled she took a handful of the pine needles she had collected and chopped them against a stone with her pocket knife and added them to the water to simmer and she enjoyed the aroma because she knew it would smell better than it tasted and she was right.

Ennor rested her head and watched the clouds thicken into a jumble of jigsaw-puzzle outlines and some were plain white and some were grey but most were teal and rust orange. She sat with her legs outstretched and drank her tea with snow falling all around as if it were the most natural thing in the world.

The snowflakes were as gentle as rose petals and they drifted and rocked on the breeze like miniature rowing boats and they moored on her cheeks and in her lap, empty vessels there, and then gone.

Her mind was heavy from earlier fear and stringy remnants of a hangover and she closed her eyes to settle her thoughts and put her mind's eye on the task of finding her mother.

She took her notebook from the side pocket of the rucksack and, sheltering it from the snow, read over her notes. She stared at the pages and reread the fumbling words but nothing was of any use and she snapped it shut and returned it to the bag.

Half asleep she finished the strange tea and warmed herself as close as she dared to the fire. She was dog bone tired and, no matter how much she wanted to blaze a trail through the snow, there was no escaping the fact that she'd had little sleep last night. She took up her things and crept down into the mouth of the mineshaft with her torch cranked and stuck forth like a sword. Underground, out of the snow and wind, she found herself a dry square of nothing and she lay down her tarp and blanket and wrapped her coat around the rucksack for a too-high pillow. Just an hour of rest to see out the worst of the storm and she'd be ready for anything.

Daylight faded fast from the entrance of the mine as though a stone had been rolled across it, but Ennor didn't notice because she had fallen asleep, hypnotised by the drip of fractal snow seeping into bedrock cracks.

Outside the snow fell fast in the wind and landed in heavy dumps at all angles against the moor and the silence cocooned the girl deeper underground. A subterranean pocket of safety emanating from a past world that carried her unwittingly through the long dark night.

At first the faint chip-chip of knocking was a mere scratch in Ennor's ear and she turned on the hard ground with the memory of home's bed and for a brief moment she was back there and she pushed the itchy army coat to her face as if it were a duck-down pillow.

Maybe the knocking was her dad summoning her to his room, or Trip throwing stones against the trailer wall. She'd warned him about that. She shouted, then woke with a start and reached for her gun and she came close to swearing when she realised she'd left it in Sonny's bedroom.

Ennor sat tight and listened against the dark and was suddenly aware of the salty sting in the mine air that dried her nostrils and sanded her lips.

'Hello?' she shouted. 'Anyone there?' Her brittle fear-lessness was short-lived when the knocking returned. She ran blind and screaming out of the mine with a kind of laughter chasing her through a wall of snow and smashing her into daylight.

'I got you, dint I? Don't tell me I dint get you cus I did, hell.'

140

Sonny stood larger than life in the entrance of the mine and she held her sides as she laughed half in pain from her antics.

'I'm the funny one, int I?' She grinned.

'You're a crazy witch, is what you are. I thought you were the knockers.' Ennor lurched towards Sonny with all her strength and she pulled her down into the snow where yesterday's fire hand been and smacked her face until her nose was level with the snowline.

'Why'd you have to scare me half to death?' The fear and worry of past days turned to anger and she pulled Sonny from the ground, sparks of blood and spit flashing from her mouth and patterning the snow. She looked down at her hands red and ugly against the white and she wanted to rewind time but it was too late, she was transforming into someone unrecognisable.

The two girls locked eyes and Ennor waited for retaliation and when it came she let it wash over her with a tsunami crash and they fell bundled into one. They rolled head and tail down the bank of snow and took turns to leap their bundle of blood forward and back until buckled legs and deflated lungs had them still and quiet and sprawled out on the ground.

Ennor rested up on her elbows and she looked across to Sonny and they both started to laugh. 'You look like road kill.'

'So do you and worse. Only tracked you down to give back your rifle.'

'Dint have to scare me half to death in the process, did you?'

'Thought you could take it, put a bit of fun in your humdrum. Anyway what the hell are the knockers?'

'Mine spirits.'

'Like ghosts?'

Ennor shrugged.

They sat up against one of the mine's collapsed walls and took turns to cuff snow to each other's wounds.

Sonny told Ennor to be proud of the black eye she'd given her because it was some punch but Ennor had never hit anyone in her life except the boy Rabbit and her apologies kept running until Sonny threatened to knock her teeth out.

'Why you goin on? I'm near KO'd. That don't happen every day.'

'Neither does me fightin.'

'Let me see your hand.'

Ennor wiggled her fingers. 'It's fine, see.'

'Push it deep into the snow for the cold just in case.'

Ennor did what she was told and she closed her eyes to the brief startling pain.

'I'm injury prone just bout.'

'Why what else you got?'

'Twisted me ankle few days back and these things come in threes.'

'You're stupid superstitious.'

'Whatever.'

'So what you do to fix it?'

'An old woman took me in and cared for me a bit.'

'Just like that?'

'Why not?'

'Dint ask nothin of you? Kind or money or nothin?'

'Nope.'

'Was she mad?'

'A little, I think.'

'Guessed as much.'

'You took me in. Makes you mad the same.'

Sonny agreed and she disappeared behind the mine and then reappeared with an armful of wood. 'We gonna eat or what? Carried this wood with me. Better than nosin for twigs.'

'I've got porridge.'

'Well I see your porridge and I'll raise you a chunk of leftover pork and a cut of lard to fry it in.'

Sonny set about making the fire. She didn't use the lucky seven rocks that Ennor had recovered from beneath the fresh snow and it was ten times the size of a regular cooking fire. Soon the meat was frying and the smell mixed with wood smoke had the girls a little giddy and Ennor could not help but ask about the police.

'They were just nosin. Why?'

'Just askin.'

'Why?'

'Just askin to ask.'

'You want some of this grub or no?'

'Wouldn't mind.'

Sonny picked the fried meat apart with her fingers. They sat opposite each other across the fire and ate slowly to make it last.

'They were askin all sorts of questions actually.'

'Yeah? Like what?'

'Suspicious stuff out on the moor, things like that.'

'Suspicious like what?'

'Anyone actin strange. Strange comins and goins.'

'Like what?'

'Somethin bout a strange kind of girl, a real shortarse roamin the moor, just countin things over and over.'

'That's not funny.' Ennor flicked snow across the fire and sat back.

'Friend of the ghostly knockers.'

'Shut up.'

'There's somethin you're not tellin me, I know that all right.' She moved around the fire and sat next to Ennor. 'What you done? Why did you leg it this mornin?'

Ennor took a deep breath. She supposed it didn't matter to tell her story from the slip and fall and the old lady in the cottage and she went into detail because it was good to walk events over in her own mind and Sonny kept quiet beside her until the story was told.

'You think he's dead?'

'I know it.'

'For definite?'

Ennor shrugged. 'I saw him flat out and I saw the blood runnin and continuin from his head.'

'Was he breathin?'

'Don't think so.'

Sonny pushed a boot into the fire to steady a fallen log. 'You can't beat yourself up over a maybe, maybe not.'

'What you mean?'

'Maybe you gave the bastard a headache and nothin more.'

'You think? You think he deserved it?'

'Course he did. Self-defence is what that is.'

'I don't wanna go back.'

Sonny shrugged. 'Who said you have to? A thing like that gets carried around for ever unless you decide not to let it. For ever is a long time for a heavy-weight burden.' She looked in her bumbag and pulled out a square of crumpled paper.

'What's that?'

'A map. Help you get to findin that mother of yours since you lost your own.'

She opened it over and over until fully spread and she laid it against the wall and let Ennor trace her footsteps from home to the tor where she had fallen and she guessed at the location of the cottage and the cairn. She smoothed the map to the wall and felt the tiny bumps of granite sand poke through the paper and she walked her fingers with stepping-stone hops up and down and around the moor.

'It's not so big, is it?'

'Ten by ten miles if you want to count them, but it's not so easy when you're walkin the rough and the snow and everythin.'

'A hundred miles of dirt roads and snow.'

'Somethin like that. You can keep the map.' Sonny bent to clean the pan and plates in the snow and she got up as if to leave.

'You goin then?' Ennor asked.

'Looks like it, why?'

'Just with your map and everythin, you might want it back.'

'Maybe, what's your point?'

'Nothin, I'll see you round.'

'You got somethin to ask, just ask it.'

'Just if he's alive, what then?'

'Dunno, finish the job?' Sonny laughed and when she saw how serious Ennor was she laughed even more.

'If you ask me, I'll say yes. But you gotta ask me.'

'Ask you what?'

'You know what. Just ask me.'

Ennor sighed. 'Will you come with me? Help me find Mum?'

Sonny kicked her boot into the snow to pretend she was having a think. 'Well some kind of magic word would be nice, hell.'

'For God's sake, *please*.'

'Why not? Headin to the north moor, int you?'

Ennor nodded.

Sonny took back the map and smiled. 'We'll find her, greenhorn. Aunty Sonny knows a short cut by a lake.'

'Which lake?'

'Siblyback.'

'You think?'

'I know. Get packed up and I'll show you.'

CHAPTER EIGHT

Ennor watched Sonny stride towards the horizon and she shouted for her to wait. 'What makes you think you're right in any case?'

'Cus I got smarts plus I got the map.'

Ennor rushed to pack up her things and she wished she had a streak of nerve that would have her turning in the other direction, but Sonny was right. She was a greenhorn.

She stood with her hands on her hips and waited for her to look back and when she was nothing but a head bounce on the snow horizon she shouted for her to wait and ran after her.

'I was waitin but now I int. Come on,' Sonny shouted back.

'Why you comin if you gotta be so mean?'

'I said I'd help you and I will, but you gotta put a little faith in me. Besides, this way we get to go fishin.'

'You better not be leadin me all ways for your own entertainin.'

'It's a short cut. Hell, loosen a little, won't you? We'll be there in an hour.'

They walked side by side where the land allowed and Ennor half-eared Sonny's elaborate fishing stories. Her other half of listening was to her natter-chat mind and she wondered which was worse, this or Sonny.

When Sonny stopped to read the map Ennor stood idly by and watched shadow upon shadow of cloud eclipse each other in a race for dominance.

In those clouds she saw faces she knew and ones she didn't. The familiarity of kin and the menace of strangers, all sluiced together like pigswill.

Sonny was telling her something and she nodded and smiled.

'You listnin or no?' Sonny asked.

'Course, you were sayin bout the fishin.'

'What about the fishin.'

Ennor smiled. 'Just that.'

Sonny put the map away and said her way was definitely the quickest and she set a course to skirt a cluster of trees.

Ennor didn't have the energy for arguing. She was aching from their fight that morning and she thought she might be getting a cold. She followed behind like a half-obedient dog, dragging her heels a little to hint at her mood. She blew her nose into her glove to keep the run from freezing into icicles and she thought maybe the dry sting in her throat was the beginnings of a cough.

'I think I'm gettin a cold,' she shouted into thin air. 'I've got a sore throat, you hear me?'

'I hear somethin.'

'It's hard to talk.'

'Then don't. It's really no biggy.'

Sonny climbed a line of barbed wire and Ennor followed and she made sure to keep to the track the girl was stomping through the undergrowth. Both girls carried sticks and they thrashed the briar that snatched at their legs with violent blows.

Ennor counted out each smack of her stick and she told herself that when she reached a hundred they would be standing at the edge of the lake and she was right.

'What you reckon?' shouted Sonny. 'The lake's big, int it?'

Ennor nodded. 'Half frozen too.'

'Don't be such a killer. We got ways to fish, hell.'

They crouched in the undergrowth and Sonny made them snap thorns from the twisted bramble vines.

'You think these'll stand for fish hooks?' asked Ennor.

'Course.'

'Only my fingers are bleedin and I hope not for nothin.' She flicked the droplets of blood on to the snow.

'Watch what you're doin then. I'm not bleedin.'

'What you got for line?'

'Baler twine.'

Ennor thought for a minute. 'Int that too thick?'

'I'll split it course. Come on, I'll show you.'

They dumped their things high up on the thin pin shoreline and Sonny made a square for sitting in the snow. She used a flat rock to scrape it clear and not until the pretty shingle stones blinked up at them did she allow them to sit down.

'They're like jewels,' said Ennor as she knelt to them with a crunch. 'Trip would love these.' She turned them over in her hands and counted out seven of the prettiest and put them in her pocket.

'How's your fish-hooks workin out?' she asked.

'Shut up. I'm concentratin.'

'How you makin a hole in the barb?'

'With another barb.'

'Genius, int you?'

'Yep and really I am.'

Ennor sat back and watched Sonny split the twine into lengths of fishing line as thin as cotton.

She threaded half a dozen of the biggest thorns they'd collected and wound each one round a section of her walking stick.

'You wanna go find us some rods?' she asked. 'That's if you're not weighted down by them stones in your pockets.'

Ennor climbed up the bank of snow and looked down over the lake that skated out before her in a spin of spectrum blues and the clay sediment that lay on the lake's bed flashed turquoise. A tropical island shore in the middle of the cold moor that made Ennor smile and close her eyes to an imaginary sun.

If she concentrated hard enough, she could hear the warm water inch up the shoreline and feel it lap around her ankles and she wiggled her toes, remembering a memory that wasn't and never would be hers.

She heard squawking crows swing close above her head, seven parrots red and green across the deep blue sky, and she watched them swoop over the beach where her parents were laughing, playing with Trip. Everyone smiling and healthy like in photos, snapshot happy.

Ennor thought she might sit down on one of the sand dunes and write herself a poem, but her mother was calling her and then the calling turned to shouting.

'Ennor, hell.'

She snapped open her eyes and the bright of winter made her squint.

'What you doin, girl?' Sonny stomped up the bank of snow and stood squarely in front of her.

'What?' asked Ennor.

'You got the sticks?'

Ennor looked blank.

'The sticks for the fishin rods?'

'I was just goin to –'

'No don't worry your pretty fussy head bout it, I'll do it.'

Sonny stormed off into the undergrowth and Ennor watched her and listened to the snap of branches peppered with swear words.

She tried to recreate the daydream but it had all but disappeared and the beautiful azure shore that stretched before her was now just an optical illusion. The crows circled the lake one more time before moving on. Ennor counted them over and over until they dipped from view and there were six and only six, no matter how many times she went over it.

When Sonny reappeared with two thick poles of greenwood they walked down to the shoreline, Ennor tying the thread into a knife split at the end of each stick while Sonny needled a nip of pork rind for bait.

Ennor waited for Sonny to take the first step on to the ice and when she was ten steps out she followed.

'This is safe, int it?' she asked.

'Course.'

'You're not goin to get us killed, are you?'

'Course not.'

'Cus all for one fish, I'd rather try for a rabbit or a squirrel.'

Sonny stopped abruptly like she always did when acting outraged but she continued to slide forward on the ice. 'A squirrel?'

'Just sayin, a rat then, whatever.'

Sonny shook her head and waited until her skidding slowed to a stop.

'Why you stopped?'

'I've lost my flow, I was following the patterns in the ice and now I've lost it.'

She crouched to the ice and rubbed the thick frosted glass with her glove, then stood up and Ennor stood beside her.

'Beautiful, int it?' Sonny looked around at their surroundings as if noticing it for the first time.

'Like another country,' said Ennor.

'Another world entirely.'

The two girls stood shoulder to shoulder and almost breathless against the cold and beauty of the lake and Ennor realised they had walked a good bit out.

'You could kind of die right now, couldn't you?' said Sonny. 'Like right now, it wouldn't be so bad.'

Ennor didn't speak. She didn't want to spoil this one moment of being, but she knew exactly what Sonny meant. Maybe things weren't so bad if you knew you could stop time, settle yourself into somewhere perfect, if you knew death and disaster were heading and say, 'I'm here, I'm ready and I'm not scared.' A moment of clarity, preparation.

Something made her take hold of Sonny's arm and it felt good to be close to someone, an anchor out there on the water.

'Let's catch ourselves some fish,' said Sonny as she pulled away. 'The quicker we get fishin, the quicker we'll be sittin by a fire eatin the buggers.'

It was hard work gauging the best place to stop to test the ice. Each footstep creaked and fractured and Ennor felt like she was walking a fine line tightrope between laughing and crying.

They crouched together and Sonny drew a deep circle in the ice with the axe she wore looped into her belt. 'I'll chop into it the best I can.'

She told Ennor to sit back and to grab her feet if she fell in and they both laughed because they painted a funny scene no matter which way you looked at it.

The ice-chipping went without a hitch and they took it in turns to cup their ungloved hands into the moon of water and splash their faces and each other. The cold water brought rosy apples to their cheeks and burning warmth to their fingers. They made sure the bait was secure and for weights they used irregular-shaped stones that Sonny had picked from their circle on the shore and they tied the string a hundred times tight.

'This better hold,' said Ennor.

'It will, have a little faith is all.'

They lowered the weights and the knotted meat into the water and sat back on the ice.

'Two regular Eskimos, int we?' Ennor grinned.

'Could do with one of them fluffy leather hats, made from a seal pup or somethin.'

'And them stitched shoes,' agreed Ennor. 'What they called?'

'Moccasins.'

'Int they slippers?'

Sonny nodded and laughed out loud. 'Could just see us sittin here with slippers on our feet.'

'And pyjamas,' added Ennor. 'Slippers and pyjamas and a dressing gown.'

They laughed until tears fell from their eyes and their throats choked with childish squeals of delight and they were two girls out on a school field trip, messing around, with nothing serious about them except fooling.

When the first bite tugged at Ennor's makeshift fishing rod she ignored it because this was the last thing she was expecting. She held the stick casually in one hand and watched it bow with absent-minded amusement and Sonny watched too.

They had been discussing fish recipes and speculated on the best way of cooking but neither of them expected to catch an actual fish.

'What now?'

'Pull it, wind it and pull it.'

'It's a big un. He's pullin me in.' Ennor leant backwards and so did Sonny and they pushed their feet together as she pulled the stick backwards and twisted the cord around it.

'Keep it up,' shouted Sonny. 'If you lose it, I'll kill you and I mean it.'

'Can't do more than what I'm doin,' shouted Ennor as she lay back on the ice. 'I tell you the stick's goin to break and it'll be your fault.'

She pulled and twisted until her shoulders wrenched from their sockets and her forearms burnt with fatigue but still she pulled because the pain wasn't as bad as the thought of a lecture from Sonny.

When she thought she might pass out the fish fired from the hole like a rocket and sent Ennor flat-backed and skidding across the ice.

'That's it,' shouted Sonny. 'You done it, girl.'

Ennor lay where she fell, with the fish flapping close by and her heart in her mouth, and she stared up into the sky and could have sworn she saw a chink of sunlight flash at her through the clouds.

'What we get?' shouted Sonny.

Ennor looked across at the fish and the fish one-eyed her back. 'A fish.'

'What kind of fish?'

'Ugly one.'

Sonny reached out a hand and pulled her to her knees and then went to the fish.

She sat cross-legged and smashed its head on the ice to knock it out, then attempted to dislodge the barb from its throat. 'He's a big bugger, only thing is, the meat got stuck in his throat and now I can't get the bloody thing out.'

Ennor got to her feet. 'Let me have a go.'

'No.'

'Well cut its head off then.'

'Damn, I wanted to cook it whole.'

'Cut the head off. It's my fish.'

Sonny continued to wrestle with the hook then finally conceded and unhooked her knife from her belt. 'Only cus I'm hungry.'

She nestled the knife into the flesh above the gills and smashed her hand down on to the back of the blade, then gutted it and washed it clean in the circle of water that became a full blood moon.

Ennor sat on the square of pebbles that Sonny had cleared earlier and held the fish in her lap. She thought about the head skating out there on the ice somewhere and guessed it wouldn't be long before some bird or other swooped down to peck at the bloody lip of flesh where the body had been and its one exposed eye.

She felt the cut with her thumbs and opened it up to inspect its belly and insides and she told Sonny she'd done a good job.

'You sittin starin at that thing till dusk or you gonna help fetch firewood?' Sonny asked.

'I'm comin.'

'Dark will be comin in soon and if we don't find wood we won't be able to cook fish and you know what that means.'

'What?'

'Sushi. You ever tried eat raw fish?'

'No, you?'

'Nope and don't want to start tryin neither so let's go.'

They carried two lengths of rope with them and made their way back towards the woods they'd skirted earlier and although there wasn't much in the way of trees, standing or otherwise, they managed to lift enough wood for a cooking and sleeping fire.

'Good job,' smiled Sonny when they returned to their camp. 'Good job all ways, I reckon.'

Sonny nodded her way and Ennor knew she was close to saying something nice about the big fish without actually saying it and Ennor felt herself steam with pride when she looked at her catch.

Sonny built her spit above the damp smoky fire and both girls bent and coaxed the flames until the glow came back to their faces and Ennor finally passed over the fish.

She wished she had a camera to take its photo so she could show Dad when she got home. He would be so proud of her. Maybe even give her one of his trophies like he used to when she was a kid.

She watched Sonny thread a thin greenwood spear into its muscular side with a satisfying stitch. 'You want to put it on the spit? Say goodbye in your own special?'

'No you can do it. I've done enough, catchin it and everythin.'

They sat and coaxed the fire some more and Ennor made pine-needle tea as they waited for what seemed like for ever for the fish to cook.

There was still a little light to the sky and they watched as a kestrel circled the lake, suddenly dropping like a weight to claw up the fish head.

'We were a long way out, weren't we?' said Ennor.

'Maybe too far out, when you look at that bird, just a speck in the dust.'

'Poor bugger.'

'Who?'

'The fish. One minute he's swimmin in his own glory and then bam.'

'Flat on his back same as you,' laughed Sonny. 'Good fun though, weren't it?'

Ennor poured the tea and turned the fish and she agreed that she quite enjoyed fishing. 'Guess I'm lucky you came along.'

'I had to help you out. Couldn't stomach comin cross your crow-pecked corpse when spring arrived.'

'That the reason you come?'

'Bit of adventure, why? What you pokin at?'

'Just wonderin stuff, your home life and that.'

'Well don't.' Sonny leant forward to turn the fish to a position that was more suitable and she kept from looking at Ennor.

'You miss your family yet?'

'Course not. You?'

'Yes.'

'Well what that say?'

Ennor sipped her tea and settled the metal plate near

the fire to warm. 'Says I should probably mind my own business.'

'Correct.'

'I can't wait to find Mum. Can hardly think about it for wantin it so much.' Ennor could see Sonny nodding but she knew she was thinking about something else.

The kestrel finished scavenging all things wet from the fish head and it looped up into the air, caught a ride with the rising wind and was gone.

Ennor looked at the fish fattening and flaking above the flames and tried not to think about the hunger cramping in her stomach.

'Wind's comin up,' said Sonny. 'Comin up pretty fast in fact.'

'Maybe it'll bring warmer weather.'

Sonny stood and looked to where the last slither of daylight crumpled against the moorland.

She licked a finger and held it up to feel for the cold wind and then shook her head.

'North, north-east, I'd say.'

'Always,' said Ennor. 'I think the planet's got stuck somehow. Keeps on blowin from the north no matter what. Can't we just say hell to it and eat the thing?'

Sonny shrugged. 'Spose. You did catch it.' She released the fish from the heat and carried it to Ennor and the plate.

They sat like birds of prey hooked in the moment of a

good kill and an even better feed, their fingers pulling at the white flesh like barbarians.

Ennor felt full before she knew it and she cursed her shrunken stomach and continued to eat, the pleasure of food on her tongue and pressed against her gums, and she acknowledged another moment when she would have been happy to die.

She sat back with the last chew of fish in her mouth and watched Sonny wipe the plate clean with her fingers.

'Fat cats.' Sonny grinned when she saw her looking. 'The cats that got the cream.'

'The fish.'

'The cats that got the fish, int got such a ring to it, has it?' She wiped her fingers on her jeans and pulled up next to Ennor. 'Dint need nothin addin to it.'

They sat with the dregs of tea in mugs on their laps and watched the fire dance the day into total darkness.

No guiding stars hung in the sky and there was no bright farm window light on the horizon to point a wayward traveller towards civilisation.

Two girls in the black of a moorland night with the worrying wind and nothing but conversation to keep them from thinking negative detail.

Sonny asked Ennor if she planned to live the rest of her days where she was born and raised and she said she guessed she would. 'When everythin's fixed the way it's supposed and everyone's happy.'

'Family-wise?'

'Family-wise and money-wise with everyone gettin on.'

'No fightin and lootin and the rest.'

'And you can go and do anythin and not worry that you might never come home.'

'That'd be somethin,' Sonny agreed. 'Although I'd probably miss the fightin bit.'

'Int there somethin you'd rather do besides?'

Sonny shrugged. 'Like it cus it's the only thing I'm good at. When I turn pro, cage fightin and that, I'll get myself a stage name and a character, become someone else.'

'Where'd you go?'

'LA, New York, see the world if it's still there.'

'That's ambition you got.'

'It's more than that. It's in the marrow of my bones to travel. I can't wait, hell.'

Ennor laughed. She liked it when Sonny got going; she kind of knew what she was going to say before she said it and this made them like old friends.

'I like to write.'

'Lists? Girl, I know that. I've seen you scratchin away.'

'Not just lists. Poems and stuff.'

'Feelins stuff?'

'Sometimes.'

Sonny shook her head. 'What's the point in that?'

'Dunno, always done it.'

'And who reads your mushy bosh? Hell, who'd want to?'

'Nobody, just me.'

'Why?'

'Dunno.'

Sonny looked confused and this made Ennor laugh even more.

'Can I read it?'

'My mushy bosh? No.'

'Anythin in there bout me?'

'No, why would there be?'

'You might have had mean thoughts then writ them.'

'Don't look so worried. There's more interestin things to write bout than you.'

'Good cus don't.'

'I can write what I like. It's called artistic licence.'

'Autistic more like.'

'Shut up. Don't say that.'

As usual congeniality was soon spoiled by arguing followed by silence and this time it was Ennor's turn to do the sulking.

She thought about Trip and how excited he had been with the Christmas talk and she prayed that all this would be over soon.

If there was a God, and she believed there was, now was the time for some good luck payback. She prayed that the country was so skewed that Trip would be forgotten in the mess of it.

When Sonny asked her if she was moping and tried

to soften the darkness by cracking jokes Ennor told her she was tired.

She wrapped her blanket tight around herself like a sleeping bag and lay propped against the rucksack to get the best of the heat. Through the flames she watched Sonny's silhouette shadow-box at the water's edge and guilt and affection made her want to shout that she wasn't really cross with her but melancholy pinched her mouth shut.

CHAPTER NINE

Ennor lay as still as a dog-buried bone and really this was just what she was. She opened an eye to the outside world, expecting to see some colour in the dying fire but saw none. The black of night straddled her and pinned her down with its weight, brushing her face with feather fingers, settling, unsettling. She went to scream but her mouth was dumbstruck shut, a frozen zip rendered useless in the cold.

'Sonny,' she tried to shout, her mouth filling up like a balloon. 'Mm mm.' She pulled her arms from the hard blanket and reached for her friend.

'What? What is it?' shouted Sonny.

'Mm mm,' said Ennor.

Sonny gunned the torch and swung the beam towards Ennor.

'Hell.'

'Mm?'

'Your mouth's frozen shut. Hold the torch so I can look.'

Sonny poked at Ennor's mouth and tried prizing it open but it didn't work.

'It's frozen,' she said simply 'What did I say bout keepin your face covered?'

Ennor nodded and tried to smile.

'I'm gonna have to warm you up. Don't want to, but I have to.' She clapped a hand over Ennor's mouth and blew a gutful of hot air through her fingers.

Ennor could see she was trying not to laugh and she too felt the beginnings of a giggle somewhere deep in her belly and her ears tickled from the pressure.

She looked into the warm circle of torchlight and saw that their blankets were fluffy white from the snow. Everywhere she looked was white and snowing and she watched it build the fire into a wigwam and turn Sonny into an old maid with white eyebrows and hair.

'What you smirkin at?' she asked.

'Mm mm.'

'Nothin?'

'Mm.'

'Maybe I should leave you stitched. It's lovely and quiet round here.'

She kept up the blowing for some time and Ennor could feel a tingling sensation return to her lips.

'Can you open them yet?'

Ennor tried and then shook her head.

'Let me try.' Sonny pinched the upper and lower lip and then pulled and they came apart with a rip.

'Aw!' shouted Ennor. 'Did you have to make it hurt so much?'

'Yep, here, take this.' Sonny handed her the handkerchief from her pocket. 'You're bleedin.'

They packed up their few belongings as quickly as they could and ran towards the nearby woods. The snow was falling fast and crossways to the lake and the two girls hung on to each other to keep from tumbling. The blizzard wind slapped and pushed from all angles and bit at Ennor's mouth with barbed kisses. She thought she might faint or cry from the pain, maybe both.

Sonny was shouting something and she nodded. Whatever she was saying was just that, whatever. Wherever they were going, whatever they were doing was fine by her. She dabbed her lips until the tissue no longer showed red and she kept her hand over her mouth like a keeper of secrets. She kept hold of Sonny's jacket when she climbed the fence and stomped the snow-laden bracken flat and Ennor did the same, turning her face out of the bully wind to keep an eye on their path.

In the woods the trees gave partial shelter from the driving snow and Sonny shouted that she wanted to keep walking until they were out of the wind.

The small outcrop of trees seemed to double in size as they got nearer and had grown into tall, thick woodland. The snow had crept into the tree line and slunk vertical to each exposed tree and Ennor wondered if anyone had ever been trapped in a snow-banked wood or forest? Tonight it could happen. She looked out into the shaded wilderness for something to count, anything to keep her mind from the claustrophobic fear, but there was nothing but dark and she started to sing instead.

When she counted down to ninety green bottles she realised she was not alone in singing and she smiled despite the cracking sting of her lips. Sonny was a little scared too and this made her feel better. They were equal.

Together they reached sixty bottles and Sonny stopped singing and turned to Ennor.

'We should stop, if we go any further we'll be back in the storm.' Sonny waved the torchlight through the trees and then back at Ennor.

'Your mouth looks bad.'

'How bad?'

'Like proper bad. You got any balm?'

'No, you?'

'Don't be daft. You'll have to rub it with ear wax.'

'Get lost.'

'The SAS do it in jungles. If it's good enough for them.'

Ennor sighed. She didn't want to do it; she knew what ear wax tasted like and it tasted bad.

Sonny was sitting on the tarp she'd laid out on the ground and she was watching Ennor with intent.

'Turn that light away, will you?'

'Why? It int no dirty act.'

'Just let me do it.' Ennor stuck both index fingers into her ears and wriggled them in deep.

The momentary silence was a relief from the rush of wind through the trees and she closed her eyes to enjoy the peace. Her mind travelled back to the tropical shores of fantasy but this time she was aboard a fishing boat.

The rise and fall of undercurrent was like a gently rocking hammock adrift on a warm summer breeze. Ennor could smell the saltwater, could taste it on her lips, soothing.

She lay back in the boat and looked up at the sky and could have sworn she saw God in the smiling sun.

'Get up,' shouted Sonny. 'Are you hurt? Hell, you int hurt, are you?'

'I'm not hurt,' said Ennor. She lay on her back and looked up into the black canopy of trees and wondered if she looked hard enough she might see more of a devil place waiting for her.

'What's wrong with you, are you sick?'

'No why? What now?'

'You fell over.'

'No I dint.'

'You did. You were diggin for wax and then slam.'

Ennor sat up and wiped her fingers over her lips and she tried not to lick them.

'What's it taste of?'

'Sick, only not sick but that yellow stuff that comes after.'

Sonny smiled. 'How many fingers am I holdin up?'

'Two and two thumbs.'

'What's the date?'

Ennor shrugged. 'Twenty-third I think.'

'What's your name?'

'Ennor Carne.'

'What's my name?'

'Sonny somethin.'

'My real name.'

'Summer somethin.'

'OK, I guess you'll survive, for now anyway.'

Ennor got up and attempted to brush herself off, then sat down on the tarp. 'What now?'

'We wait till mornin. Stupid question but still.' She shook the last of the snow from their blankets and pegged them to branches she'd snapped into spikes to act as hooks.

'These'll stop the wind and dry out a bit,' she nodded to herself. 'If they don't, we're buggered cus I'm not draggin wet wool round with us.' She turned to Ennor and clapped her hands. 'You listnin to me?'

'Course.'

'I'm not draggin them wet blankets round with us.'

'I heard you. What we goin to use tonight?' Ennor asked.

'We'll have to pilchard up in the tarp.'

'It's freezin.'

'Tell me somethin I don't know.'

They lay rolled in the tarpaulin sheet like frozen sardines stranded on the shore and Ennor thought about fish. Caught, eaten and gone from the earth. She thought about her own meat hanging from her bones and all the wild things that might make a meal of her. Ennor Carne was half-dead anyway, a soon-to-be skeleton sinking into the ground. She imagined the slow decay and the tiny lives that might move in there, the worms and the maggots and the mites you couldn't even name or see with the naked eye, chewing the rot.

She wondered if Sonny had the same thought and she would have asked but knew the answer well enough.

Ennor commenced singing under her breath. Ten green bottles down from sixty and she wouldn't stop until she got down to none. No mean feat when your brain was closing down to hypothermia. Sometimes she missed whole chunks of numbers and had to go back to the beginning and sometimes she fell briefly to sleep, one lonely number stuck to her grizzly lips, on hold.

Ennor counted out her heartbeat, 'One banana, two banana, three banana.' She wondered what number banana would be its last and hoped to reach one hundred. A good clean number, a good one to go on. Number one hundred was a 'finished business' number and she counted out her bananas like a market trader, hoping to clear the table before closing time.

'What's with all the bananas?' asked Sonny.

'I'm countin my heartbeat.'

'Do you have to do it out loud?'

'I wasn't.'

'So how'd I know bout the bananas?'

'Sorry I woke you.'

'It's too late now. I got bananas everywhere I look.'

'You goin bananas?'

'Gone,' giggled Sonny. 'Bleedin fruit-loop bananas.'

The girl's splintered laughter warmed them a little and Sonny wondered if she might light a fire.

'If you got the spirit to do it, then do it. Otherwise don't.' said Ennor.

'Once it's done it's done, and it's heat and light and tea in the mornin.'

'Do it if you want to do it.'

Sonny sighed and then she buried her head under the tarp. 'Hell, I'll do it and then it's done. It's not as if we int shy of wood.'

'Take the torch.'

'Course.'

'Don't be long.'

Sonny rolled out of the rough-ready bed and Ennor

watched her fade into the woods with the tying rope slung across her shoulders and the wind-up torch revving in her hand.

She must have fallen asleep because the sun had returned to her dreamscape and she could feel the heat on her face. Maybe this was death, or heaven. The smiling sun of God or the furnaces of hell, either way it was warm.

'You asleep?' asked Sonny. 'Eh, bananas, you asleep?'

Ennor rubbed her eyes and then opened them. 'You made a fire.' She smiled.

Sonny nodded.

'You made a big fire.'

'I'll burn this whole wood down if I have to. The downdraught's blowin it good.'

Ennor sat up. 'Maybe we won't die after all.'

Sonny laughed. 'Never thought we would. Did you really think that?'

Ennor shrugged. 'Could be as easy as that. You fall asleep, then dead.'

'Or you fall asleep and wake to a raging fire.'

'Lucky.'

'Luck's got nothin to do with it. Called common sense if you int noticed. Dint I tell you I'd look out for you till you found your mum?'

Ennor nodded. 'I'll make some tea, got some pine needles left.'

'I wish we had teabags and milk and sugar. Hell, if we had coffee, I'd probably die in ecstasy.'

Ennor looked in her rucksack for the pan and then looked in Sonny's. 'Where's the pan?' she asked. 'My everyday pan, the one I use for boilin snow. We'll die without it.'

Sonny agreed. 'Can't live on snow, get hypothermia that way. You sure it's not in your huge everyday bag?'

'No.'

'In mine?'

'I've looked. We must have left it on the shore. Damn, no hot water means no water at all.'

'I'll go,' said Sonny. 'It's not far.'

'No I'll go, you collected the wood.' She stood up and stretched the cold from her legs and took up the torch.

'I won't be long. It's probably buried in the snow by the fire.'

She adjusted the scarf around her face and pulled the woolly hat down past her ears. 'Wish me luck.' She smiled.

'Don't believe in luck. Have fun.'

Ennor followed their tracks back through the woods towards the lake. Every now and then she'd look back to check that she could still see the home-fire burning and she could.

She walked with the torch in one hand and a stick in the other and she beat at the space in front.

The further she walked the stronger the wind became and their earlier tracks were close to gone as she neared the tree line.

Ennor took off her scarf and tied it to a tree as a guide for her return.

The storm would not get the better of her, not tonight and not ever. She climbed the fence and stepped out on to the wash of thick snow where the jewel stones lay like fossils beneath and headed towards the ice lake.

Exposure to the blizzard had caused all trace of their footsteps to disappear and even the lake was buried beneath a flat white skid of white.

Ennor dared herself to step out on to the ice and she stood to enjoy the luxury of having her boots and shins out of the freezing suck. She skidded her feet a little to feel the motion and when she stepped forward the wind pushed her back on to the snow shore of her desert island, stranded. She tried to guess where they had made their camp and poked her stick, kicking at irregular shapes in the snow until finally her foot sunk into the ashy remnants of the dead fire.

She dropped to her knees and with one hand clawed at the snow and pulled at the half-burnt timber until she found the pan. She raked through the frozen ashes for any other objects they might have lost.

In the debris of the fire she felt the ribbed zip of the fish backbone and yanked it clear of the snow. The fish that made Ennor eternally grateful. Life for a life. It had given her strength, strength to keep her heart beating, her mind from going mad. She snapped off the tailbone and cleaned it in the snow. A found object, beautiful, and she pressed it to her lips to make a wish.

When she returned to the woods Ennor realised she had been gone some time. Sonny was standing black against the huge dancing flames and she had her hands square on her hips.

'You were ages.'

'Sorry. It took time lookin.'

'I was worried.'

'Sorry, least I found the pan.' She waved it in the air as proof. 'Even filled it with fresh snow.' She nestled the pan near to the fire and sat back on the tarp. 'Snowin mad out there, worse than before.'

'Don't doubt it.'

'It's like all the planet's snow quota got dumped on Cornwall in one swoop. I hope Trip and Dad are all right and Butch of course.' Ennor had wished this when she kissed the fishtail, but it didn't hurt to say it out loud.

'What you got there?' asked Sonny.

'Bit of the fish. Part of the tail I think.'

'Why?'

'It's my wishbone. Gonna bring me luck, like catchin the fish was luck.'

Sonny added branches to the fire and sat down beside Ennor. 'You finally losin your mind?'

'Maybe. Don't hurt to have hopes and dreams, does it?'

'Let me look.'

Ennor handed over the wishbone and Sonny turned it over in her hands. 'It's got a nice weight to it, nice and smooth too, make a good mini-dagger.' She nodded and reached into her bumbag.

'What you doin?'

'Wait.'

'Don't carve it or nothin.'

Sonny pulled out the ball of baler twine and unclipped her knife to cut off a good length. 'See this hole here?'

Ennor nodded.

'It's perfect for a necklace, int it? That way you won't lose it.' She wound the string twice through the hole and tied a double knot at the end.

'There, now you can make wishes all day long.' She smiled as she passed it over and Ennor put it on.

'What's it look like?'

'Like a bit of fish caught on some twine.'

'Like how I caught it.'

Sonny nodded her head. 'Somethin like that.'

'You int so bad, are you?'

'Worse.'

'All hard but soft in the middle.'

'Shut up. Just dint want you to lose the bloody thing, hell. Couldn't stand you all weepy and feelin sorry.'

'Feelin sorry is your job,' said Ennor as she moved to make the tea, 'that and buildin fires.'

'Yours is feelin sorry and makin tea.'

'We got most things covered then.'

'Guess so.'

Ennor passed her a mug of tea and sat back with her own and they watched the fire burn almost out of control.

'I thought I was gonna die back there,' said Ennor.

'Where?'

'Earlier, before the fire.'

'But you dint.'

'Dint but I might of.'

'That's two of our lives gone, first the frozen lake, then here in the blizzard.'

'How many lives we got?'

'You got three.'

'How many you got?'

'Nine, like a cat.'

'Why'd you get nine? That int fair.'

'Girl, life int fair.'

'How'd I get nine? Some kind of gypo spell or somethin?'

Sonny shrugged 'Maybe. Maybe you should get wishin on that fishbone of yours.'

'All right I will. How many wishes make up one new life credit?'

'Bout a thousand, just to be safe. Nine thousand in all should do it.'

'You don't think I'd do it?'

'Don't really care to be honest, but for a girl who likes countin, it's somethin to do.'

Ennor smiled. 'You're right, best go for ten thousand though.'

'Why?'

'It's a good clean number, a good one to start on.'

CHAPTER TEN

Some kind of lesser sun limped ragged and untrusting towards dawn and crept up on the girls as they walked through fresh drifts of snow. Sonny called it an early bird start and that was exactly what it was.

She was convincing her new friend that nothing was without reason and if it wasn't for certain circumstances they would never have met. She walked with wide determined strides out from the woods and held the paper map in one hand and a rope for tying found timber in the other.

'You walkin slow for a reason?' she asked.

'Course not.'

'Guess you only got biddy legs but still.'

'Guess so.'

'Still you could pick um up a little, put some gumph into the thing.'

'I'm goin as fast as I can, I'm stiff from the cold.'

Ennor laughed at Sonny's big hair bouncing wild as she walked. Her leather jacket tight and too short for her arms and ancient biker boots split sideways and hard as nails. She wanted to ask her if she was cold but couldn't stomach another sideswipe and she wondered if the temperature was anything above freezing.

'How cold you think it is?'

'Cold.'

'No, really.'

'Really cold.'

'Why you in a mood?'

'I'm not, I'm concentratin on the route. You wanna find your mum before Christmas or no?'

'Course. I was just askin.'

'It's about seven or eight below.'

They walked in silence and Ennor settled her mind to counting steps and she kept her eyes on the thick-set snow around her. She lengthened her stride and stepped into Sonny's footsteps and she looked at the other prints running alongside them.

'Sonny?'

'What now?'

'We bin here before?'

Sonny stopped to look at her. 'Hello? No. Other side of the woods, int we?'

'You sure?'

'Course, why?'

Ennor pointed to the patch of snow beside them.

'You think it's that mad old woman? After me cus I killed her son?'

'Don't be daft,' said Sonny. 'There's two sets of prints circlin there. She int got four legs, has she?'

'Don't joke.'

'I int. Probably just people passin, same as us.'

'What kind of people?'

'People, just people.'

'Police?'

Sonny started to laugh. 'When was the last time you saw a bobby on the beat? Don't walk roads or lanes or nothin, do they? Not likely they're out on a hike.'

'Spose,' said Ennor.

'Double spose,' said Sonny. 'Now come on.'

They continued north following the bearing Sonny had set them and there were times when the footsteps vanished and times when they were in there walking between them.

Two ghosts making tracks and two girls following. Ennor didn't like it. The moor wasn't for sharing, not any more.

'They started to slow,' said Sonny. 'The footsteps are closer together.'

'We gonna catch um up? I don't want to catch um up.'

'Too late, look.' Sonny pointed towards two dark figures studded black in the dip of valley below.

'Hello?' she bellowed.

'Don't call um!'

'Why not, hello?' She waved both arms and jumped crazy until the figures stopped and turned.

'Come on. Let's say hi, looks like one of um's a kid.' She got out her telescope. 'Yep, a boy type kid.'

Ennor snatched the telescope and hurried to find familiar faces in the magnified white. She had a feeling, a good one.

'Trip!' she shouted. 'Butch!' She ran down the hill and called out their names until her own name rolled back with a bounce.

'Ennor,' Trip shouted. 'We bin lookin everywhere for you.'

Ennor bent to catch her brother and they hugged so tight they squeezed tears from each other's eyes.

'I missed you, sister,' he cried. 'I missed you lots.'

Ennor smiled as she knelt in the snow and she kissed both his cheeks. 'I missed you so much, buddy.'

'Anyone mind explainin?' asked Sonny.

Ennor hugged Butch and then pushed him away so she could look at him. 'What you doin here?'

'I kept runnin away.' Trip grinned. 'Just kept runnin, dint I, Butch?'

Butch nodded. 'He kept runnin off at night. I had to lock his bedroom door but he'd jump from the window and run.'

Ennor crouched to hold Trip in her arms and she stroked his hair back from his face. 'You stayed up at the farmhouse, did you?'

'Yep and buddy horse.'

'Well this is a regular mystery, int it?' laughed Sonny. 'Like a bloody whodunnit or somethin, this is.'

'Sonny, don't swear in front of my brother.'

'Sorry, brother. So anyone mind tellin what you're doin out here?'

Butch looked at Ennor. 'Things are gettin worse. We had to leave.'

'Worse how?' asked Ennor.

'They're takin kids from all over, good and bad. Detainin them in centres, for our own good they say but it don't sound right.'

'I int stoppin in no young offenders!' said Sonny and she looked down at Trip. 'What you lookin at?'

'Nothin.'

'Well that's good.'

'You're weird.'

'So are you.' She poked out her tongue and he laughed and said he didn't like her.

'What about everyone else, what about Dad?' asked Ennor.

'The cities are the worst; they got the army drafted in to keep the peace.'

'How you know all this?' asked Sonny as she stuck out her hand to shake.

'Radio. It's all they talk about, that and the weather.'

'This is Sonny by the way,' said Ennor. 'Sonny, this is my brother, Trip, and my friend, Butch.'

'So this is the famous Butch? I had you painted as a macho. Name don't really suit, does it?' Sonny laughed and continued to grip his hand.

'Why you laughin?' asked Butch.

'Well no offence but you're a skinny little rag, int you? No disrespect mind.'

'Looks like you got my share and more.'

Ennor told them to stop sniping. She wanted to ask Butch about Dad but there was no right time with all the fussing and goings-on and she told herself the reason he wasn't saying wasn't bad news but news of a kind. She closed her eyes and pictured herself back at the farm, walking with Dad out in the best fields. She watched him herd the cows with his walking stick and she remembered how when nobody was looking she'd practise on the chickens in the yard.

Loaded dread swamped her and she opened her eyes to stop it but it was too late because she pictured him dead in bed with his cheeks ballooned further from the drugs and his eyes opaque smudges with the twinkle all gone.

'You OK?' asked Butch.

'Course she's OK. What, you her babysitter?'

Ennor told him she was fine and she asked him how he knew where to look for them.

'Kept a copy of your route.' He shrugged. 'Just kept walkin. I knew I'd find you.'

'You did?' Ennor smiled. He knew he'd find her; she liked that.

'We bin walkin for ages,' said Trip. 'I got sores on my feet.'

'I'll have a look at them later.' Ennor went to put her arm around him but he took off down into the valley.

'Hey!' he shouted. 'A dog!'

Buddy dog was named by Trip and was immediately given best friend status.

A sheepdog mixed with something else nobody could call, he was spotted on that first morning the gang set forth into the blizzard.

'Come on, buddy dog,' laughed Trip.

'Stop with the salt crackers, dogs don't eat salt crackers,' said Ennor.

'This one do.'

'If you feed him, he'll follow us for ever.'

'Good, he's my best friend.'

Sonny patted the dog's head and ruffled his coat. 'I like him, and if we can't feed him, we'll eat him.' She smiled at Trip and winked but he pulled the dog away.

'Storm's gettin worse,' shouted Butch from up ahead.

'Jeez, you think? Hell.' Sonny turned to Ennor and made a face. 'Your boyfriend's a regular genius.'

'He's not my boyfriend.'

'Friend who's a boy, whatever. Hey, Butchy boy, where you headin?'

'North,' he shouted.

'I'm the one with the map.'

'Map int worth much without a compass.'

There was a serious air about them that was grownup and silent, the storms had brought the moor to a white- wallpapered stop. They walked in one another's footsteps and called out their names when they wandered left or right. Every breath taken was painful and brittle in the chest.

Landmarks they had circled on the map were useless to them in the suffocating snow and they hung to the plastic Christmas-cracker compass Butch had brought with him like their lives depended upon it because it did.

'If we keep headin north, we'll be fine,' Butch said to Ennor.

'And when the storm eases we'll be able to pick up our route,' shouted Sonny.

'I hope so,' said Ennor. 'I'm gettin tired of this.'

Butch shook his head. 'I told you, dint I? You got to take account of everythin.'

Ennor knew he was right because he was always right. There was a time when she took comfort from this, but they were in a new world now, her world. His righteousness bugged her when everything was so skewed.

Earlier she had wanted to take hold of his arm, allow herself to be guided, protected from the grinding worry that turned her thoughts to dust.

But now she harboured an overwhelming desire to tell him to get stuffed. She'd survived the journey so far, hadn't she? Maybe some of Sonny's attitude had rubbed off on her and maybe that was a good thing.

She wanted to ask him if he'd rather leave them to it and turn back but knew this would only hurt his feelings. He was sensitive for all his arrogance. His job was unfaltering help and protection and she'd always needed him but maybe he needed her more, a weak boy and a beaten boy, who was strong for her. She felt bad for thinking bad and when he started coughing she felt bad for that too.

She linked his arm and smiled. In her mouth there were a million words stored for asking about Dad, but when she went to speak spitting grit jammed her throat tight.

'What?' he asked.

'You goin to be all right?'

'Course, why?'

'Your cough and all.'

'I'm fine.'

'But your chest infection?'

'Don't worry bout it. It's the least of my worries. It's cleared anyhow. Just got the cough now.' He pulled away from her and stopped to reach into his rucksack for the water bottle and Ennor stopped too.

She looked back and waited for Sonny and Trip to catch up and she laughed at the dog jumping crazily between them.

'Stupid dog tryin to trip me up,' shouted Sonny. 'What have I ever done to you? Grizzly cloth-eared mongrel.'

'He likes you,' said Ennor, still smiling.

'Glad I can provide you with some entertainment, hell.'

'Maybe he can smell the fish on you?'

'What fish?' asked Butch.

'The fish I caught on Siblyback.'

'Big bugger,' added Sonny.

'You eat it?' he asked.

'Course we did,' laughed Sonny. 'What you think we did with it? Fashion it into a hat?'

'You got any left?'

'Nope.'

'Shame.'

'Not for us.'

Ennor told them to shut up and for Butch to ignore Sonny because she always won with wind-ups.

'It's true,' grinned Sonny. 'Just try it and you'll see.'

Occasionally the dog ran into the abyss with Trip in pursuit and Sonny made a lead with great lengths of the baler twine she still had balled in her bumbag, plaiting it in her mouth as they walked.

'If the dog goes to make a dash, you give this a sharp tug,' she shouted as she tied the lead securely around the dog's scruff and she let Ennor tie it around Trip's wrist.

'What you say to Sonny?'

Trip stroked the rope and they all stood sideways in the gale while he thought for a moment and then he thanked her.

'You're welcome. There's nothin Sonny Pengelly can't make out of twine, I know all the knots.' She smiled at the others but nobody was looking and nobody was listening and she got out the map instead.

'According to this there's a farm near bout.'

'If we pass it, we're doin well,' yelled Butch through the wind.

'If we pass it, we're goin in,' Sonny replied.

'We can't go knockin on every door we see, it's Christmas. People will think we're on the rob.'

'Well I'm gonna find me a barn cus this is ridiculous and it'll be dark before long. You've not spent much time out here, have you, skinny boy?'

'Just shut up, you two. If we get to a farm and it's gettin dark, we'll ask if we can stay,' said Ennor.

Sonny laughed. 'Just ask? You two are as green. Buddy dog's got more smarts than you.'

She looked at the dog and looked at Trip and he smiled and told her he had a horse too.

'Really? What's his name?'

'Buddy horse.'

Sonny laughed. 'And you're buddy boy, I spose.'

'No.'

'Hell, come on, buddy boy, tell me about your horse. How many hands is he?'

'He don't have hands, stupid. He's got hooves.'

'He big or small?'

'Small, smaller than buddy dog.'

'Really? Like one of those micro pigs but a horse.'

Ennor grabbed her arm and whispered in her ear that the horse was a toy that lived in his pocket and to shut up.

'A toy horse, buddy boy?'

'No.'

'Sonny, shut up.' Ennor dug her fingers into her arm. She would have to tell her about Trip's autism when they had a proper minute because if she kept on winding he'd lose his temper and she didn't trust Sonny not to lose hers.

'What you laughin at?' asked Sonny.

'Nothin.'

'I know you're thinkin somethin and now you're laughin.'

'No I int.'

'You're like a bully but worse cus you don't say it.'

'What goes on in my head is my own business.'

'Not when it's bout someone else.'

'It's my head.'

It was Butch's turn to raise his voice and he told them to shut up and look ahead and they huddled together and squinted towards middle ground at a wall and a gate and nothing much else besides.

'What you think?' he asked.

'Looks like a ram-shack field to me, let's go in.' Ennor stepped forward and held the gate open and she told Trip to hold the dog lead tight in case of livestock.

'This is a crappy high place to have a farm,' she said and everyone agreed and they dragged their heels through the field of thick snow until they found another gate and then another.

'So what's the plan?' asked Sonny.

'We'll go to the house and knock.'

'Just like that? Gonna spin any kind of story? Might help.'

'Nope, I'll tell the truth or thereabouts. You two can stand back and I'll go with Trip.'

'And buddy dog?' asked Trip.

'Fine and the dog.'

It took time to find the farmhouse because it was hidden in the crack back of yet another valley and shrouded in an icy fog. Sonny and Butch kept out of sight from the front door and listened with their fingers crossed while Ennor and Trip stepped the whitewashed yard and approached the house.

She stood on the stoop and rang the doorbell and when nobody came to the door she knocked and stood back to look at the closed curtains of the living room. She saw a shadow grow large in the frosted pane of the hallway window and she tidied her hair into her bobble hat and told Trip to do the same.

'Who's that?' asked a man's voice through the letterbox.

'Hello, sir. my name is Ennor and this here is my brother, Trip.'

'What you want?'

She cleared her throat and counted to three. 'Some food maybe and a night's shelter. We're on a kind of mission.'

'We've had your kind recent, cracked religious fanatics sendin in the kids. Where your parents at? I'd like a word.'

Ennor went to explain her predicament but the chewed two-eye of a sawn double barrel poking out the letterbox was enough to render her speechless and she grabbed Trip's arm and pulled him running.

'Buddy dog,' he shouted as the dog pulled the lead from off his arm and they all ran any which way until they buckled panting out of view of the house.

'That was fun,' laughed Sonny. 'Guess I was right bout hidin out in the barn.Could be gettin a fire goin by now, if anyone bothered listnin.'

'Shut up, Sonny,' Ennor and Butch said at once. They sat up against a half-torn fence to catch their breath and watched Sonny tear at the wood with fierce determination.

'What you doin?' asked Trip.

'Firewood, come and help.'

The boy got up and helped her rip the thin tooth planks from rusty nails and fence posts and they called for buddy dog between breaths and eventually he returned.

'He likes you,' she said.

'How'd you know?' he asked.

194

'Cus he came back, dint he? Knows his name and everythin.'

Trip smiled with pride and Sonny could see he was finally coming around to the idea of her.

'You really pullin down somebody's fence?' shouted Butch.

'Course she is,' said Ennor.

'I'm thinkin practical. Must be minus ten out here and it's gettin dark or dint you realise?' She told Trip to stand steady with his arms outstretched and she piled the timber lengthways and she bundled whole planks into her own arms and said anyone who was cold and hungry to follow her and she walked back towards the farm.

'We int goin back down there,' shouted Butch.

'Course not, just near enough to it. Don't forget we got a gun ourselves, don't we? We'll set the kid to stand guard.' She looked to see if Ennor would bite but she didn't.

They followed their coming and going spin footsteps and diverted from the course towards a clutch of outbuildings that sat further along the valley and out of view of the house.

'Don't look like these get used much at all. Could probably move in and nobody would know.' Sonny rattled a corroded lock and when it wouldn't twist free she kicked at the door until the hinges loosened and it fell to the ground.

'She's like some kind of warrior,' Butch whispered to Ennor and they both laughed.

'Put the wood over there,' she shouted as they entered the cramped brick building. 'This place was used for curing ham; I can smell it, smell the hickory smoke.'

She pushed wooden crates into a circle with her boot and set about making a fire. 'It might get a little smoky but we're beggars here so can't go choosin.'

'You gonna do everythin or can we help?' asked Butch.

'Other than gigglin with your girlfriend? Work out a watch rota for the three of us if you want.'

'You serious? I don't want to shoot anyone. We are tresspassin.'

'It's no biggy when you're the hunted, believe me.' Sonny sat cross-legged on the dirt floor and showed Trip the quickest way to a successful fire and he watched her hands intently and sat the same with half the wood piled in his lap.

'You ever killed someone?' he asked.

'Only with my dazzlin good looks.'

'You're funny.'

'I know it.'

'You're crazy.'

Sonny laughed. 'I know that un all.'

Ennor and Butch went to look for useful things at the end of the small barn and Sonny told Trip they were excusing themselves because they wanted to get up to lovebird stuff and when Ennor protested she told him that was a sure sign.

'Where did you meet her?' asked Butch when they were out of earshot.

'Gypsy camp west of home. I got into some trouble and came across this camp and Sonny just kind of took me in.'

'What kind of trouble?'

'Nothin, nothin I want to talk bout. Anyway she's OK really. Grows on you even.'

'I doubt it, so what we lookin for exactly?'

'Anythin useful, won't know till we see it.'

They pushed about the dust and the dry and Ennor finally got to ask about Dad.

'I couldn't find the right time to say, with the others and everythin.' Butch upturned some kind of rust rack and they sat on its backboard while he rolled them a cigarette and he lit up and took a deep drag and then coughed.

Silence was a blood drum banging in her ears and was deafening. 'He's dead,' she said.

Butch looked at her and nodded and he handed her the cigarette. 'Died in his sleep, kind of.'

'What's kind of?'

'Overdose. Accidental, they said.'

'Who said?'

'That retired doctor from the village.'

Ennor stood bolt upright. 'That bloke that come visitin last week weren't no friend at all, I bet.'

She paced a little and upset was quickly snuffed and replaced by anger. 'If only I knew.'

'Butch got up and stood as if to hug her but rested a hand on her shoulder instead. 'Don't beat yourself over. His days were numbered and you know it.'

'Did he die peaceful, they reckon?'

Butch nodded and squeezed her shoulder tight. 'I'm sure he did.'

Ennor smiled just a little and she pictured her dad gathered and shrinking in the bed. 'High as a kite, I bet, flyin out over the fields like a bird. He always said he wanted to come back as a bird of prey. Maybe he will.'

'Where they take him?'

Butch shrugged. 'Hospital I spose.' He felt in his pocket and pulled out her dad's bootlace with the ring on it.

'I guessed he'd want you to have this.'

'Mum's ring.' She opened her hand and gripped it tight. 'The ring he gave to her when they got engaged.'

'Sorry,' said Butch.

'Don't be sorry.' She smiled and squeezed her eyes tight to keep the tears from falling. The whole of life and death smelted down to a simple curl of gold in her hand.

She passed the butt to Butch and looked around. 'There's nothin here but junk and more junk. Let's leave it, I int got the energy in any case.'

They returned to the fire to find that Sonny and Trip had disapeared and they read the message Sonny had scratched on to the stone floor to say they'd gone for food.

'Damn,' shouted Ennor. 'Gone where?'

'Back to the house?'

'Sonny int that stupid, not quite anyway.' She sat at the fire and rolled the ring around in her hand and she watched as the flames brought it to life. 'I spose a black mood int goin to cure anythin.'

'You allowed feelin sad. Trip int here to make a show for,' said Butch.

'Still, it won't bring him back.' She put the bootlace over her head and put on her coat and hat and told Butch to tend the fire and she pushed out into the squally snow.

'They won't have gone far,' shouted Butch but she had disappeared and he stood and finished the cigarette in the space where the door once stood.

Ennor followed the four footsteps that ran skidding between the half-cut buildings and she replaced sadness with anger because Sonny was a big dumb kid.

The wind spun punching around hard corners and at times lifted her off her feet and she cursed and bent to the ground to follow the boot prints until they disappeared behind a low creeping wall.

'Don't move,' came a serious voice. 'Keep still and don't move a muscle or you're dead.'

'Sonny?' she whispered. 'I int in the mood for this.'

A hand appeared at the top of the wall and pointed

towards an empty pigpen and whipped into a sudden exclamation mark towards Ennor.

She stood skeletal and shaking in the wind and looked the pen over and she kept her eyes peeled until a chicken poked its head through the bars and winked and Ennor thought maybe it was her dad returned as a chicken and she winked back.

'Why you winkin at the chicken?' asked Trip from behind the wall.

'The chicken winked at me.'

'You don't wink at home's chickens.'

'Well maybe this is a new thing to be doin, winkin.'

'Buddy dog winks.'

'There you go.'

'Can everyone shut up about the winkin? Hell, I'm tryin to catch grub here!' shouted Sonny.

'You won't catch anythin with a raised voice. Can I move yet? Before I freeze to the spot.'

'One more minute, just wait.' Sonny appeared at the far side of the wall and she told Trip to run when she did and on three they fired towards the bird like hot lead with Trip blocking the fence and Sonny jumping the pen wall.

Ennor petted the dog and watched feathers rise from the enclosure and she shouted for them both not to swear.

'Gothcha,' shouted Sonny with the chicken dangling from its feet. 'The incredible winkin chicken.'

They carried it back to Butch and the fire and Ennor was struck by the absurdity of life and death. Her dad and a boy and a fish and a chicken, all dead because of her.

'I'll show you how to kill it and pluck it,' Sonny promised Trip, 'if your sister don't go all soppy and bow it up like a dolly.'

'I int soppy, I'm hungry.'

Inside the barn Ennor sat with Butch at the fire in silence and they drank the tea he had made.

Hunger was no longer something but everything and their lives were dictated by it.

They listened to the death choke of the chicken from outside the door and the homely rattle of Sonny's bad singing as she plucked it to skin; this was as close to normal living as any of them could wish.

CHAPTER ELEVEN

Rapture was an unknown something Ennor's mother used to talk up when she helped peg out the washing or dig the garden over. It was something to be sung and something to smile at suddenly but the girl never knew its reason and was never told the why.

She thought maybe the four of them circled loosely about the fire had a little rapture to them. Even the dog had a half-dizzy smile wrapped around it and he listened and nodded to the conversation with one ear on the storm and one eye on the roasting chicken. Sonny was talking through the best way to roast a bird and the dog listened with a kind of seriousness as if it were about to be quizzed.

She turned the body slowly on the makeshift spit and smiled when it made the rotation without falling into the flames.

'Anyone want to know how to make the perfect spit?'

She looked over at Ennor and Butch and they shook their heads.

'Whatever, you two got no sense of spirit to you. I get more interest from the bloody kid and the dog.'

'Don't swear.'

'Dint.'

She cobbled a shelf out of a few discarded concrete blocks and a plank of wood not yet picked for the fire and she set what metal plates they had between them into a line and she mumbled a wish for spuds.

'Chicken's just fine,' said Butch.

'Fine for a bird boy like you but chicken's just chicken and won't go far. How you come by that ridiculous name anyway?'

'My dad.'

'Joke was it?' She called Trip close to the fire and told him to kneel so he could turn the spit every five minutes and said she wouldn't be long.

'Where you headin now?' asked Ennor.

'Out, won't be long.'

'Then take the gun.'

'Don't need no gun. Keep it, you've got a regular family here to protect.' She put Ennor's army coat over her own and stumbled through the door.

'Where she goin?' asked Trip.

'Round the bend,' laughed Butch. 'Let's eat the chicken before she gets back.'

Ennor poked him in the ribs. 'If it weren't for Sonny, I'd be dead in the ground.'

'I'd be plenty able to supply if it weren't for her hangin round.'

Trip told Butch to shut up because Sonny was his friend and Ennor said he was only fooling and she thought about the rapture right there and then because she was flirting with Butch just a little and she wondered if he'd noticed.

She looked at him occasionally when his eyes sank sleepy to the fire and the heat bundled him silent, his secretive eyes dancing the flames alive with uncharacteristic passion.

'How long's she bin gone?' he asked.

'Five, ten minutes maybe.'

'Ten,' said Trip, turning the chicken.

'You think someone should go lookin for her?'

'Not yet, she'll only go mental.'

'How long until she'd go mental if we dint go lookin?'

'Few hours?'

They both started laughing but soon stopped when Sonny threw a turnip at them through the open door. 'Peel that and dice it tiny cus its animal feed and chewy. That's if you got nothin better to do.' She sat cross-legged with a pan of fresh snow and rested it snugly into the embers of the fire.

She sang a song about a time before poverty and disaster and half the words she made up and when the chorus came around the third time the others joined in.

She boiled the chew from the turnip and strained it to plate and carved the chicken four ways equal because Trip was growing and needed sustenance the same as the others.

They ate noisily but in silence and when the chicken was picked through they broke bones from it and tossed them to the dog and he smiled the evening through.

That night darkness came as a different kind of dark and was heavy and bright with the non-stop snow.

It seemed as if a lifetime of winters had arrived at once and settled on that little peak of Cornwall known as Bodmin moor.

The snow at the door had risen into a step and Sonny carried concrete blocks and stacked them against the doorframe to keep it at bay.

'We won't get snowed in, will we?' asked Butch. 'If it keeps snowin the way it's snowin?'

They sat in a line with their backs against crates and the fire and the changing world between them and watched the entrance diminish.

'If it gets to the middle, I'll climb out and start shovellin,' said Sonny.

'What with?'

'I dunno. There must be somethin in this tip we can make a spade with if we need to.'

Ennor settled herself to looking deep into the heart of the fire and every time she thought of Dad she thought of Mum instead. She put her hand to her chest to feel the bootlace ring press against her skin and closed her eyes and prayed Dad into heaven and Mum into her arms.

Butch made more tea by scraping snow from the ice-wall with a knife and all blankets were piled by the fire for a bed and Trip and the dog lay snuggled to the heat and listened to the comfort of older conversation.

They all agreed the chicken was the best they'd ever eaten and even the turnip added a certain something to the meal.

'Where'd you find it?' asked Butch.

'Floor of that barn by the pig sty.'

'Pig feed?'

'Anyone's feed when you're hungry, you did eat it, dint you?'

Butch shrugged.

'There you go then. Dint Mummy put turnip in your pasties?'

'Course.'

'Course, turnips are turnips and food is food whether it's out the ground, the sky or a bin, hell.'

She went and found herself a piece of thick wood from the junk which she hoped to whittle into a paddle for shovelling and she built herself a step at the door out of crates so she could see over the snow and sat with her hunting knife in hand.

'What you kids don't realise is I've seen the world and thereabouts and I know that sailin int as plain as you think. Crisis is whole world or don't you listen to the news?'

'Course,' said Butch. 'Radio won't shut up bout city riots and good people runnin scared to the country. Said it's gonna take a whole lot of time to get back to somethin that resembles normal.'

'When you hear that?' asked Ennor.

'Before I came away.'

A menacing silence settled between them, interspersed occasionally by Butch's coughing.

'Can't we just bed down now?' Ennor asked Butch. 'You're on the next watch and need to rest.'

Trip and the dog lay fast asleep and Butch and Ennor got beneath the blankets and Sonny added a little of the fence wood to the fire to keep it ticking over.

Time stopped and drew back and forth through the night and Ennor was aware of the fire crackling with damp wood and of Sonny's silhouette shaping the paddle through the low dancing flames. She dreamt they all lived in a big house the shape and size of the farmhouse back home but within it echoed the open rattle of the barn. Everything make and mend and almost perfect from a lifetime of living and making do, anything and everything fixed and fiddled and found a use for.

Ennor could imagine the world changed in her dream and it was no longer anyone's concern who was or who wasn't sent to institutions and or whether adults played their part in the lives of their children or if they were out fighting mad. The war that people fought in her dream was like the ones in the history books with guns and uniforms painting the picture and she woke almost believing that those old wars in history were somehow better to have lived through because they had boundaries and sides and everything made sense in a roundabout way.

She sat up and saw that Butch was now sitting guard and it was Sonny who slept peacefully beside her and she smiled and nodded at him and bundled back down beneath the blankets before the cold had her rattling.

When it was her turn for guarding she sat and peeked over the snow line and waited for her eyes to adjust to the strange snow light and was glad to see snowflakes had been replaced by fog. She watched the veil lick the stone and slate of farm buildings and pull up short to the door frame to look at her and it filled the half-square with daring front.

Ennor had an urge to bat it away with the shovel or draw the gun to shoot into the void because it told her that her dad was dead and it demanded she show some emotion.

She bit back the tears until her face ached with the pain of defiance and it caught in her throat like a bone that had grown long into the flesh.

One flash of emotion multiplied like spores gathering on the wind and her dad's voice drowned her ears and she could see his face clear as youth and it filled the square of fog like a painting and smiled and joked and whooshed with a thousand memories.

Re-enactments of happier times and made-up times merged into fantasy and Ennor slapped her face to keep back the tears but they bubbled beneath her fingers. They travelled down her neck and into her shirt collar and splashed on to her lap and she crawled out on to the level snow just to feel something tangible and outside of herself.

The fog left her where she lay and moved on to other places and she pressed her face to the snow and waited for the sting of tears to harden into tiny salt crystals on her cheeks.

If this was grief, she was better off not getting close to anyone ever because it hurt more than you could think or say or know.

Ennor rolled on to her back and she flapped her arms and legs as a trick way into thinking she was fine but the snow was frozen hard and she merely lay there spent and stupid with anger rising and overflowing inside.

She jumped to her feet and ran a little way out from the complex of buildings and through the unfamiliar field. The moor was like an enemy and she stamped it dead with all the strength she'd been building and hiding all her life and she screamed and cried until the long-stuck bone snapped and fell from her throat.

She could no longer hear her dad's voice but the shrill power of her own and she kept at it until the snow inched back below her feet and the fog retreated to the coast.

There was nothing left to stamp or scream about and Ennor bent to catch her breath back into her lungs and she smiled at the craziness of it all.

When her heart beat normal and she stood normal to the world her smile became a giggle and the giggle became healing laughter.

Ennor Carne's dad was dead and that was a fact no matter which way she turned to look at it and life would move on the way God intended.

To the east, light was threatening to rise and a string of muted colour traced the cross-border landscape in an arc from Bodmin Moor to Dartmoor.

She made her way back to the barn and was mindful to keep her wits close because with the coming light and without the veil of falling snow there was every possibility that she would be seen.

She walked close to walls and edged her way forward and she realised the snow was planted with everywhere footsteps that a farmer with half an eye and half a brain would notice. They would have to get moving as soon as they were able and she wondered how to say she'd gone for a dawn walk without sounding like the crazy she was.

'The wanderer returns.'

Sonny sat on a crate outside the half-blocked doorway and she clapped and nodded some kind of appreciation.

'Glad you could join us.' She smiled.

'Don't start, I was gone no more than half an hour.'

'More like two and a half. I saw you goin and then heard you runnin off into the night, I was concerned.'

'I needed to be on my own. You goin to let me in?'

Sonny stood to let Ennor pass and she followed her down into the cubby.

'I had to relight the fire.'

'You shouldn't have bothered. I made fresh footprints all round, we'll have to go.'

'I guessed that, but the kid needs to eat somethin besides chicken bones.' Sonny sat and tended a pan of porridge and she said they weren't going anywhere until it was eaten because it was their last.

'What are you two hammerin on about?' asked Butch and he sat up and blinked towards the light.

'Your girlfriend here decided to go for a jog in the early's and set a trail every which way to our door. You better sit with the gun till we're done.'

'I'll do it,' said Ennor. 'It's my problem anyway.' She sat with the barrel poking and she watched Sonny stir the porridge until it was cement thick.

'What we gonna do with no food?' she asked.

'That's a stupid question I won't be answerin.'

'She'll steal some,' said Butch. 'Break down that farm-house door and stamp right into the kitchen demandin and goin on.'

Sonny laughed. 'Not such a bad idea. You offerin to come with?'

Ennor stopped listening because they were beginning the first bicker of the day and it was interfering with the calm buzz she'd gleaned from earlier. She sat in the doorway and watched the sky develop and bend into lighter hues of grey outside and allowed herself to wonder briefly if today was the day for rekindling something with Mum.

'You gone over the plan?' she asked Sonny. 'You know how to get to that Treburdon place, you reckon?'

'Course.' Sonny smiled.

'Good,' Ennor nodded. 'That's good.'

CHAPTER TWELVE

The ragtag crew of five crept from the barn and went silently through gates and fields until they were back on open moorland with the morning light a dazzling surprise.

The temperature slunk below freezing and the group knew it would stay that way. There was no wind coming from the south to push it warm, but neither were there snow clouds rising from the north and that was something to be grateful for. In any case north was where they were heading and they rough-sketched the day's route in their collective mind.

The crazies that had Ennor running mad earlier that morning had settled into a warm, content buzz.

'What you smilin bout?' asked Sonny. 'Grinnin like an idiot.'

'I'm not.'

'You are. Big stupid grin slapped across your face like a nutcase.'

'Just happy a while, what's wrong with that?'

'Don't seem happy. You might be smilin but . . .'
Sonny shrugged and ran off to tease Trip and the dog.

'What's her problem?' asked Butch.

'What?'

'She's always at you.'

'Just her way. Kind of like havin fun I spose.'
Butch laughed through a cough.

'How's you?'

'OK.'

'Your chest?'

'You don't have to keep askin, I'm fine.'

They walked shoulder close and Ennor could imagine them holding hands. They walked slow and steady on the hard frozen snow and were careful not to slip. Broken bones were not an option in the middle of the frozen wilderness.

Sonny and Trip kept stopping and waiting for them to catch up, their heads shaking and toes tapping in impatience.

'You two slow on purpose?' shouted Sonny.

'Yep,' said Butch. 'We love slippin and slidin roundabout in the freezin cold.'

'Looks like it,' she smiled. 'Only if you put some speed into the thing you might find you warm up. Just a suggestion, no offence like.'

'None taken,' he smiled back. 'Only mind you don't go fallin and breakin your back with all your runnin around. We'd have to leave you and you'd soon freeze to death, no offence.'

Sonny laughed. 'None taken, hell.'

'Sister, my eyes are burnin out my head,' said Trip.

'What you mean?'

'It's too bright.'

They all agreed it was a bright white day. Despite the cloud the sun was up there somewhere, making hollow promises.

'I'll make you some sunnies,' said Sonny. 'Got some pine bark I bin savin.'

'Savin for what?'

'You'll see later.'

They stopped for a break while Sonny made sunglasses out of a strip of bark and twine and Butch rolled them a cigarette for sharing.

'How will I see?' asked Trip.

'Through a slit.' Sonny unclipped her knife from her belt and cut a centimetre strip in the middle of the bark and tied it around the back of his head.

'It feels weird,' he said.

'You'll get used to it.' She nodded. 'Suits you.'

They continued on their journey, occasionally skidding across the sheet of thick ice and using each other as buffers. Ennor's legs hurt from sliding one foot in front of the other and her feet throbbed where new blisters formed on the old.

'How much longer of this?' she moaned. 'It int worse

than the snow but still it's bad enough. Mum won't believe this when she hears it.'

Butch passed her the cigarette and she sucked the warm air deep down into her lungs.

'Hope you find her,' he said.

'Course I will. Why? What you know?'

'Nothin, but neither do you.'

Ennor dug her heels into the ice and sighed. 'I got my ideas and leads and stuff.'

'What that old bird told you is probably a pile of bull, you know that, right?'

'Well thanks Butch, thanks for the downer.'

'I int puttin a downer on you, but you got to be realistic, prepared just in case.'

They watched Sonny and Trip run about up ahead and Ennor wished Butch were more positive sometimes, even if just a little. She knew he had stinking crap in both hands with his dad's violence and his mum's ignorance but didn't they all have their hands full of something they'd rather they didn't?

'You in a mood with me now?' he asked.

'Nope.' She didn't look at him because if she did he'd do the eyes that made her forgive him. Ennor didn't want to forgive him. He was forever dumping on her dreams while she had to bolster him up when he talked about studying and university dreams.

Since meeting Sonny she'd realised there was nothing wrong with a little optimism no matter how crazy.

Life was going to go one of two ways anyway so why not make the best of it? This was what she wanted to say to Butch, but it would have come out at all angles, like always when she tried to be serious.

Up ahead Sonny shouted that they needed to make progress while there was no northerly wind to push them backwards.

They continued their journey into the vast blue-white plains of the moor. From a distance they must have looked like a family of hardened travellers as they walked with determination across the changing land-scape, but up close they wore the faces of bewildered children, lost between two worlds. They were kids just walking.

The weather was still at odds with itself with thick bundles of drifting cloud that could answer neither snow nor rain.

Ennor mentioned the early hour fog that came from the north that morning and they all agreed that if it had come in once it would come in again.

The north moor lay flat and tired in areas sprawled between solemn tors and Ennor tried to remember what it was she wanted to say to Mum because she had to get it right.

They stood a moment and looked across at the bubble of granite that burst from across the valley and Sonny said she was sure they were at the highest point of the moor.

'We close to the village?' asked Butch.'Cus if you said we were lost I'd believe you.'

'We int lost,' said Sonny.

'Sure? Cus you know between us all we bin walkin past a week.'

Ennor put her arm around Trip's shoulder and they continued to head towards the valley.

'Well done, big mouth,' shouted Sonny and she stopped him in his tracks. 'Why you come out here at all is beyond my reckonin.'

She pushed him to make herself feel better and he fell on to his back. 'What's wrong with a little hope or what else is there?'

She left him sitting in the snow with shock gritting his teeth and ran after the others.

'Sonny, what you done to him?' asked Ennor when she looked behind and saw him sitting in the snow with his arms crossed over his knees.

'Gave him a little push is all. Don't worry, I dint hit him.'

'His dad hits him,' said Trip. 'Hits him black and blue some days.'

'Well that's not my fault. Not my problem neither, come to that.'

They waited for him to appear at the crown of the hill and watched him follow them down into the valley and Sonny shouted to hurry up before the fog had them pinned.

They followed each other with loose space between them. The dog leading the way, his head barely lifted from off his chest.

They were heading to the village they'd marked on the map, the village where the old woman had told Ennor her mother lived, Treburdon. The closer they got, the more Ennor's stomach filled with scree and stones and she prayed and wished and tried to scrape her mood from off the ground. If she'd been on her own, she would have been bursting with excitement and she'd have gone through her mother questions with bouncing anticipation instead of dampened doubt.

They got to the lane that would lead them to the village and Sonny said from thereon in they should keep their wits about them.

'What are the chances that this village Treburdon has a shop?' she asked. 'I mean a shop that's open. It's not Christmas yet, is it?' Ennor counted the days out from the day she left home and there were nights that she couldn't remember and others that she counted twice. She looked at Sonny.

'Might be.'

Sonny shrugged.

'It's not, is it?' Trip looked up at his sister and she was reminded of all the things she'd promised him and the weight in her stomach lunged to the ground.

'We got no food or presents or nothin.' He looked

shocked as if the reality of walking blind cross-country had suddenly dawned on him and his cheeks and forehead bunched in confusion around the mask.

'Don't worry, buddy.' She smiled. 'We're really close to Mum now, I promise.'

'You promised things before and nothin.'

'That's cus your sister don't know everythin cus she can't. It's just the way of things.' Sonny smiled and clipped him under the chin and when he said he wanted to go home she told him to grow up and be strong and Ennor was surprised to see her harsh words worked.

The lane they walked was narrow and meandering with thick high hedges closed to the speeding wind. For the first time that day and for many days they could speak without having to shout above the din and Sonny sang her happy song and marched up ahead with the gun swinging crossways.

Occasionally they came to signposts forked in the road and through the graffiti they read the miles and Ennor counted them down into single digits.

'There's no cars or nothin,' she said to Butch. 'It's as if everyone went to bed and forgot to get up again.'

Butch agreed. 'You wouldn't get too far drivin on this ice rink, unless you had chains strapped to the wheels.' He ran a little to test the road and skidded into the hedge. 'What I wouldn't give for a comfy four-wheel drive with chains.'

'A full tank of fuel,' agreed Ennor. 'We could get to where we're goin and back with no worries or anythin, imagine that.'

'We could have beddin in the back and a fridge full of beer,' added Sonny, who had stopped to add two pennies to the conversation, 'and a trailer full of firewood so we don't have to go haulin everythin we find.'

They walked side by side and Trip and the dog skipped ahead and they smiled because the mood had lifted briefly.

'Can buddy dog and buddy horse go in the trailer?' he asked.

'Course,' laughed Sonny. 'And maybe we'll get us some real horses as well, like in the good old days, real gypsies on the road. All of us teens with good solid plans while the world's broken with adults lost and limpin everywhere you turn. I wanna keep movin, keep movin and never stop, ever.' She ran up the lane and the dog barked after her with Trip skidding behind and Ennor laughed and looked at Butch and she imagined there was something close to love between them again.

'I see it!' shouted Sonny from way up the lane. 'Down below, I see the village, come on.'

They grouped on the brow of the hill and Sonny hatched a plan that would have them looking and acting in a way that she hoped was near enough normal.

'One of us needs to hide out with the bags and it can't

be Ennor cus she's got to ask after her mum and it can't be me cus my light fingers need an outin.'

'You can't go stealin from strangers,' said Ennor.

'What as opposed to friends and family? Get with it, greenhorn.'

Butch said he didn't mind hiding out. In any case, his cough was getting worse with the current drop in temperature and he said he'd hide somewhere away from the road in a field with Trip and the dog. They found him a spot of dead hedge and Sonny pulled it clear so they could sit inside.

'Now don't go wanderin, not even for a wee.' Ennor pointed at Trip and made the face that grown-ups made when they needed to be taken serious.

'How will I know that you're OK?' asked Butch.

'When you see us,' said Sonny and she gave Ennor the gun.

'I hate this gun. I won't shoot unless I have to.'

'Obviously, it's a precaution. If someone draws on you, what you goin to do?'

'Run away.'

'Hell you are. You're gonna fight cus flight gets you dead.'

They left Butch and Trip putting rocks out for seats and a table for playing cards and they walked through the gate and back on to the lane.

'How long you think we'll be?'

'Depends, don't it. You nervous?'

'A bit. Don't feel right now we're here.'

'What don't?'

'What the old maid said. You think she was bullin me some kind?'

'Dunno, won't know till we find that yellow door of yours.'

'I hope we won't be long in any case. Trip don't seem right, he's got a mood comin, I know it.'

'Don't worry bout him. Concentrate on findin your mum or askin bout your mum. What you gonna say?'

'A hundred things and I don't know.'

'Just remember, we gotta seem just like two friends out and about who don't know how bad things have got in a week, so keep your wits.'

'So how'd I say I'm lookin for my mum if she int around?'

'Let's just knock on some door.' Sonny shrugged and thought for a minute. 'Say she's gone missin and put the sad and innocent thing on thick, that'll help.'

'Maybe I should say we int eaten in a while.'

'That's good, now you're thinkin like a pro.'

Ennor smiled and Sonny said it was a rare thing to see but a nice thing all the same.

'What I had to smile bout recently?'

'I dunno, we finally reached the north moor, everyone's still alive, just. If there's somethin you're not tellin, just spit it out. Have it said just to say it or stop your maudlin.'

Ennor didn't know how to say the words and she tried and shook her head. She wanted to keep from talking about Dad to Sonny. She was all things that were good and positive about the world.

'Tell me,' Sonny said.

Ennor took a deep breath. 'It's my dad, he's dead.'

Sonny stopped to look at her. 'How d'you know?'

'Butch, that was half his reason to come lookin for me.'

'That's nice of him, hell.'

'He knew I'd want to know.'

'And now you know?'

Ennor nodded her head and they picked up walking again and soon they were entering the village. Her dad was dead and here she was looking for her mum. Life was a flipped coin that just happened to spin this way and then that.

Sonny said she'd taken to praying for some kind of shop to appear as they slowed past a line of untended gardens. They painted their faces to look friendly and smiled at the windows of the terraced cottages in case anyone was looking.

'Some of the downstairs windows are boarded up,' said Ennor.

'They've been smashed, I reckon. Keep your mind on that gun.'

In one of the windows stood a boy not much older than Trip and Sonny shouted if there was a shop and he nodded and pointed to a whitewashed chapel at the far end of the village.

'I think God answered my prayer,' she laughed. 'As good a place as any I spose, hell.'

'Don't make jokes bout these things. That's where it's all gone mad. Emmets buying chapels for holiday homes cus nobody can be bothered to sit down and pray no more.'

'I int seen you prayin all that much.'

'Don't mean I don't.'

They reached the gate leading to the graveyard and a serious man stood across the threshold and he asked them their business.

'I hear you're some kind of charity,' lied Sonny.

'Well you heard wrong, there's no charity here, unless you got somethin to barter.'

Sonny coughed and cleared her throat. 'We're just kids, sir. What we got to barter with?'

'You'd be surprised,' he grinned.

'Sir.' Ennor edged forward and the man opened his coat for a peek of his gun.

'I was wonderin if you could help me. It's my mother, she's gone missin.'

'Not my problem.'

'Please, I'm worried sick. She's bin livin in this village.'

'You're not the first to lose someone or somethin. People bin displaced all over the last two weeks.'

'You don't understand. She's bin gone sometime.'

'Girl,' he shouted. 'Just leave it, eh?'

Ennor watched his fat lips rub dry against his teeth and she could sense Sonny was winding herself up into doing or saying something crazy.

'So you got somethin more than a dumb sob story to sell or no?'

'I got gold,' said Sonny, reaching into her bumbag. 'Real good gold.'

'Let's see it,' he barked.

'Give me a minute, Christ's sake,' Sonny barked back.

She looked at what she had hidden out of sight from both Ennor and the man and produced an ornate gold ring.

'It was my dear departed grandmother's, God rest her soul.'

'Let's look at it then.' The man clubbed a plump hand over the railings and Sonny snatched it back.

'What you got yourself?'

The man laughed as if he were enjoying an afternoon of pub banter. 'Dried stuff mostly – rice, pasta, lentils. No more flour but we got tins of veg and beans and some half-rot apples if you've a hand for makin cider, but sorry, no lost mothers.'

Sonny nodded. 'I like the sound of rice and beans, got any coffee?'

'Decaffeinated.'

'Yuck, that's no good, no point to that at all. Got any hot choc sachets? The ones that don't need milk.'

'Depends.'

'On what?'

'Might cost you more. I'd have to show that ring to the wife. She's jewellery and miscellaneous.'

They were asked to step through the gate and stand in the porch while he stood behind them and shouted his wife out of hiding.

Inside the chapel Ennor felt like she was a young girl again. The pristine walls with hardwood trim and simple unadorned altar were like the chapel they used to attend as a family.

The pew on the right had food stacked like shelves in a shop blown outwards and felled to the ground and on the left were car parts and household randoms stacked into towers like junk sculptures.

The man secured the door with sliding bolts and Ennor counted them five and he stood to their left and the wife to the right like guardians to a lost kingdom.

'Let's see it then,' said the wife.

Sonny handed her the ring. 'It's antique, real old.'

'I'll be the judge of that,' she spat.

'It was my dear departed grandmother's, God rest her soul.' Sonny looked around at the colour and sparkle of food and she asked if it was Christmas Day yet.

'Darlin, every day's Christmas in this business.'

'Well is it?'

'Couldn't tell you. Couldn't care less either.' The

woman took the ring to a window to study it up close. 'What you want for it?'

'Four tins of beans, kidney or red, and a five-hundred gram bag of rice and some hot choc sachets.'

'How many sachets?'

'Ten.'

'Ten? You can have the sachets but nothing else. There's toffee flavour, mint and all sorts.'

'I don't want all sorts. They taste like plastic and rubber and worse. I want just chocolate.'

Ennor looked at Sonny in disbelief as the woman walked towards them and then back to the window. 'I'll give you three.'

'Four and we got ourselves a deal.'

'Cocky little scrag, int you?'

Sonny smiled and nodded. 'And my friend here's got a question that needs answerin and we're not goin till it's answered.'

'Spit it out then, girl, and make it quick. We got a business to run here.'

Ennor told the woman about her missing mother and she described her from distant memory.

'She's got eyes like mine, look.' She opened her eyes wide.

'Sounds like a million crazies that fall our way. My starvin kid this, my dying kid that.'

'No she int as normal as that,' added Sonny. 'She's like a bit of a religious freak.' She apologised to Ennor. 'It's true,' and she continued to connect all the dots that made up the woman and when Ennor said something about the yellow door the woman's ears pricked up.

'What's it worth if I know somethin?'

'Tin of beans.'

The woman nodded. 'She's close all right, well she was. Got a few followers turns out. Tried to drive us out of here, dint she, Bob? Used to squat in a cottage up the back lane, yellow door and peelin. She's gone now mind.'

Ennor moved forward suddenly and the man picked his gun from its holster and smiled.

'You know where they were headin?'

The woman took Ennor's face into her two hands. 'You sure you want to be chasin a woman like that?'

'Like what?'

'Wrap your wares in your coat or you won't get back to wherever you came from.' She walked down the isle and when Ennor shouted for her to come back she turned briefly.

'Bude, they were heading to the coast, to Bude and good riddance cus I don't like the place.'

Outside the chapel they adjusted themselves and Sonny wore the gun out over her jacket and she said things were totally worse than she had thought.

'At least we know where we're headin. How far you think?'

'Hell, I don't know, another ten, twelve miles if the weather holds back. Should get there tomorrow.'

'And we got food.'

Sonny nodded.

'This is it, we're nearly there.' Ennor smiled.

'What about what that woman said. Bit weird the way she said it.'

Ennor laughed away the doubt she shared with Sonny and waved a dismissive hand in the air. 'So what, she was crazy herself, weren't she?'

'I guess.'

Ennor could see Sonny wasn't convinced and they walked back through the village and up the lane towards the others with worry and relief and everything else mixed and confused and the thought of hot chocolate almost too much to contain.

They found the field with the cubby cut into the hedge and the rucksacks and bedrolls bundled neatly but there was no sign of Butch or Trip.

They stood in the ice-field and shouted and listened for anything that resembled voices catching on the wind.

'You hear anythin?' asked Sonny.

They held their breath and turned their ears to every corner of land and Ennor thought she heard something in the fields beyond. They ran the hedge and criss-crossed through the field, stepping high to avoid the razor-sharp peaks of ploughed earth that sprung from the snow like fins.

'It's Butch!' shouted Trip as they climbed the gate.

'Buddy dog ran off and Butch ran after him and he fell.'

The girls sprinted towards him and fell and sat like props as he lay in the snow and Ennor bundled her coat into a cushion for his head.

'Anythin broke?' asked Sonny.

'Don't be stupid,' said Ennor. 'It's his chest. He's got a bad chest.'

She asked if he could sit up and he nodded and they two-arm pulled him into sitting and the runaway dog came and sat beside him as he fought to control his breathing.

'When did this happen?' she asked her brother.

'Just. Buddy dog ran and I ran and Butch ran, just runnin and then coughin and then he fell.'

'Any blood?' she asked Butch.

He pointed to a splash of speckled red on the trampled snow.

'Is he goin to die?' Trip asked and Butch tried to laugh.

'He'll be all right, just needs to catch his breath, int that right?' shouted Sonny and she turned to Trip and said she had a treat if he wanted it.

'I want it, what is it?' shouted Trip.

'Hot chocolate, with milk and sugar ready mixed.' They helped Butch to his feet and he said he was fine to walk but the girls knew from his wheezing that he was anything but.

'We'll make an early camp,' decided Sonny. They

gathered their things and walked three fields deep from the road for safety and settled in a corner of a good flat field flanked by tall hedges on all sides.

'Come on, Trip, we need to scout for firewood. Butch needs to get warm and by warm I mean roastin.'

'Roasty toasty?' he asked.

'That's right.' They walked the field's perimeter and pulled branches from trees in the hedgerows by twisting them backwards and forwards until they ripped.

Ennor sat close to Butch and she petted him with warmth and kindness whether he wanted it or not.

'You got me worried,' she said at last. 'Somethin int right with you and you won't say.' She looked at him and wished he'd tell her his secrets, she knew he had many.

'What you want from me? How d'you want me to paint it? Cus whatever it is you know it's not what you want to hear.'

'I int askin for nothin, just for you to admit you're not well would be somethin.'

'You don't know the half of it.' He coughed.

'So tell me some of it so I know somethin. Give me a clue at least.'

Ennor could see he was turning something over in his head; something was being chewed and she wanted to coax it out of him, get him to spit it out so she could dissect it. She looked out across the field, and land and sky were just the same, dazzling and confusing. Up was

down and down was for ever miles, uncharted. She
fiddled with her hands and the bitten corners of nail
around her fingers.

'It's me dad,' he said.

'He OK? I forgot to ask with all my goins-on.'

Butch shook his head. 'He's not OK and not in the
way you think.'

'What way then, the depression?'

'More, since I found him in the barn plus everythin.
He wants me to be somethin that I int.'

Ennor shrugged. 'He's always gainst you one way or
other. What you gettin at?'

Butch undid the zip on his jacket and pulled out the
layers of clothing that stuck there and he lifted them
over his head. 'Take a look,' he said.

Ennor knelt close and her instinct was to touch the
purple bands of bruising in some way of healing but
instead her hands hovered dumbly between them.

'Butch, that's bad,' she whispered.

He let his clothes drop and stared blankly ahead.

Ennor felt her throat tighten and threaten tears and
she swallowed with defiance. She had to be strong for
him.

'You think anythin's broken? Your ribs, I mean?'

Butch shrugged and said maybe, maybe not. 'All I
know is it hurts like a bastard.'

Ennor shook her head and put her arm around his
shoulder and held him close. 'Should have left him

swingin in the barn, should have cut him down days later and fed him to the pigs.'

Butch laughed. 'Well there int much left to say or do in regards to him now.'

'What you mean?'

'Means I've ran away from home, way he sees it anyway. Ran away with a seven-year-old boy, int that somethin?'

'He dint beat you cus of Trip stayin over, did he?'

'Cus of everythin and nothin, don't worry bout it. There was always somethin to beat on me bout, always. Just got worse recent.'

He looked at Ennor and patted her hand that rested on his shoulder. 'He threatened to tell the social bout Trip, but I'm glad I left. For all this, it's better than that.'

Ennor didn't know what to say and that was something too. She stopped with the hugging and asked about his mother.

'What about her?'

'He can't stop you seein her.'

'I'll wish him dead and then let's see what happens.'

'When the world turns right.'

'When the world turns right and I'm studyin and learnin all there is to know. Clever stuff, not livestock market prices like Dad.'

They watched Sonny load oddments of wood into Trip's tiny arms and they both laughed and Ennor told Butch she thought him too clever for her world.

'You'll come back and see me, won't you? When you're a big-shot lawyer or doctor or somethin.'

Butch nodded. He fancied himself as a big-shot something all right. 'Course I'll come back to see you. I'd be an idiot not to.'

'You mean it?'

'We're joined up somehow, int we? Stitched together someway or other.'

He looked at her and smiled and she smiled too. Something akin to honesty was sitting there between them and it felt like the return of a missing link. A link they'd lost on the way growing from run-around kids up until now.

Sonny and Trip were bringing the wood over to their corner camp and Ennor remembered she had a little of the dried gorse left for tinder and it wasn't long before they were gathered around a growing fire.

Butch's wheezing had lessened to a crackling bubble and he thanked them in a roundabout way and Ennor could see he felt stupid being the boy and everything and perhaps a little useless and she volunteered him to cook the rice and the beans.

Ennor told him about Bude and they sat with the map between them and traced the next step in their journey and made it quick by deciding they would go by road.

'I'm not goin by road. There's danger everywhere,' said Sonny.

'Like what?' asked Trip.

'Like everythin you could imagine.'

'I want to go with Sonny,' he said.

'You're welcome, boy, and the dog can come. And we got rice and beans and hot chocolate, and the biscuits will go far between us.'

'What biscuits?' asked Ennor.

Sonny produced two packets of custard creams from inside her jacket pocket and everyone fell silent with flashing greed.

When the rice was cooked and the beans heated through in the can Butch spooned the food out equally plus rice for the dog and they ate like wild animals and licked their plates clean.

They washed the dishes by scrubbing them in the snow and Sonny heated all the hot chocolate together with snow water and counted out one pack of biscuits five ways.

The fog returned and thickened with the fall of evening and it snagged itself in the corner hedges like a canopy roof and the warmth of the fire bounced against and all around.

Rapture had returned with the eating of food and the sugar of biscuits and chocolate combined had turned everyone hot and frenzied about the fire.

They sang loud and clapped rhythms on each other's knees and legends were told and made in the running and each story was more elaborate than the last.

Trip taught the dog to dance and Sonny made ribbon

strips from the food wrappers and tied them to his collar.

'We'll be headin to the circus at this rate,' she laughed, and the dog danced and showed his teeth because he too was in rapture and they sang and cheered long into the night.

CHAPTER THIRTEEN

With the passing of the fog came the exposed gape of morning and Ennor lay on her back and looked briefly at heaven through a gash in the clouds that healed like a miracle before her eyes.

It didn't seem like long ago that they had settled down to sleep and it probably wasn't because the fire still pushed out a little heat from hidden embers.

She rolled towards Trip to wake him and then to Sonny and laughed when they complained in unison.

'You missed it.'

'What?' said Trip.

'A sign.'

'For what?'

'Not sure but somethin good's headin our way.'

She sat huddled to the fire and coaxed it back into being, boiling snow and adding the last of the tea bags, and when Butch woke up she poured it and shared out the second pack of custard creams, taking comfort in the counting of things.

'Ennor's had one of her signs,' said Sonny. 'Somethin good's headin apparently.'

'Maybe we'll stay off the moor for ever,' wheezed Butch. 'That would be a somethin.'

He swallowed down the hot tea and Ennor knew not to make a big thing about it but she couldn't help but wonder if he should see a doctor and she said as much.

'I'm fine. It's just a cold type cough.'

'Leave him, Ennor. He said he's fine so maybe he's fine.' Sonny looked at him and shrugged. 'He'll either get worse or he'll get better.'

The decision to walk to Bude by road had been made and Ennor could tell Sonny was still brooding about it but with Butch ill and her mum so close she couldn't imagine trekking cross country any more than they had to.

They packed up camp and kicked the fire with snow and followed the lane down to the village and past the half-cocked cottages and the chapel with the man standing guard and Sonny bid him good morning and she smiled and waved like it was any normal day in any normal Cornish village. She walked up ahead with Trip and the dog with the wrapper ribbons still attached to his string lead and she let Trip hold the map so he could follow the thin blue line of the lane.

Ennor knew they had become close and Trip looked

up to Sonny in a way that was different to his life else-where. She was strong and resourceful and she made him laugh with a sarcastic tongue that was beyond humour and because of his ways he wasn't supposed to get sarcasm but he did.

'Road gets wider soon,' he shouted back to them. 'The blue line gets wider on the paper.'

'I wonder if we'll see any cars to cadge a lift,' said Ennor.

'Like anyone's goin to lift us?' shouted Sonny from further up the lane. 'We're black from the fire and blue from the cold and we stink a whole rainbow of colours.'

They walked slowly because the cold split Butch's chest occasionally and they stopped and started with a hundred niggling problems and concerns but still Ennor told herself they would be entering the town by sundown.

Hours slipped by unnoticed and at lunchtime they passed around a can of beans between them to ease the burn of hunger and they discussed their favourite meals in such detail that they were soon starving all over again.

With their minds taken up with food and the taste and memory of better times they didn't hear the shout-ing in the road up ahead until it was almost too late.

Sonny pulled Trip to the ground and she waved behind to the others to do the same. Two men were jousting and spearing threats and all ears knew there was only one way to settle the thing.

Sonny gathered Trip into her arms and sprinted as fast as she could towards Butch and Ennor and they ran with their thighs burning back down the lane and into a field far enough away so they could whisper and as they went a lonely burst of gunfire carried with them on the wind.

'Now what?' panted Butch.

'We gotta stay calm,' said Ennor. 'Calm and quiet.'

'We gotta get goin quick,' said Sonny. ' Take a wide chunk out of these fields, skirt um or head cross to the moor.'

'Whatever we do, let's just get goin,' said Butch and they backed up into the field and followed a wall, high and half crippled with weather, that wound and tumbled this way and that and they were about to look for other routes when it finally gave way and they headed west once more.

The top line of the moor was near and a step back into the open plains was welcomed.

Occasionally the edge of moorland traced villages and roads and such was their fear of the unknown they backtracked more and more until they were deep in the wild again.

'I don't care how long it takes to get from A to B long as I dodge a bullet in the process,' said Sonny and she wondered if they thought everyone had gone bad.

'Can't have,' answered Ennor. 'Must be people same as us roamin round.'

Butch agreed but decided they weren't as stupid because they were sat with some comfort at least in their boarded-up houses riding out the storm.

Trip startled them by saying maybe this was the end of the world and they all nodded and felt the cold air twice over and doubled with added doom because maybe he was right.

Ennor counted the clouds in the sky for a good number and sighed and she looked on as Sonny and Trip passed the telescope between them.

'What now?' she said to Butch when she saw Sonny pointing towards the horizon. 'Int there always somethin to follow somethin?'

'We got horse wranglers up ahead. Them poor buggers don't stand a chance.' Sonny passed the telescope to Ennor and she adjusted it and changed eyes until she saw the dance of two men on horseback chasing and roping wild ponies and banking them into a makeshift corral.

'Are they the same men from earlier?' asked Trip. 'The fightin men?'

'No,' said Sonny. 'Don't worry. They might not be so bad.'

'What do they want with the horses? Practically skin and bone,' said Ennor.

'Meat.' Sonny nodded to herself. 'I bet you. Cheap meat but they'll offload it for somethin better.'

They walked a little closer and Ennor didn't notice the look twisting across Trip's face until it was too late and he bent to the ground and ran towards the men at full tilt.

Ennor ditched her rucksack and ran to catch him but it was too late because the men had seen them.

'Don't you dare touch him!' she screamed. 'He's just a kid!'

The men sat back in their saddles and watched the riotous children with amusement. One of them held his hands in the air when he saw Sonny point the gun, but soon started laughing so hard he had to pull the baseball cap he was wearing off his head to fan himself.

'I've seen it all now,' he shouted. 'And I've seen some crazy things I can tell you.'

He jumped from the horse and told Sonny to put down the gun and he ruffled the dog's head and called it 'mutt' when it ran over.

'He int mutt, he's buddy dog,' cried Trip.

'All right, boy, don't wet your Y-fronts.'

'You're gonna eat horses. You're gonna kill um and then eat um.'

The two men stood side by side with their horses behind them and they held straight faces long enough to put some explaining out there and the man with the cap said they were animal activists and were saving them from death.

'How?' asked Trip.

'By takin um to the barn we got lined up. Warm and cosy with hay and everythin.'

Everyone knew this was a lie except Trip and they waited for him to accept what was said. The men talked of other things to sweep the situation over and they invited the five of them to their camp beside the stick-fence corral.

'What are we doin wastin time with strangers?' whispered Ennor to Sonny. 'I don't trust um.'

'I've got a sudden plan.'

Every time Sonny had a plan it ended in a maze of complication but there was something in her eyes that seemed set.

'I don't like um,' said Butch as they circled to a dying fire, but Sonny told him to trust her and she gave him the gun to cradle in his lap.

The men refuelled the fire and Sonny offered them the remaining rice and the two tins of beans and they were grateful and cooked them with some kind of stew that looked like it was on its tenth reheating and they passed around a large earthen pot of cider.

'You kids look like you could do with some lookin after,' the man with the baseball cap said and he smiled and nodded towards the snow.

'It's a regular badlands out here, int it? Gotta keep movin just to keep from freezin to death.'

'And not get shot,' added the other man.

They questioned each of the men in turn regarding their comings and goings. Sonny did the talking and answered their questions with more questions to keep from revealing anything much. The tough skin she had worn when she first met Ennor was zipped tight and her friends sat back and enjoyed the interrogation because it was not aimed at them.

The cider was strong and warm and wonderful and Ennor listened to the banter with an ounce of comfort in her heart; it was something just to listen to words other than her thoughts. The men talked of losing jobs at Falmouth docks, which had led to government handouts and then no handouts and finally each and every man for himself. They'd travelled the three corners of Cornwall and had a go at getting to Devon but the bridge had been blocked with abandoned trucks and guarded by tooled-up truckers asking for levy to pass and the man with the cap said he wished they had a boat again but they had swapped it for the horses.

Sonny gleaned that they were brothers with only a year between and they had a younger sister back in Falmouth with a baby. 'She spends all hours walkin the streets for food enough for one more day walkin. What's the point in that?'

When the food was ready Ennor was half drunk and the food was the best she'd ever tasted because the men had added salt and the flavours mixed and sprang to life in one square meal.

The men had stretched a square of plastic sheeting between three stick trees and pulled it tight above them and said they were welcome to spend the night there.

Ennor snuggled Trip into a blanket where they were to sleep and he soon fell asleep with the dog as a pillow and Butch settled close by. She guessed that they would be staying the night and thought how short and passing the days had become.

Another jug circled the group and snowflakes became stars on the night air and licked the old snow with a fresh coat of brilliant white.

The strong drink and fresh snow had Ennor thinking of new beginnings and she asked if Christmas had come and gone and nobody could say for sure.

She walked her memory past every day and every night since she'd met Sonny and she confirmed that they had missed it altogether. Everyone laughed and those who had tin mugs raised them towards the fire and a somewhere someplace New Year.

The man in the cap had an eye for Sonny and Ennor hoped his brother didn't plan to slink her way because she would have to make some kind of a scene and then they'd all be back walking in the black and white.

She watched Sonny and caught her eye with a question in hers and Sonny shook her head a little to stop her worrying but still she wanted to distract the man away from her friend.

Words stuck in her throat and she wanted to say something to smack him back but strong words didn't belong to her and when his eyes and hands roamed further she got up and sat next to Sonny. There was a green streak cracking inside her that she was not used to. She wanted to tell the man that Sonny belonged to her in some way, but instead she said it was time to get some rest.

'You her mother?' asked his brother and both men laughed.

'More than, actually.' Ennor stood up and steadied herself against a tree. 'She's my best friend.'

They continued to laugh and Sonny thanked them for the drink and said something about an early start. The two girls left the men drunk and laughing by the fire and went to join Butch and Trip.

'Hell,' laughed Sonny. 'Dint know you cared.'

'I don't.'

'So why with the best friend act?'

'Had to think of somethin to get that sleaze off you. He was probably three times your age.'

They sat rested against a jut of granite and pulled one of the blankets over and up to their chins.

'I was loosenin him up, makin sure he drank his fill. I got a plan, remember?'

'What plan? Better be good cus most so far bin otherwise.'

'You'll see in the mornin.'

'You playin complex again?' asked Ennor.

'No, just normal.'

They nestled down into the blanket and Ennor said there was nothing normal about her and she agreed.

'That's why you like me.' She smiled. 'Everyone likes Sonny Pengelly.'

'OK, you keep dreamin if that's what makes you happy.'

They listened to the crackle of the fire as it slowed in its tracks and Ennor checked to see if the men were making any moves towards sleep and they looked settled enough where they were.

'Dint think I was goin off with him, did you?'

'Guess not.'

'What you take me for?'

Ennor didn't know how to say what she was feeling just now. She told Sonny she was worried and asked her friend what she might do once they reached Bude.

'Just see you right, I guess. Did promise, I think.'

'Then what?'

'Dunno, I int thought that far ahead. Just keep walkin. Maybe go back to camp, maybe not.'

'Sonny.'

'Yep.'

'You scared?'

'Bout what?'

'Everythin.'

'Nope. Don't do scared.'

'Don't lie. Everyone gets scared.'

'Bout what?'

'You know what, the future and stuff.'

Sonny thought for a minute and Ennor knew talking

candid was not one of Sonny's strong points and was
going to tell her to leave it when she said she was scared
of being scared.

'I guess that sounds as stupid as.'

'No it don't.'

'Sure? Cus I can try and make it make sense.'

'It makes enough sense to me.'

'Sure?'

Ennor poked her in the back. 'You can go to sleep
now. I'm done quizzin.'

'You know what you said bout best friends?' asked
Sonny.

'Yep.'

'You mean it, kind of?'

'I mean it proper. Said it, dint I?'

'That's funny.'

'Why?'

'Cus you're my best friend too.'

'I'm glad that's established,' wheezed Butch from
beneath his blanket.

They laughed and Ennor remarked on what a ragtag
family they made and her words brought comfort to the
others because that was what they had become. No
matter what the future held, they would have that for
ever and always stitched between them.

CHAPTER FOURTEEN

Early morning and the fog had returned and had staked the snow thick and heavy to the ground.

Ennor could hear Sonny whispering her name behind her but she stayed drifting in that loose space in time that was the edge of dreams in the hope that she could fall back to sleep.

'Ennor, wake up. We gotta get goin.'

She opened her eyes to see Sonny squatting in front of her with her boots on.

'I'm doin my plan. Wake the others but keep it quiet.'

'What's goin on, Sonny?'

'We're out of here, that's what.' Sonny pointed to the two horses she had saddled and coupled to a tree and told her to hurry up.

They crept from the moorland camp with Sonny leading the horses ahead of the others. She watched her whispering to the horses and smiled because she knew her friend was telling them to be quiet. Trip walked with his hand cupped over his mouth because he didn't trust himself not to blurt out words and Butch coughed into his scarf and his eyes watered with restraint.

The silence of that great place and all its history and tales caught Ennor in the heart and she made a place for it there and the landscape became something majestic and no longer to be feared.

She had slept it and breathed it and drunk it and lived it a lifetime over. She had grown up into ways she thought she had already grown and found some way of being that was the child she had lost. Innocence had returned despite and because of everything and to the moor she would be for ever grateful and grateful too to the great leap into chaos that was Sonny.

When they were safely hidden from the sleeping men's view Sonny emptied the panniers she'd stolen from the camp of anything not useful and loaded them with their things and lashed the empty rucksacks to one of the saddles and a bundle of roped wood and they rode out into the fog.

'You sure we're headin right?' Butch asked Sonny from his perch behind Ennor.

'Course I am, we'll be back on route and flyin in no time.'

'Forever optimistic.'

'That's right and we'll be in Bude in a matter of hours cus of me.'

'Cus of the horses.'

'Cus of the horses, cus of me.'

'Buddy horse!' shouted an excited Trip and Sonny had to tell him once more to hold on to her waist.

Ennor watched him pat the horse's rump with delight and she realised how thin he had become, shrunken down to a size way younger than his years. 'At least he's enjoyin himself,' she said.

'He'll be on the ground in a minute if he don't hold on,' said Sonny.

They rode at a slow pace and the dog danced between them, barking with excitement.

'You don't think the men will come after us, do you?' asked Ennor.

'What on, them old nags?' asked Sonny.

'They long gone,' giggled Trip. 'Don't you worry bout them. I let um go just before.'

'That's my boy,' laughed Sonny and she reached around to pat him on the arm. 'Followin in Aunty Sonny's footsteps, int you?'

Ennor couldn't pinpoint the exact moment the bit of wind that skirted the horses legs and the bit of snow that caught in her eyelashes became blizzard weather. They'd been engaged in the usual favourite meal conversation and the thought of food had risen to hallucination status. She'd been deciding between pasty and chips and egg and chips as her all time favourite when she looked back at Sonny and Trip and was startled to see they were no longer there.

'Sonny?' she shouted, standing the horse in the snow.

'Over here!' Sonny replied. 'Where you at?'

'It's snowin again,' said Trip as they emerged from the heavy falling white, 'and the horses don't like it.'

This was true. The animals had become skittish, unresponsive mules.

'You gotta be hard on um,' wheezed Butch. 'If you're afraid, they're afraid.'

'I int afraid,' said Ennor. 'Just can't see nothin. Where's the compass?'

'Here,' said Sonny and she led her horse up next to Ennor's. 'We just gotta keep headin straight. We int far. Don't think anyway.'

Ennor closed her eyes to help her think. She didn't like sitting on a horse in these conditions, she felt vulnerable, easily pushed. Butch was coughing up his own storm behind her. She could feel the tightness in his chest against her back, his fingers gripped around her waist to keep him upright. 'We gotta find shelter,' she shouted. 'Sit out the storm.'

'We gotta keep goin is what,' shouted Sonny. 'Where you think we're gonna find shelter? We can't even see each other.'

'I can see sister,' said Trip.

Sonny told Trip to zip it and Ennor told her to do the same. 'We keep goin and if we find shelter we take it.'

Sonny nodded towards Butch. 'He looks bad.'

Ennor looked over her shoulder and saw that he had fallen into a half-sleep. 'I know.'

'What we gonna do?' asked Sonny.

'Make it to Bude and go get a doctor.'

'Whereabouts?'

'Mum will know.'

Sonny nodded and she looked into the blizzard.

'What you lookin at? There int nothin to see.'

'That hawthorn bush.' She pointed to a charcoal sketch of tree so faint it was as if it had been pencilled on to tracing paper. 'The comb-over, it's aimin north-east.'

'How'd you know?'

'The wind, mostly a sou'wester, int it?'

'Not these days.'

'But general, so if that's north-east and that's sou'west then that's north-west.'

Sonny held her horse steady with one hand as she pointed around them. 'Come on, we gotta keep movin.'

'Before we freeze to death,' shouted Trip.

Ennor watched Sonny and Trip move on and she told Butch they'd soon find a doctor and she patted his hand a little and there was nothing of the living about it. They would find their way at some point, or find someplace fit enough to wait out the storm. She was getting tired and weak enough that her bones felt like magnets drawn downwards. It was something just to keep her head steady on her neck, her eyes peeled and stuck on the horse up ahead with the raping wind the only thing to occupy her mind. She listened for the familiar warmth of Trip and Sonny's chatter but there was none. Nothing but the fingering worm of winter, its damage done.

Ennor wished she'd cut some bits of rag to poke in her ears. Another 'just in case' thing she should have had stuffed in her pocket. If she'd thought things through, she would have packed earmuffs, she had some somewhere in the trailer back home. But everything was an afterthought now, an afterthought and a 'never mind' and a 'too bloody late'. She turned her face to look at Butch and she asked him if he was OK and he nodded yes but she knew he meant no. He was sick and worse and it was her fault.

'Sonny!' she shouted. 'Sonny, stop!'

'What?'

'We gotta find someplace fast.'

Sonny led her horse up alongside and Ennor waited for her to complain but when she looked at Butch she just nodded.

They pushed forward, scanning the white for anything that resembled colour or shape with the hours pulling and passing them by.

What Ennor would have given for a hole in the ground, a gully to lie down in with the tarp turned over, anything. She kicked the horse and rode up beside the others, smiling at Trip when he looked out at her from his snug behind Sonny.

'You OK, buddy?' she shouted downwind.

Trip shook his head.

'What's up?'

'I'm cold and more.'

'What else?'

'Hungry too.'

'You ever eaten bark crisps?' asked Sonny.

Trip shook his head.

'Well you're in for a treat, that's all I'll say.'

Ennor smiled and in her mind she told herself Sonny was a good friend because she was. She was more than a good friend; she really was her best friend, perhaps more than Butch. The kind of friend you hear about but don't believe exists, with good sense and calm and a mind for things same as yourself.

'What's up with you?' Sonny shouted.

'Why?'

'You got a face on. Misery's sittin close I spose.'

'I got a lot to be miserable bout.'

'True, you seen anythin worth stoppin for?'

'Nope. Int nothin but snow.'

Sonny turned her horse close to Ennor's and they rode tight like they were hitching a carriage.

'We could make an igloo.'

'Don't be daft.'

'I might set my mind to thinkin bout it.'

'Save your energy.'

'I can't, there int nothin else to do.'

Ennor shouted for her to keep her eyes skinned. 'We can't ride out this storm much longer.'

The wind was pushing past gale force and it twisted the riders and the horses into a meandering muddle. If they were making progress, it wasn't a known thing. She leant into the horse and whispered encouragement and she dusted the snow from its mane.

If there was something positive to tell it, she'd say but there was nothing but the hum of white noise. It blocked her ears and burnt her eyes and she felt it crack and snap every bone as the horse soldiered on with tentative steps.

She heard screaming and closed her mouth and she let go of the reins to block her ears with her forearms but the pitch was in her and all around. She looked over at Sonny and saw her head back and mouth ripped wide.

'Stop it,' she shouted. 'You're scarin Trip.'

She rode close and stretched out a hand to touch her brother and she shouted to Sonny to shut up or she'd hit her.

'Try it,' Sonny shouted back.

'I've done it before. Gave you a black un, dint I?'

'Only cus I let you.'

'You talk bull, Sonny Pengelly.'

Sonny started to laugh and so did Ennor. They laughed until their jaws hurt and their lips split and bled. Trip laughed too and Butch looked up from his huddle and shook his head.

'We've finally lost it, Butchy boy,' shouted Sonny. 'You always said it and now it's true. Sonny and Ennor are officially fruit loops.'

'Fruit loop loopy,' laughed Ennor.

'And Trip,' shouted Trip.

'And buddy dog,' shouted Sonny. 'And buddy horse and all the horses and just about every poor mongrel creature out here teeterin on the ridge of civilisation lookin in.'

They shouted anything that came to mind and cheap jokes were laughed into the blizzard.

They had given up caring, Ennor knew this and so did Sonny and Butch. Probably even Trip and the animals knew this. Fate was loping round in circles waiting and they were waiting for luck or death or another day of the same. If they lasted another night, it would be because of partial hope, piecemeal giving.

The only thing good to come from giving in to fate was fear no longer bothered Ennor. It had baited her all her life but now she could not even remember what it felt like.

Nothing scared her because nothing mattered.

Given her mindset Ennor didn't believe her brother when he screamed he'd seen a car, and she ignored him.

'I seen it back there.'

'No you dint,' shouted Sonny.

'I did, go back.'

Sonny stopped the horse and looked across at Ennor 'Did you see a car?'

Ennor shook her head.

'I dint either. You playin us?'

'No,' he shouted. 'I promise.'

'There int no cars out here, Trip,' said Ennor. 'There's no cars cus there's no roads.'

'I seen it, sister, honest to God and everythin.'

'Where then, where?'

'Back there.' He pointed to the left a little way behind them.'Just there, promise.'

The two girls looked at each other and shrugged.

'Spose it won't hurt,' said Sonny as she spun her horse round and she told Trip if he was wrong he'd be taking turns on a spit across the fire tonight.

'You'll see.' He nodded. 'It's just there.'

A forty-metre turn and Trip was screaming that he was right and the two girls sat the horses dead in the snow and adjusted their eyesight to what it was he was looking at.

'Is that a car?' said Sonny. 'Hell, it *is* a car.'

'A bad burnt-out one,' said Ennor.

'Can we drive it?' asked Trip as they jumped from their saddles.

'No, buddy, but we can sit out the storm.'

'I did good, sister?'

'You did great, buddy. Come on, let's unpack.'

Sonny hobbled the horses' legs together and Ennor

helped Butch down and settled him on the back seat of the car.

'You're lucky, boy,' said Sonny. 'Still got a bit of spring and paddin to it.'

'Lucky me,' he whispered.

They covered the north and east sides of the car with the tarp and secured it to the roof with scavenged rocks to mask the blown-out windows and Sonny stacked the rucksacks and panniers into the front window, then sat back in the passenger seat with Trip in her lap 'Where you takin us?' she laughed. 'I wouldn't mind somewhere warm.'

'Anywhere but here, wheezed Butch.

Ennor looked around from her place behind the wheel and she laughed at him and the dog snuggled beneath the blanket.

She put her hands on the steering wheel and looked straight ahead and she replaced the dark wall of luggage with a desolate winding road circling a warm blue sky.

Ennor Carne and her mix-match family, riding out through a hot foreign country, cruising and in control.

'We could do with makin a fire,' said Sonny. 'It'll be dark soon and colder than ever. I just know it.'

'Could do with somethin to cook on it,' added Ennor. 'You make the fire with the stolen wood and I'll go lookin.'

'Don't wander far.'

'I won't, I'll just sit out a little. Might get a crow or a rabbit or somethin.'

Sonny shook her head and laughed. 'Maybe a squirrel.'

'What'll I do?' asked Trip.

'You can dig round for more rocks for the fire pit. Jiggin will warm you up a bit.'

Ennor took the gun and a stick and walked a little way out into the curtain of white. She stayed within shouting distance and stood stony with the gun in her arms and her back to the wind. They had found shelter in the seventh circle and this made her smile. Maybe they would find food too. She had given in to fate, but that didn't mean she'd given up on hope.

Sonny called to check she was there and she shouted for her to shut up. She wished for a skin and bone pony or a Galloway calf to stumble her way. She knew they were out there because she'd seen them all over when she wasn't looking.

She should have shot at something earlier, anything with a pulse enough to call fresh, to give them one more chance at keeping going. The cold had them emptied, they'd been upended and shook so hard there was nothing but rattling bones between them.

In the space Ennor used to keep for prayers she cleared her mind and let the moment carry her, closing her eyes and settling herself into the void. Several minutes passed and she thought she heard Sonny call her name and she looked up and saw a shadow cross her path.

It was too small for a cow or a horse and too skinny for a sheep and she tightened her grip on the rifle and crept forward.

The shadow turned and made a noise that was alien to her and she questioned whether she'd seen anything at all. Her mind was playing tricks, tripping her. She whispered a stupid, 'Hello,' and edged forward, her trigger finger ready, twitching.

The shadow didn't speak and it didn't move and Ennor crouched to its level for a clean shot. She would count to three.

She jammed the butt-stock of the rifle against her shoulder and knelt into the sinking snow counting, one and two, as beautiful eyes swung upon her from out of the startling snow and blinked. 'Three,' she whispered and her finger twitched the trigger into action.

'What you got?' shouted Sonny from out the ether.

Ennor dropped the rifle and waited for the deer to stop kicking and she didn't speak until she'd stopped crying.

'Ennor?'

'Dinner,' she shouted. 'That's what I got, dinner.'

They sat bundled in the car and watched the young flesh crackle and spit above the fire. Its legs bound and its guts in the dog and everyone with their eyes feasted upon it.

'It would have died out there tonight,' said Sonny. 'Probably thought you were its mama.'

Ennor sighed. 'It don't make me feel any better knowin that.' She told Trip to stop calling it Bambi and sat back against the car door to drink her mug of hot water.

'It needed doin and I did it.' She sipped at the nothing tea and watched the flames fill the hole where the other car door used to be, a feel-good movie warming her through. They chewed on the bark chips Sonny had fried in the heat of the fire and sang songs for cheering.

Darkness and snow circled them in a noose and nobody cared because they had a roof and good things coming. When the deer was near enough done Sonny ripped and cut it a hundred ways and piled it on to a saddle propped up in the entrance of the missing door. They grabbed what they could hold and it was hard not to yelp and stuff themselves like wild animals. Wild children lost to civilisation, lost in the kill.

The meat kept coming and they ate until everything was chewed and stripped and when the wind threatened to overturn the car they huddled tight and let themselves know what it was like to be content. A full stomach, warmth and then sleep.

Ennor dreamt she was alone in a forest. It was dark but somehow she knew her whereabouts, the smell of fresh river water racing to the sea and the back-throat tang of pine sap rising from memory. She stood idle among the trees and her hands gripped sticky deep in her pockets. She was waiting for something or thinking about something, or both.

The night air was a comfort to her, had warmth greased through it as though the forest had been poured with liquid shine and was full to the canopy with heat. Sparks of colour like Christmas lights flashed in the forest and raced the night wind and Ennor was taken by the busy of heat and colour, another world but her world the same.

She smelt the sharp sting of burning all around. The cooking and scorching of flesh and the stench of foliage blackening and she turned to see the dead boy grinning close by with fire in his eyes. She ran gasping in a chase, the burning night fumes filling her head as she raced the flames, the ash-ember floor swept and moving like a hearth beneath her. Christmas come and Christmas gone. The fire chased itself out towards the treeline and Ennor imagined it staring at the snow, whip-cuffed and dumb, struck down by its own rage, a fire just trying to stay alive same as everything.

Ennor knew if she could just get out of the woods, jump the ring fire fence and run home to wash the blood from her hands, everything would be OK. The snow melted and the fire dampened and green shoots returned to the forest floor. Little green shoots of hope to cover up the fear.

'It'll be better then,' she said.

'What?'

'After the snow and the fire.'

'What you talkin bout? Ennor?'

'What?'

'You dreamin?'

Ennor opened her eyes and there was fire and snow but she was not in the forest next to home.

She rubbed her face. 'I was dreamin.'

'What about?' asked Sonny.

Ennor shook her head. 'Can't say I know what about.'

'You were sayin bout things gettin better.'

Ennor laughed. 'Can't get any worse now, can they?'

'Not by my reckonin.'

'How'd it get so bad?'

Sonny shrugged. 'You should of gone mother huntin in the summer months.'

They both laughed.

'Can you imagine?' said Ennor. 'It would be easy as, wouldn't it? Hot days and swimmin and bathin in the sun.'

'Maybe we'll do it sometime. Go back to Siblyback where we got that fish and swim with his rellies.'

'We could get a boat. That would be somethin, wouldn't it? The two of us bobbin and fishin with no cares in the world.'

They snuggled deep into the front seats and were warmed by the idling fantasy of being kids closer to their age, and Ennor soon fell back to dreaming and in this dream the snow had fully gone and the sun was high and blasting in the sky. She was sitting in the car with her mother sat next to her and she was singing and clapping mad on the steering wheel.

'Come on, Ennor girl,' she shouted above the blast of choral music. 'You remember this one, don't you?'

Ennor pretended to sing along but the words escaped her and there was a part of her that wondered if she was singing outside the dream.

'Louder,' Mum shouted.

'I can't remember it.'

'Yes you do. I used to sing it to you to keep the wind from out your ears.'

She looked across at her daughter. 'Don't you remember anythin bout me?'

'Course.' Ennor smiled. 'You're my mum.'

Her mother turned off the music and they sat in silence. From the passenger seat Ennor watched the A30 slice the moor and she wondered when exactly they had crossed it in her other life, the life without weather except for snow and nothing but friends for family.

'Where we goin?' she asked.

'What you mean where we goin?'

Ennor shrugged.

'We're goin for a ride, silly.'

'Where?'

'Round the bend and back again.' She looked at Ennor and laughed and she dug her fingers into Ennor's ribs until she laughed too.

They were driving fast, too fast, and Ennor felt the rise and rinse of cloying sick in her throat and she clenched her jaw shut.

'Right little quiet bird, you are. What's that father bin sayin bout me, eh? Tellin lies as usual? I'll stop you seein him if he's got your ear.'

Ennor was confused. She waited until the sick settled back in her stomach and then asked her mother where she lived.

'With me, you sure you're all right?'

'Where with you?'

'Bude of course. I bin visitin Nana Burley and you bin to that dump truck your dad calls home.'

'The trailer?'

'Tin shack, more like it.'

Ennor wanted to ask about Trip but the car was getting faster and her head thumped with confusion.

'You gotta slow down,' she shouted. 'Please, Mum, I can't bear it.'

'Quit your whinin, girl. Gotta get home. Time's passin us by.' She turned to Ennor and took her hands off the steering wheel. 'Tick-tock, tick-tock.'

She put her foot flat smack to the floor and screamed up a storm that had sleet back in the sky and ice on the road. Ennor reached to take the wheel but it wouldn't move and she shouted at her mum to stop from racing but it was too late. She was gone and Ennor was left spinning out on the ice.

The car turned somersaults and skidded and raced some more and crashed into a spiralling burn.

Ennor sat and looked the road over and up and down. There were no signs to guide her north or south and nothing of any significance except she was still alive. She glanced over at the driver's seat and watched Sonny sleeping wide-mouthed and peaceful and she sighed. It was morning and she was pleased to be there.

Behind them bundled on the back seat Butch and Trip and buddy dog slept happy and she thought to pick over her dreams like scavenged bones and then wondered why bother. She leant over Sonny and tapped her on the leg.

'What?'

'Wake up.'

'No.'

'It's mornin.'

'Big whoopee-do, I'm sleepin.'

Ennor huffed and folded her arms.

'Don't tell me,' said Sonny. 'You gotta feelin that this is the day.' She sat up and stretched and looked behind at Butch. 'He's still breathin then.'

Ennor nodded. 'I hope we find a doctor; more than Mum, I hope to find one.'

'Maybe he just needs a bit of civilised livin, drag him back to normal.'

'I'm fine,' coughed Butch.

Ennor turned and stretched out a hand to pat him

and she patted Trip too. 'How you feelin this mornin?'

Butch shrugged and stretched out. 'Bit better spose. Chest don't hurt so much.'

'That's good.' She smiled and she asked Trip how he was.

'Hungry.'

'After last night's feast?' asked Sonny. 'Where you hidin it?'

Trip sat up. 'Not hidin nothin. Where's the horses?'

They looked out of the side windows and Sonny got out of the car and went looking. 'They're here,' she shouted. 'They'd be stupid to wander far.' She walked them back to the car and she tied their reins together and got back into the driver's seat and put her hands on the steering wheel. 'Where we goin today then?'

'Where we goin, sister?' asked Trip.

'Bude.' She nodded. 'We're goin to Bude.'

'Finally,' he shouted and they all laughed.

CHAPTER FIFTEEN

They travelled north-west by the compass and when they saw the fat dark line of a hedge or wall appear in the fog they dropped back a little to keep from being seen because they were riding commodities and food all wrapped up into one.

'Nobody's goin to see us,' whispered Butch. 'We can barely see each other.'

'Just concentrate on preservin your energy,' said Ennor. 'It wouldn't hurt to pray that there's a doctor in the town either.'

'I'm all out of prayers.'

'Shame you're not all out of moanin,' said Sonny. 'We could leave you out here for the buzzards and kestrels if you'd like.'

They bickered through the snow and fog like it was a regular family day trip to the sea and arguments were peppered with nervous songs and jokes and long sombre silences.

'Is it Christmas yet?' asked Trip.

'We'll talk bout it later, buddy,' said Ennor.

'Christmas has been and gone,' said Sonny.

'Don't tell him that.'

'Well it's the truth, int it? And while we're at it there's no Father Christmas either.'

'Sonny!'

'Dint think so,' said Trip. 'What about the piskies?'

'Definitely piskies exist. They're all around if you know where to look.'

'Where?'

'Roundabout, but they don't like snow so don't go botherin just yet.'

'What bout the Easter Bunny?' he asked.

'What bout him?'

'He exist?'

'Don't be stupid, course not. Whoever heard of a ten-foot bunny hidin chocolate eggs for piggy kids? It's rubbish.'

The moment chocolate was mentioned the riders became children and Ennor started off a list of the top ten chocolate bars to keep from worrying. For the first time since journeying from home, moor time was running as it should be. The horses stood side by side and along with their riders and the dog they looked on towards the silent road and all waited for someone to take the first step.

'This is us,' said Sonny. 'This is our road if we're headin to Bude.'

'How far?' asked Ennor.

'Few miles but ridin on roads shouldn't take long if we're goin. We still got the gun.'

'There's no way round, is there?' asked Ennor. 'So we just gotta head, bandits or no bandits.'

They all agreed but there was apprehension settling among them up there on the horses; they were near the end of the journey and they sat and thought out the possibilities of a future they could not control.

In the end it was the dog with the colourful wrapper bows that stepped out into the road and the horses followed without a word.

Ennor's horse led the way with Butch holding the rifle and they set a single-file trail down the lane that fingered its way on to bigger roads and the fog hid them from danger and carried them safely to the north coast.

They came into the town with the tide drawing and sketching like normal and they stopped to watch it smack against the shore and each one greeted it like an old friend.

The town lay spewed and spent as they rode along the front. The buildings crouched crumpled and low to the sea, and everything was washed pure grey or thereabouts.

'Nothin but a ghost town,' said Sonny. 'Used to come up here most summers backalong, spose it's a shame.'

They looked about them, at the wild ocean crashing and the boarded-up arcades and surf stores half lifted with snow, a prophetic frontier town.

Signposts were graffiti-tagged with codes and pointers hinting at underground factions and the boarded windows were flyer thick with faces lost and forgotten names and everything melted with the cold and the wet.

'Now what?' asked Sonny.

Ennor shook her head and said she didn't know and she turned and asked Butch how he was feeling. He didn't answer.

His wheezing was back and he whispered to save himself from coughing.

'Where is everyone?' asked Sonny. 'Hello? Anyone?'

'Shush, we don't want to draw attention.'

'Yeah we do. Hello? Got a two-litre of scrumpy for anyone willin to talk.'

She sat back and looked over at Ennor with a smile. 'Best way is the loud way.'

'Did you nick them men's cider?'

'Among other things, why?'

'You're somethin else.'

'I know. Might just have that written on me grave.'

They about-turned the horses and were going to risk riding through the main part of town when Trip said he thought he saw someone in the bus shelter.

'Let's look,' said Sonny and she clipped the horse into a wide circle that skirted the half-cut building.

'You!' she shouted. 'Stop or we'll shoot.'

'No you won't,' came a dry raspy voice.

'How do you know I won't?'

'Cus you int got a gun.'

'My man over there does.'

A face chewed and spat, peeked through the square of light where the glass used to be and opened wide into a toothless laugh.

'What you laughin at, old boy?' demanded Sonny.

'Can he even lift the damn thing? Cus from where I'm standin I doubt it.'

'You want him to try?' asked Sonny and she reminded him he was the one sitting.

The old man got to his feet and stretched in a snap.

Sonny pulled the plastic milk carton filled with orange-coloured liquid and sat up to the pommel of the saddle.

'How much?' he asked. 'Only I int got much.'

'Not askin for much 'cept what you might know.'

'How'd you know if what I know is what you want to know?'

'Well try shuttin the hell up and I'll ask you.'

'How'd I know that there int just pee?'

'I'll splash you a mouthful, how bout that?'

The old man shrugged and sat down on the stone plinth that was part home and said he'd answer the questions if he knew the answers.

As it turned out the old man lived his life just as it was

and how it had always been, out of bins and on a bench by the sea. He'd seen everything that turned and changed in the town and knew everything that was about to.

With every answer given Sonny cupped a sip of cider into her dirt-black hand and reached down from the horse so he could lap at it like a dog and it was soon Ennor's turn to ask questions and she asked first about a doctor and then about her mother.

'There int no doctor willin for anythin, not by my reckonin. All rich bastards without conscience and Boots have been cleared of supplies so don't bother askin bout them.'

He told them there were groups of all persuasions forming allegiances about the town and he agreed that religious groups were very popular on account of the end-of-the-world talk.

'You heard of a group called the Sevens?' asked Ennor. 'A woman called Eleanor Carne?'

'Oh yes.' He grinned. 'Oh yes indeed.'

He danced about on the spot and whooped a little because he knew the drink would be his. 'Crazy bunch, am I right? Hard-core fanatics takin in all sorts, crackheads, rednecks, voodoo worshipers all mixed and crazy as a stew.' He told them they used to come through the town every few days on some kind of recruitment drive but not recently because everyone was gone.

'Where they gone?' asked Sonny.

'Behind closed doors just, or in their little groups hidin out. There's only a few of us out on the street and mostly we're left alone, same as always.'

'You know where the Sevens are based?' asked Ennor and she felt the number fizz on her lips with pleasure because it belonged to Mum and it belonged to her, a lucky number.

'The castle heritage place on the hill. I know that definite.'

Ennor's heart beat hard with a flash of fear and excitement and she told Sonny to give the man his drink because she had heard all she needed to know.

'You better not be sellin fibs,' shouted Sonny as she tossed the carton into his arms. 'We'll be back else.'

Ennor thanked him and they rode on towards where he had pointed.

'We goin to see Mother?' asked Trip.

'We'll see. Don't put your hopes too high.'

'Why not?'

'For a million reasons.'

Sonny took the gun from Butch and she told him they'd find a doctor soon enough and they followed the signs for the castle.

There were bags of rubbish built up in the street and the contents were strewn into a stinking carpet of colours where dogs and foxes had been.

They rode through the stench with their backs to

the wind and when they neared the castle they dismounted out in the road and waited. Dumb kids with hope dangling and falling from their hearts like ticker-tape.

'You here to convert?' asked a teenage boy through the bars of the front gate.

'Nope,' shouted Sonny. 'We're here to see the boss lady.'

'Don't say it like that,' snapped Ennor .'We're here to see my mum,' and she said her name and the boy went away and then came back.

'The boss lady is busy.' He smiled.

'But she's my mother. I've spent weeks lookin for her.'

'She's everyone's mother, if you want to convert to the Sevens, that is. Otherwise go swing.'

'OK, we'll convert,' grinned Sonny. 'I've come over all holy all of a sudden.'

'Well now I don't believe you.'

'Believe what you want.'

'You got a big mouth, int you?'

'They let you in, dint they? Just let us in or I'll blow your smug mug to bits.'

Sonny took the gun from Butch and raised it and fixed the cross hairs to his head and winked.

'No need for violence,' called a woman's voice. 'God made us equal and all that.'

The voice became a face and Ennor stared into the

dull arched corridor to search the woman's features for something that might resemble her own.

'Mum?' she asked, her heart a plump stifling pillow in her mouth.

'Don't think so, dear.'

'It's me, Ennor.'

'Never heard of you. Who's these?'

'My friends and this here is Trip. You remember him? He was just a baby but –'

'What do you want? I'm busy.'

Ennor thought it a funny thing to ask because what was it all children wanted from their parents.

'Are you Mother?' asked Trip.

'Only to my flock. You talk funny, boy. Are you joinin us? Cus like I said . . .'

Ennor passed the horse's reins to Butch and she wanted to shout out her confusion and ask the list of questions for ever but instead she approached in silence and stood with heavy hands swinging and a mouth full of feathers. The questions she had carried across the moor had deserted her.

'I got a photo.'

'Tell your friend there to lower her gun.'

Sonny nodded and swung the rifle on its strap so that it hung from her shoulder and they all watched maybe daughter and maybe mother stand face to face and silent. Ennor took the picture frame from the saddle bag and she held it up to the gate.

The woman shook her head. 'Who is it you're lookin for, kid?'

'Eleanor Carne.'

'She's gone.'

'Where.'

'Search me. People come and go and she's gone for ever, I'd say.'

Ennor wondered if she'd gone in the physical sense or perhaps the spiritual and she gave the woman a good looking over and recognised nothing but glimmers like shockwaves through and part was voice and part was something else. She stepped forward.

'So you convertin or no? Come on, girl, tick-tock.'

Ennor looked at the photo and then at the woman and she searched for the cogs of recognition to turn sparks into fire but anything that might once have burnt there had died long ago. She thought about showing the ring and decided against.

'No,' she said.

'You sure?' She pushed a hand through the metal bars and touched Ennor briefly on her face and a small tick-lish laugh escaped her lips that was both heaven and hell.

'I gotta go.' Ennor turned and mounted the horse with Trip behind and the woman said her name and told her to take care of herself and when she looked down at the gate she had gone.

She rode the horse ahead of Sonny and Butch and

they were quiet with the sting of sudden smacks still fresh on their faces.

Nobody spoke because there was nothing left to say and there was nothing worth listening to except the blunt hum of chatterbox minds.

They went single file through the littered streets and the dog jigged and barked at the rubbish like he had reached heaven and looked prepared to stay there.

Ennor rode to the harbour and she stood the horse in the surf to close her eyes to everything and the sea spray and it was Sonny as always who had the courage to confront the uncomfortable silence and she asked what next.

Ennor shrugged.

'She your mother or no?'

'Don't know.'

'You want her to be your mother even if she is? Not sure I would.'

'Well you've got your parents alive and sane so don't start wonderin.'

'Not sure bout the sane part but, anyway, just tryin to make it so it don't hurt so much.'

'I know.'

Ennor stared into the flat smack sea and everything in her wanted to kick the horse into running. Towards the waves and out into the for ever horizon, keep going, sink or swim.

'Where we goin, sister?' asked Trip.

Ennor didn't answer; she didn't know.

'I'm scared.'

'I know, buddy.' She reached around to pat him on the leg. 'Sister's scared too.'

CHAPTER SIXTEEN

There was nothing that could be said and nothing that could be done but roam the streets for signs of life and they went back through the town and called out for a doctor.

'I gotta get down,' coughed Butch. 'Just set me down a while, please.'

'We're gettin you a doctor,' said Sonny. 'Got to be one hidin somewhere.'

'Let me lie down, just for a minute.'

The two girls looked at each other and Ennor said they could sit him on a bench while they continued looking.

'Won't be long,' she told him. 'We'll go once more round town, then back.'

Butch tried to smile and it broke her heart all over again to see him huddled over the dog like a deadbeat.

They rode through the streets and looped back along

the beach front and one or other of them called out until their throats itched with hopeless words.

'Let's stop a minute,' said Sonny. 'Where's that tramp gone? He might know more than he's lettin on. I got more to sell.'

'I'd say he's settled into that bottle of cider you gave him,' said Ennor and she turned to look at Sonny. 'What's that?' She pointed towards a placard poking out from the sand behind her.

Sonny turned and they both read it out loud.

'What is it?' asked Trip. 'What's it mean?'

'Says bout a boat goin tomorrow, goin to the Scillies.'

'Why?' he asked.

'The promised land,' laughed Sonny. 'Fancy that.'

They rode their horses on to the sand to read the sign up close and a fisherman stepped out from behind the rocks.

'You kids interested?' he asked.

'What's great about the Scillies?' asked Sonny. 'What's different?'

'They got a self-sufficient community goin out there. Food and business near to normal.'

The girls looked at each other.

'How'd we know?'

The man smiled. 'You don't. That's where the world's gone wrong. No trust left.'

'How much?' asked Ennor.

The man came close and he felt the horse's legs down to the sand. 'These horses yours?'

Sonny looked at Ennor and then told him they were.

'Well I'd say that might swing it.'

'Got room for four?'

'Might well, be here by ten tomorrow. See what we can do.'

Ennor nodded and asked if he knew of any doctors in the town but he just shook his head. 'Scillies got doctors, got teachers, the lot. Don't forget, ten in the morning. Don't be late.'

They rode back to town and Ennor counted two magpies, one two, for luck as they circled the main square up ahead of them. One more night in the rough and they would be on their way: a doctor for Butch, teachers for Trip and a new life for them all.

At first she didn't notice the commotion. A little fantasy had wormed its way into her thinking and happiness was close by.

'What's goin on?' she asked. 'What's all the yappin bout?'

The pack of feral dogs stood barking mad in the road, clambering over each other in a fight to get to the prize. Family pets turned to wolves in just a few weeks of neglect. Sonny held out the rifle and fired a bullet into the air and when they didn't move she fired another at their feet and had them scattered, regretful to have to leave blood behind.

'You killed buddy dog!' shouted Trip as one of the dogs howled out in pain. 'You killed buddy dog!'

Sonny jumped from her horse and ran towards the lifeless body in the road.

'Is he hurt?' shouted Ennor. 'Please, God, tell me he int hurt.' She slid from her own horse and ran to Butch, a high-pitched ping resonating in her ears from Trip's screaming.

'He's breathin,' said Sonny.

'Is he bit?'

'Just torn clothes, let me look.' Sonny pulled up his jacket sleeves and peered into the chewed holes of his jeans. 'Grazes mostly. It's his breathin that's the worry.'

Ennor cradled his head and asked him if he could hear her and he blinked and tried to smile, his pale skin as white as the snow that skidded crossways on the road beneath him.

'He needs a doctor.'

'There int none,' said Sonny.

Ennor looked around for assistance and she called out for help just as if they lived in a regular world. A gang of youths stood watching from the bend in the road and she called for them to get a doctor.

'They don't look right, leave um,' said Sonny. 'Looks like they're settlin to rob us.'

'Stuff um,' shouted Ennor. 'What we got to rob?'

Sonny shook her head. 'We need to get Butch on the back of the horse quick and shut your brother up, would you?'

Trip was still screaming at the sight of blood on the snow and he punched the saddle in anger.

'Trip, you need to be a good lad. This is very important, Butch is poorly,' shouted Ennor.

'Buddy dog is dead!' he yelled. 'Sonny killed buddy dog!'

'Trip, please.' Ennor helped Sonny lift Butch towards the jittery horse. 'For fuck's sake Trip, shut up.'

The gang were getting closer, calling Ennor to come over, jesting that they wouldn't bite.

When Butch was hanging securely over the rump of the horse Sonny swung the rifle into full view of the boys and turned to face them.

'Dare me,' she shouted. 'Just go ahead and dare me.'

'Just being friendly,' one of them smirked.

Sonny ignored him and held the gun firmly in both hands. 'Who's first?' she asked, guiding the double barrel from one face to the next.

'You wouldn't do it.'

'Wouldn't I?'

'You int got the guts. Besides, there int more than two bullets a go in that gun and you've had your share of firin.'

'Int there now?'

The mouthy boy edged forward so he was face to face with the barrel. 'Nope.'

'Wanna take the chance?'

'You're bluffin.' He grinned.

Sonny winked. 'Your funeral.'

She unlooped the strap and flicked the rifle into the air, catching it by the barrel in time to smash the butt into the side of his face.

'Anyone else?' she yelled.

Ennor looked down at the boy, blood from his head seeped into the snow and mingled with that of the injured dog and it was all red just the same. 'Let's go,' she shouted.

The remaining three boys stepped back and so did Sonny and she jumped up in front of Butch. 'Don't even think bout followin us!' she shouted. 'We got bullets and it takes a second to reload.'

Sonny reached behind her and felt for Butch's neck, he was breathing but only just and his skin was ice cold.

'We need to get him warmed up,' she shouted across to Ennor on the other horse. 'Gotta get out of town and get a fire goin.'

Ennor looked at Sonny through a blur of silent tears. She wanted to ask if everything would be all right like she always did but the look on Sonny's face told her it was anything but.

Something she knew in any case: something she'd known all along.

They rode in silence and with purpose to put a little distance between them and the town, with Sonny sitting stiff from the cold and Butch stretched out behind her like a deer corpse after a hunt.

Ennor felt Trip's small warm body snuggle tight against her back, his crying nothing more than random gasps for air.

'You OK, buddy?' she asked and felt him shake his head.

'You gotta be strong. I'm countin on you.'

'Sonny,' he gargled. 'Sonny killed buddy dog.'

Ennor reached around and patted one dangling leg. 'The dogs had got into a pack like a gang. They were attackin Butch.'

'Why?'

'Cus they're animals and were hungry.'

'Why what Sonny done?'

'She had to stop them.'

'I hate her.'

'No you don't.'

'Do,' he shouted. 'I hate you!'

Sonny looked over her shoulder at them and her silence unnerved Ennor.

'Shut up, Trip,' said Ennor. 'Please, just shut up.'

They rode on towards higher ground and Sonny led her horse into a small crop field overlooking the bay and dismounted.

'Lay out your tarp and I'll pull him down.'

Ennor did what she was told and when they settled Butch on to it she covered him with all their blankets.

'Kid,' shouted Sonny. 'Stop your dribblin, you're comin to fetch wood with me.' She grabbed his arm and pulled him towards the hedgerow.

Ennor took off her coat and bundled it into a pillow for Butch. 'We'll soon get you warmed up.' She looked into his eyes and ran her fingertips across his cheek.

His breathing was thin and worn like it had journeyed a million miles to get from his lungs to his mouth and she pulled his collar tight and told him everything would be OK. This was the only time she would ever lie to him. He was not OK and things weren't OK. Butch was dying, the first of them to be heading the way all of them would be heading soon enough.

'Sonny's gone for some wood. Only thing she's good for, right?'

Butch smiled and he tried to speak.

'What is it?' She leant forward until her ear was close to the sucking that was his breathing.

'Thank you,' he whispered.

Ennor's eyes filled with tears and they dropped heavy on to his cheeks.

'What you got to thank me for? Should be me thankin you,' she sobbed. 'Stupid boy.'

Butch shook his head. 'Thank you,' he said again. 'For bein you.' He started to cough and his hands went to his chest, every word, every breath an excruciating punch of pain, too much.

Ennor must have screamed out loud because Sonny and Trip came running towards her and she shouted a jumble of words that were both comforting and startling but it was too late. Butch was dead.

Hours, days and weeks could have passed her by and Ennor wouldn't have noticed them or counted them. There was no luck in counting, no lucky seven and no good fortune in the colour red. She lay on her back and saw crows circling the dead hour before bed and she knew they were the lucky ones, the free. Sonny gave her the blankets that they had piled on to Butch but had left him one. He lay beside her as still and as cold as a pebble washed up from the shore.

'He'd bin ill a long time,' said Sonny from out of the darkness. 'Trip said.'

'What he know?'

'A lot, sister. I know everythin.'

Ennor sat up and saw that they had made a fire and were sitting awkwardly beside it. She must have passed out. Two children with faces like cold-bitten tramps, resigned and dirty and worn. Children used to the rhythm of winter's homeless bash and bang and all of them broken souls with one dead awaiting the ground.

'This is my fault,' she said. 'All this and everythin up to this. I should have known. He'd bin badly beat cus of me.'

Sonny shook her head. 'I int listnin. Trip, block your ears.'

'Not talkin to you,' he said.

'Dint ask you to. Block your ears cus your sister's talkin bull.'

Ennor moved closer to the fire and gave them back their blankets. 'Don't swear.'

'You did,' said Trip.

'When?'

'Said "for fuck's sake, Trip, shut up."'

'That's different.'

'Why?'

Ennor took a deep breath. She knew there were things Trip didn't understand, couldn't. Butch was lying dead on the tarp between them and here he was with the usual hair-splitting questions.

'Just leave her be,' said Sonny and she put a finger up to his mouth. 'Leave it.'

'We'll have to bury him,' said Ennor.

Sonny nodded.

'Put him in the ground one way or the other.'

'Yep.'

'You got ideas?'

Sonny shrugged. 'I guess diggin would do it.'

'The ground's hard as rock.'

'I got me axe.'

'It'll take for ever.'

'Then for ever is how long it'll take.'

Ennor gripped hold of Sonny's arm, she wanted to thank her but despair caught in her throat.

'I know,' said Sonny as she stood up and she wrapped her blanket around Ennor and Trip's shoulders.

'Might start diggin down there by that tree.' She

pointed towards the bottom edge of the field and nodded. 'Next to the hedge. Farmers don't plough that far out.'

Ennor watched her lead the horses down the field with the axe handle sticking from her jeans pocket and a little lump rose up in her throat.

'What's Sonny doin?' asked Trip.

'She's diggin Butch a grave.'

'Why?'

'Cus he's dead, buddy.'

'What she doin with the horses?'

Sonny was hammering at the frozen snow and scraping it clear with her boot. 'She's feedin the horses,' she nodded. 'Findin them grass.'

'What we got to eat, sister? We int eaten all day.'

Ennor thought for a minute and wondered if Sonny had anything left over from the bartering.

'Pass me that bag,' she said to Trip.

'It's Sonny's.'

'Just pass it, would you?'

Trip pulled the rucksack from off the snow and on to the tarpaulin sheet. 'What's in it?'

'Food, I hope.'

'Please, God.'

'Please, God, is right,' and for once their prayers were answered. They had two tins of beans left, plus two tins of stolen spam and a packet of custard creams.

'Savin the best for last.' She smiled.

'Thank God.' Trip smiled.

'Thank God. We'll have a feast now, won't we, buddy?'

'For Butch,' said Trip. 'Before he goes to heaven.'

Ennor wiped her eyes and told Trip to go and help Sonny and to tell her she was cooking everything they had. The tears were starting to fall in heavy splashes down her face and she didn't want Trip to see, not again. They would have a feast and toast Butch and everything that was good about him. Toast him into heaven.

She set about opening the tins with her knife and adding the last of the wood to the fire, enough to heat things through. She thought about their adventure because that was what it was and wondered if Butch's destiny was written to end like this all along. They would never know, but known things were ending in any case.

When the beans were spitting from the tins and the two slabs of spam heated in the pan she called Sonny and Trip.

It felt strange to be eating when Butch was stretched out beside them.

'This tastes every bit as nice as anythin,' said Sonny.

'I love sister's cookin,' smiled Trip. 'Love everythin she cooks me.'

Ennor laughed. 'You always say that, buddy.'

'That's cus it's true.' He nodded. 'Shame Butch can't eat none.'

Sonny raised her plate into the air. 'To Butch.' She smiled.

'To Butch,' said Ennor and Trip in unison.

They took their time to enjoy the food and Ennor told herself that it would be their last meal together. Tomorrow Butch would be in heaven and the ground and they'd all be on their way someplace other.

'How's the diggin?' she asked.

'It's like liftin tarmac.'

'How long you think?'

Sonny shrugged. 'All night I guess.'

'We can't leave him, can we?'

'Birds will get him or them wild dogs.'

Ennor looked over at Trip to see if his ears pricked to the word dog, but he was listening to something that carried on the evening breeze.

'Buddy dog,' he said.

'I know,' she said and she put an arm around his too-thin back. 'Buddy dog's gone.'

'No, he int. Buddy dog.' He got to his feet and stood with his nose and ears pricked. 'Buddy dog,' he shouted.

The two girls looked at Trip and then at each other and Sonny put a hand on the reloaded rifle.

Barking resonated up from the valley below, a bark for every shout Trip made.

'Sit down,' said Ennor, pulling at her brother's jacket. 'It's them mad dogs.'

'It's buddy dog!' he shouted and pulled away from her grip.

'Trip, come back.' Ennor chased after him and Sonny

followed with the gun loose in her hands but it was too late to catch up.

The dog appeared in the open gate and jumped at Trip as he ran towards him. 'Buddy dog,' he shouted.

Ennor waited for the riot of screams and snapping jaws and she tried to pray but everything happened fast and confusing.

Trip lay twisted in the snow with his arms around the dog and he was crying. Tears of joy, not pain, tears that Ennor had never seen before that moment.

'It's his dog,' said Sonny and she started to laugh. 'It's his crazy mutt dog.'

Ennor bent to pat the dog. 'He's here for the biscuits,' grinned Trip. 'He can have some, can't he?'

'He can have whatever he likes,' she laughed.

'Did he come alive again? Will Butch?'

Ennor and Sonny looked at each other and then Ennor shook her head. 'Sonny must have shot a different dog, there was so many.'

'And Butch?' he asked.

'Butch is dead, buddy.'

CHAPTER SEVENTEEN

Trip sat cross-legged by the fire with the dog's head on his lap and he fed it bits of meat and biscuit. Ennor listened to him talk to it like he was his best friend, his confidant. He told the dog that he had been shot and that it was a miracle because here he was, alive and without blood.

'A miracle dog.' He nodded to himself. 'Special.'

Down at the edge of the field Sonny had made a small fire for herself, a tiny beacon to work by and perhaps a little heat. They had carried Butch's body down to where his final resting place would be, wrapped in his blanket from home, his shroud.

She hadn't wanted him to go just yet, still had things to say, chatterbox things like he was still company of a kind. Sonny said it was best, especially for Trip. 'These things stay with kids for ever,' she'd said, like she knew.

Butch's body was barely visible from where she sat. A

small grey bump in the snow, smooth and round and immovable like a rock, her rock.

She looked at Trip and smiled. He was asking her a question.

'What is it?'

'We got tea?'

'Tea's all gone, buddy, and the pine needles. You thirsty?'

Trip nodded.

'I'll boil some water.'

'Hot water to drink?'

'It's good for you, good for your tummy.'

Trip laughed and shook his head. 'You're crazy, sister.'

She lumped clean snow into the pan and wondered if she'd ever get to use a tap again, or cook on a stove, or more than anything, sleep in her own bed. She wondered if the trailer had been emptied by the landlord yet. Maybe he'd piled everything into the yard and put a match to it, or sold it. He was a mean bastard.

'We're goin in a boat tomorrow,' Trip told the dog. 'Can buddy dog come?'

Ennor shrugged. 'We'll see.'

When the water was boiling she poured it into the three tin mugs. 'You be careful drinkin this,' she said. 'Don't drink it straight away. I'm takin this one down to Sonny.'

She could hear the swearing from quite a way off. The

tiny figure bent to the ground with mud on her hands and cuss on her lips.

'How's it goin?' she asked.

'It's goin just about.'

Ennor passed her the mug and snuggled her own.

'My hands are killin.'

'You want me to take over?'

Sonny shook her head. 'No point two of us sore and dirty more than ever. Besides, you need your energy for tomorrow.'

Ennor wanted to ask Sonny if she was coming to the Scillies in the morning, but suddenly something had them distracted.

'What's that?' she said.

'Voices. Where's the gun?'

'Up by the fire.'

'Go get it quick.'

Ennor ran up the field and she told Trip to be quiet.

'What is it?' he whispered.

'Don't know, maybe strangers. Come with me.' She strapped the rifle crossways to her chest and filled her pockets with the remaining ammunition.

'Strangers who?' asked Trip.

'From the town, now come on, hurry.'

They ran down to where Sonny was standing in the dark, her fire trampled to smoke and the axe steady in both hands.

'Who d'you think it is?'

Sonny shook her head. 'Don't know. Maybe they saw the fires.'

'Will they pass?'

Sonny crouched to the ground and beckoned to the others to do the same. 'They won't pass, look.'

'What?'

'They're standin at the gate.'

'Maybe they don't see us,' said Trip.

'They see us,' said Sonny. 'Wouldn't have stopped otherwise.'

Ennor told Trip to take the dog and stand in the hedge behind the animals. 'Keep your eyes closed,' she told him, expecting the worse.

'You got bullets in that gun?' asked Sonny.

'Course.'

'You know you might have to use it?' She looked across at her friend and Ennor nodded. The two girls stood their ground and watched the boys' silhouette fill the gap in the hedge.

'It's those lads from the town.'

'I'd say so.'

'What they want with us?'

'The horses,' said Sonny as she edged forward. 'They want the horses.'

'What you want?' she shouted. 'Got nothin to give so just keep movin.'

One of them laughed. It was the mouthy one from earlier, the one Sonny had knocked out.

'Just lookin to share your fire,' he shouted. 'What's your problem?'

'You is.'

'That's not so nice. You got that pretty one with you?'

'What's it to you?'

'I'm here,' said Ennor. 'What you want?'

'Well let me see, for starters a hello would be nice.' His voice was irritating and loaded with connotations and he made the others laugh.

'Hello,' said Ennor, moving forward. 'Now go back to whatever rock you climbed out from.'

'That's not very nice.'

'It weren't meant nice.'

'Weren't nice how your friend here whacked me cross the face for nothin.'

'You asked for it.' Ennor could see Sonny looking at her from out the corner of her eye, but it was too late now, she was rolling. She let down the hammer on the gun and pointed it at him, Ennor Carne had killed once and she could kill again.

'I reckon you should probably stop walkin roundabout now and tell your boys to get from circlin. We int stupid.'

The boy smiled, said something about starting over, but Ennor wasn't for starting over any more. Not with anyone or anything.

'You seen them pack of dogs runnin mad in the town down there? Abandoned, unloved, homeless? Well

300

that's us, see?' She waved the barrel of the gun in his face. 'That's us.'

The boy put his hands into his jacket pocket and nodded. 'That's us and all,' he said.

Ennor kept hold of the gun and she screamed that she had killed a boy and could kill another and she shook so hard the barrel swung out into the darkness.

'Give me the gun,' said Sonny and she lifted the rifle over Ennor's head.

Ennor heard her say that it would be OK, that they would all be OK, but the flood of tears that engulfed her indicated it was anything but.

Sonny walked her back to the fire and she shouted to the lads that they were welcome to join them if first they scouted the hedges for firewood.

'What you say that for?' said Ennor.

Sonny shrugged. 'All the same, int we? Pack of mad dogs.' She sat Ennor close to the fire and wiped her eyes with her sleeve. 'Besides, might get um to dig the grave for us.'

'How'd you do that?'

'Payment somehow, I still got saleables in me bumbag.'

'Like what?'

'Jewellery mostly, gold and stuff.'

'Where from?'

'Home, 'cept it int home no more.'

'What you mean?'

'Went round nickin before I came after you, dint I? Thought it would be useful and it is.'

Ennor started to laugh. 'That's why you can't go back?'

Sonny nodded. 'Dint want to anyhow. Don't matter.'

The four lads went out into the dark and soon returned with roots of bracken and the occasional rotten branch and they seemed happy to be working, like they needed something to do and someone to tell them to do it.

'You can have some biscuits for your trouble,' said Sonny. 'Half a pack is all we got left.'

The boys were overjoyed, like light and life had come back into their lives in an instant.

The seven of them sat hunched to the fire eating biscuits and sharing stories and Ennor felt like she was back at school, hanging and idling with the villagers. Seven kids the same, a brotherhood, and she counted them over for the pleasure that was the number seven forming on her lips. Luck perhaps.

'You got no home to go to?' asked Lee, the big mouth one.

Ennor shook her head.

'Me neither. Only had a mother anyways.'

'What happened to her?'

'Knocked down.'

'Hit-and-run,' added a younger boy. 'She was my mum un all. What happened to your friend?'

'He died,' said Trip.

'What of? The cold?'

'Kind of,' said Ennor. 'Amongst other things.'

'The cold finished him,' added Sonny and she took the chance to ask if they would help dig the grave later and they said they would without her having to open the bumbag.

'Where you bin livin?' asked Lee through a mouthful of biscuit.

'The moor,' said Ennor. 'Can't say how long, a week, maybe two.'

'Why'd you wanna stay up there in this weather?'

Ennor smiled. 'I forget.'

'And you?' he asked Sonny.

'Live up there. Used to anyway. Everythin's changed now, we're all on the road same as.'

Ennor could tell there was more the boy wanted to ask and she said as much.

'You killed a boy?' he asked.

She shrugged.

'He was a rum un so it don't count,' said Sonny. 'A bunny boy by all accounts.'

'He had a name?'

'Rabbit,' said Ennor and she wondered if she should feel guilty, she didn't.

'Rabbit?' asked the boy. 'Funny looker with teeth like daggers?'

Ennor nodded.

'Nothin wrong with Rabbit, saw him few days back. Wanted to join up and we told him to go hang. Right odd one off the moor.' He laughed and the others joined in. 'We'll crack on with that diggin if you want. Keep us warm, won't it.'

Sonny walked them down to the grave.

'You killed a rabbit?' asked Trip.

Ennor petted his head and said they were just joking and she closed her eyes briefly to allow herself to be released from damnation. She did not kill the boy and she wanted to scream and she wanted to cry relief but instead she looked at Trip and smiled.

'Funny boys,' said Trip.

'You like um?'

'No. Are they comin on the boat?'

'Doubt it. They int got nothin to barter for the ride.'

Trip smiled. 'We do. We got horses, int we, and Sonny's gold.'

'How you know bout Sonny's gold?'

'She showed me.'

'She got a lot?'

'Loads, she gave me this.' He unbuttoned the collar of his coat and showed her the small gold pendant hanging on a chain around his neck.

'It's a Saint Christopher,' she said.

'I know.' He grinned, delighted with himself. 'Saint of travellers. Sonny said he'd look after me in the boat and all my life. She got one too cus she's a traveller.'

Ennor put an arm around him and pulled him close. 'When she give it to you?'

'Earlier, when you were sad.' He turned abruptly and looked up at her. 'You int sad no more, are you?'

Ennor shook her head. 'Not any more.' She smiled.

'Promise?'

'Promise.'

She watched Sonny boss the boys and a great ache lifted and wedged itself crossways inside her belly. Sonny had given Trip the pendant to keep him safe because she wouldn't be there to do it herself.

Ennor snuggled Trip into his blanket with the dog close by and she told him to get some sleep, they had a big day ahead of them tomorrow, a great adventure.

She sat with a burning twig between her fingers and when the flame died to smoke she put it to her mouth for familiarity and thought about the dead boy that was no longer dead. A bit of history that belonged to her with the good and the bad reversed.

At the bottom of the field Sonny and the boys were putting their backs into digging Butch's grave and they would soon have it ready. She looked out and deep into the night's sky and wondered if heaven was waiting to accept him, settling a little corner among the righteous and the concealed stars.

Ennor hadn't seen much of stars or the moon or the sun since her first day walking out on to the moor and she wondered if beneath the grub they were all pale as clean sheets.

Ghosts from out of the woodwork and beneath the snow shelf, poor imitations of their even poorer selves.

The whole of Cornwall could have been sky but for the buttons of fire that studded the black horizon. Tiny fires in the snow built for doing or saying something same as their own.

She turned an ear towards the others and they were laughing, getting on and she listened to the night air and heard shouts and the racket of street life in a country gone wrong.

The clatter and smack of people getting used to doing what they pleased.

She thought about her mother and father. Separate except in the making of her and Trip, and she reached for the rucksack and felt for the cold metal of the picture frame. In the firelight she cradled the photo in her lap, Mum and Dad. She didn't even recognise them.

She wondered about the boat ride tomorrow and their future as usual uncertain in the hands of destiny and she bent to kiss Trip's sleepy head and settled in behind him and closed her eyes. They were sore from crying and blinking in the acrid smoke and although it hurt to keep them shut she told herself to rest. Butch was dead, Dad was dead, but Ennor would be strong and go on.

Sometime in the night or maybe it was morning she woke to find Sonny's hand against her cheek and she told her they had put Butch in the ground.

'Do you want to say somethin? Prayers and stuff?'

Ennor nodded and she sat up and pulled Sonny close.

'I know,' whispered Sonny.

'What?'

'Just that, I know.'

'Sonny?'

'Don't.'

'What?'

'Ask me bout comin, it's hard enough.'

They stood and held on to each other as if they were at the edge of some precipice and in a way they were, and there was so much Ennor wanted to say that there were no words to say it.

'Why you huggin?' asked Trip. 'Why you whisperin?'

'We're goin to say goodbye to Butch,' said Ennor.

'In the grave and off to heaven?'

Sonny smiled. 'Somethin like that.'

They walked down the field and the boys took off their hats and held them in their hands out of respect. Ennor stood at the head of the grave and she closed her eyes and prayed.

She said words from the Bible that she didn't believe and words from her heart that she did and everyone was quiet and nodding. There was something about the occasion that was everyday ridiculous and it made her smile and then she laughed. The others joined in and they kicked the rock earth back into the ground with smiles on their faces, everything everyday and normal.

'He's gone now,' said Trip. 'Can I go back to sleep?'

Ennor nodded. 'Course you can, buddy. You can sleep as long as you like.'

The boys finished off the shovelling and Ennor and Sonny walked back to the dying fire.

They watched dawn break to the east of the sea and saw it blow colour in a bleed of reds and pinks across the horizon.

'You know what that is?' asked Sonny.

'What?'

'That's a good sign.'

Ennor smiled. 'How'd you know?'

'Cus I know everythin and I know a good sign when I see one.'

'Thought you dint believe in um.'

'This one's different. It's real.'

They sat and watched the world come anew and when it was time to go they rode down to the harbour in silence with the ragtag boys in tow.

The harbour was quiet apart from a family of four and they gave away the horses and sat near to the strangers, waiting for the boat to arrive.

'I saw that necklace you gave Trip,' said Ennor.

'I know, kind, int I?'

'Can't sway you to come, can I.'

Sonny shook her head. 'All that confinement and kids and the boat trip will takes days, maybe weeks, hell.'

'What you gonna do?'

Sonny shrugged. 'Hang with the lads. See if we can't reclaim our future somehow.'

'Don't get into trouble.'

Sonny raised her eyebrows and this made Ennor laugh. 'OK, don't get into *too much* trouble.'

'I won't.'

'Promise?'

'I promise.'

'I got somethin for you.' She reached under her scarf and lifted her necklace over her head.

'Your lucky fishbone,' laughed Sonny.

'You might need the luck more than me.'

Sonny nodded and she let Ennor tie it around her neck.

'I just wanna say thank you,' said Ennor.

'For what?'

'Everythin.'

'You're welcome.'

'More than that.'

'More than everythin? Hell.'

Ennor sighed. 'For teachin me stuff, bout life. You taught me to love life. I'll miss that, I'll miss you.'

Sonny smiled. 'It's true you don't make lists any more and you don't count half as much.'

Ennor agreed and she looked out to sea to watch the boat drifting towards the shore.

'This is goodbye then,' she said.

'Until the next time,' said Sonny. 'You'll see me along the line. Don't worry bout that, greenhorn.'

She hugged Ennor and then Trip and the dog and went to join the boys, who were sitting on the harbour wall.

Ennor and Trip waded out to the boat with the dog awkward between them and they sat crying and stupid among strangers. Ennor watched the beach and waited for Sonny to go and she laughed when she came back down to the shore to stand proud in the surf.

'You cryin, Sonny Pengelly?'

'Nope.'

'Looks like you are. What is it you want to say?'

Sonny shrugged. 'I guess I'll miss you un all.'

The boat was loaded and two oarsmen were set to take turns in rowing the distance.

'There's somethin else,' shouted Sonny.

'What?'

'Bout the end of the world.'

'Go on.'

'Only it's not the end, is it, it's the beginnin.'

Ennor smiled. 'I'll be seein you.'

They were both smiling and they were both crying and it was true, life would go on. Winter had its damage done but things would soon heal and be forgotten and gone.

Ennor knew this and it was not wishing or hoping or banking on luck. It was the truth and as she thought it she sank her arm into the water and let go of the picture frame, two strangers' faces, one and two, and gone for ever.